To Stacey Wesley—
a consummate reader and amazing friend.

Chemistry

KIM LOUISE

ARABESQUE®

ISBN-13: 978-1-58314-800-6
ISBN-10:   1-58314-800-0

CHEMISTRY

www.kimanipress.com

Printed in U.S.A.

Acknowledgments

A special thank-you to Rod James—computer guy extraordinaire—who sat down with me and shared his knowledge and passion for technology. You are gracious and wonderful. How do you keep all that in your head? Thanks to all those who showed up for my sign and dine: Janice and Allan, Capiz, Gwen and Retonya. And a great big ol' thanks to Kim Meyer for cooking the sign-and-dine dinner. You were marvelous and that German food is to live for! Thank you to Sherry Siwinski for putting up with me and maintaining my Web site anyway. And thank you, thank you to Patti Lynn whose creative ear is always available. As always, thank you to all the fantastic readers who continue to read my work. You are the best!

Chapter 1

"Well, what does it say?"

"It says the same thing the others said. 'No.'"

"Ky, I'm sorry. Come here. Let me hug you."

Kyra Douglas needed a hug. She'd been trying for two years to get her poetry published. She'd been rejected so many times, she had considered the idea of never writing another poem, ever. She got up from her writing table and headed straight into the arms of a handsome man.

No matter how many times Turk Mosley held her, it felt as good as the first time. In his solid and unwavering embrace, Kyra found assurance, understanding and compassion.

"Hey," she said, pushing back slightly. "What's going on down there?"

Turk flashed that devastating smile of his. "I was

thinking that if you really want some consoling, I could definitely help you out."

Kyra punched him lightly on the shoulder and sat back down at her desk.

"Why do you keep saying things like that? We don't even swing that way anymore."

Turk straddled the chair across from her. "I know. But in addition to being a computer geek with an IQ of one-sixty, I'm also a dog. So, my mind never strays far from—"

"Okay! I get it."

Kyra picked up the letter from Callaloo publishers and read it again. She couldn't understand how something that weighed less than an ounce could make her feel so heavy with sadness.

"Don't worry. Somebody out there will realize how good you are. Just keep submitting."

"I'm tired, T. I mean, I know I got this computer gig and all—and don't get me wrong, the money is way better than good—but I thought..."

"You thought you'd be the next Maya Angelou, by now."

"Something like that," she said.

She'd let her hopes run wild. Surely, she thought, after attending the month-long writer's retreat, she would come home to at least one acceptance letter. But all the letters that she'd received read the same way: Thanks, but no thanks. She thought she would have been so energized by the poets retreat that she'd be reluctant to go back to work after her sabbatical.

She was wrong.

* * *

They were in her apartment, again. It was a place she'd designed for the two sides of her that she loved: technology and creativity. Her living room, kitchen and dining area were full of bold colors and straight lines. She was aiming for B. Smith meets Bill Gates. When she invited her friends over—all of whom worked in some capacity in technology—she wanted a space that they would feel comfortable in. And she'd achieved that.

In her bedrooms, she'd gone in another direction entirely—an Erykah Badu–Jill Scott kinda groove. Her second bedroom, where she now stood with Turk, was the place she went to be creative and write all those poems she didn't seem to be able to get published. And her second bedroom, that vibe was warm, setting a different mood altogether.

And it worked. Until today. Today, she just wanted to pack up her life and start over. *Callaloo* was the last major literary magazine she could think of to send her work. She'd submitted to all the other big literary publishers, and nada.

Heck, maybe she should become a rap artist.

"Are you sure you don't want me to *tighten you up?*" He gave her his best "I'm a damn good lover" face.

"Turk, it takes more than a look and a line to get me into bed. You should remember that."

"I just thought, since we have a history—"

"Turk!"

"All right. I'll drop it, as long as you drop all this drama and get to writing. I'm not going to leave here until you write another poem."

"I don't feel inspired."

"I don't care. Write about how this rejection makes you feel. Write about a man who won't stop hounding you for sex. Just write. You have to get back on the horse, or in this case the desktop. Both of those images get me hot."

Kyra let a laugh fly. Her mood was a little over-the-top, but the rejections had pushed her there. If Turk wanted a poem, then he would get one. Maybe she would write about a horse who ran away every time the rider tried to mount it.

That's how she felt.

She reached over, grabbed a sheet of paper from the stack, and her favorite pen and inkwell, and set her emotions free.

Corporate America. The daily grind. If she didn't enjoy living the way she did, Kyra would have quit in the flap of a hummingbird wing and lived the life of a starving artist. She drove her Camry into a parking space in the company garage and got out.

Five dollars a day for this space, she thought and locked the car with the remote.

It always amazed her how many people came in at 6:00 a.m. like she did. The flexible schedules at ComTel America meant that people pretty much came and went as they pleased. Just as long as they got their work done.

It was obvious that most folks wanted to get in and out so they could get on with their lives.

"Mornin', Kyra."

"Mornin', Becky."

Kyra and the administrative assistant to the vice president of her department had had the same greeting for the entire ten years she'd worked there.

Kyra entered her cubicle thinking that it had been a long road—from help-desk specialist to senior systems engineer. She'd learned quickly and the company had rewarded her well. Now she knew ComTel's computer network as though she'd built it from the ground up. Heck, in some ways, maybe she had. She loved computers and understanding them came way too easy for her. She loved her job and after some "training," the people she worked with left her alone and let her do what she was hired to do. Now, if she could just do the same with her poetry her life would be perfect.

"How was the retreat?"

"Jesus!" Kyra said, spinning around in her seat. "You scared the HTML out of me."

"She's back!" Orlando said. Orlando Bloom. Not the actor, the ComTel computer tech who would be CIO.

"Yep. I'm back. The retreat was wonderful. I wrote so much and so fast, my hand cramped up. I think I'm getting carpal tunnel or something." She switched on her computer and watched the screen flicker as it booted up.

"I wish I had a hobby like that," he said. "All I have is computers. Oh, well. I'm on my way to a meeting. I just wanted to say, 'Welcome back!'"

"Thanks, Orlando."

Kyra logged into her e-mail. It had been idle for the past thirty days. A system-generated "Welcome Back" e-mail sat in her inbox. She dreaded seeing what a month of unanswered e-mails looked like. Instead of turning the out-of-office message off, she opened her assignment log. The level-one and -two technicians did most of the work. That freed Kyra up for companywide

IT project planning and special technical issues. Her assignment log had only one item in the queue.

Race Jennings—New Computer Install—ASAP

She read the item again, but it said the same thing. Installs were level-one jobs. Orlando would be perfect. She rushed out of her cube to see if she could catch up to him.

"Orlando!" she said.

"Yes?" He turned from where he was standing in front of an elevator.

"I guess there's a new guy—Race Jennings. Can you do the install?"

"No. Adam and Lisa won't do it, either. And Rod is on vacation."

"Have I been gone too long? What's up?"

"That guy has had four computers in four weeks. He thinks we're all idiots. It's like the Bermuda Triangle in his office. Operating systems just disappear."

The elevator doors opened and Orlando stepped in. His tall, thin frame took up practically no space in the large square compartment. "Maybe *you* can get him a computer that works."

Kyra let the doors close then checked her watch. Not quite six-thirty. She'd have enough time to print the comment file on the new installation, visit the ladies' room and get to her best friend's office for the scoop just as she came in to work.

Thirty days and the whole company had gone crazy. The twenty-eighth floor, where her best friend Chantel

Mosley worked, had been completely remodeled. In fact, some of it was still under construction. Kyra stepped around boxes, parts of unassembled cubicles and carpet fragments with amazing dexterity.

She traipsed through the obstacle course and made it to the ladies' room. At least, she thought it was the ladies' room. When she stepped inside there were urinals and more construction.

"What the...?" she began.

"I was just about to say the same thing," a man's voice said.

At the closest end of the row of urinals, a man stood finishing his business and zipped up his pants.

"Oh, my gosh! Isn't this the ladies' restroom?" she asked, embarrassed, and nearly overcome with attraction. The man, who was now washing his hands, looked like something created for sex and sex only.

"I certainly hope not," he said. He dried his hands and walked to the door while Kyra stood there waiting for her feet to work.

He pushed past her and held the door open. "Are you coming?" he asked.

"I think so," she said, walking through and deeply inhaling something that was not cologne but love potion. The fragrance practically floated her off of her feet.

Kyra forgot she had to go to the bathroom.

"Hey!" came a familiar call. Chantel came strutting around the corner looking fun and fabulous.

The two friends embraced and Kyra gave her friend a quick appraisal. Chantel was hands down the best-dressed woman at ComTel. She was tall, attractive and had a body that men swallowed their tongues over. Just

enough of everything. Although Kyra didn't dress
nearly as funky as Chantel, and was clearly a head
shorter, when the two of them were together, the men
all paused and didn't move until she and Chantel said
it was okay.

"Girl, you've been shopping!" Kyra said.

Chantel's pink-on-pink suit met the fashion style
of the day.

"You know American Express loves me! Now, come
on in here and tell me about your retreat."

Kyra looked around to see in what direction the
handsome man had gone, but he'd disappeared around
the corner. Kyra fanned herself and followed Chantel
to her office.

Chantel had managed to score one of the largest
offices in the company. Just as large as the VP's offices.
The thing was, Chantel didn't really do much of
anything. She just looked good, talked a good game,
and had all the men with influence in her hip pocket.
In exchange, she got a massive office and an administrative assistant and a microscopic to-do list.

The beautiful people, Kyra thought.

Chantel placed her briefcase on top of her immacu-
lately clean desk.

Kyra sat down in the small leather chair just across
and tried not to laugh.

"What?" Chantel asked.

"Girl, you and that briefcase. I mean, it ain't like you
work. What are you carrying around today?"

Chantel turned on her computer. When it booted up,
her Internet Explorer automatically connected to eBay.

"Fashion magazines. Gotta plan my next outfit."

The two of them burst into laughter and Kyra almost forgot why she came.

"Okay, what can you tell me about Race Jennings. He's the—"

"New guy. CFO. Word is the new subsidiary isn't doing as well as the bigwigs thought it would. It's pulling everything else in the toilet with it. So, they brought somebody in to save the Titanic before the iceberg takes us out."

"My girl!" Kyra said. When it came to corporate scoop and the office grapevine, Chantel knew it all. Everybody liked her and they knew she was the go-to person for information. In order to get information, you had to give some. And that's what kept her information network so strong and accurate.

"But you still haven't answered my question. How was the retreat? Or do I have to call Turk. I know he knows."

"You know what? Your brother is all the way off the hook. I mean his service is completely disconnected."

"Tell me something I don't know. He said he was at your place all afternoon yesterday. You didn't even bother to call me and tell me you got back."

"I know. I'm sorry. Every time I get another rejection letter, it brings me further and further down. I'm about to leave this poetry thing alone for good."

"What? Are you crazy? You're the best poet I know."

"I'm the only poet you know."

"That doesn't matter. Look, if it ain't about fashion or flaunting, I don't know much about it. But what I do know is every time I read one of your poems something inside me connects with the universe. It's spiritual, that stuff you write. You can't keep that to yourself. It would be unfair."

"No, it wouldn't. After all these years, I think it's the right thing to do."

Chantel was about so say something more, but Kyra cut her off. "But before I put down my pen for good, I have a farewell poem I want you to read."

Kyra handed over the poem she'd grabbed instead of the comment file.

Chantel took it and read it. When Kyra saw the tears form in her friend's eyes, she knew it was good. Chantel didn't have a literary background. Heck, the woman didn't even read for pleasure. But she had been Kyra's audience for the eighteen years of their friendship. Her feedback had been invaluable and right on the money every time. With Chantel's subtle suggestions, Kyra had crafted what she believed was some of her best work.

But maybe she and Chantel were the only ones who thought the work was good. Poets at the retreat seemed impressed. But what did that matter if she couldn't get published?

Chantel looked up. A single tear slid down her cheek. "You can't give this up, Ky. Not even for a minute."

But her friend's comment came too late. Kyra had already made up her mind. No more poetry.

Chapter 2

Kyra had hoped to miss the end of the office remodeling while she was away at the retreat. By the looks of things—unassembled cubicle parts, carpet remnants and the sounds of hammering and drilling—progress on the top floors of the thirty-story office building were slightly behind schedule.

A few more obstacle course maneuvers and Kyra arrived at the finance department.

"Hey, Leslie."

"Kyra, I haven't seen you in a while."

"I took a sabbatical," she replied.

Leslie sat behind a large open cubicle that was so neat and tidy, only the word *pristine* would accurately describe it. She offered Kyra a wry smile. "Two more years and I'll be eligible for that little perk. I've already decided I'm going to Europe."

"Europe sounds nice."

"So, where'd you go?"

"Flint Falls, Idaho. There's a writer's retreat there. I was there for the entire month."

"Cool!"

"Yeah, it was. Say, I'm looking for your new CFO."

"He should be in his office. Right around the corner, sweetie."

"Do I need an appointment or anything?"

"If you do, I'm sure he'll tell you."

As she walked, Kyra fanned herself at the image that had been in her head for over an hour. If she'd been a painter instead of a poet, she might have put the image on canvas and called it "Man and *Man*ificence." Because that had been a 100 percent, all-beef, real-deal, can-I-get-an-amen man standing in the john, and from what she could see of him—which was darn near everything—he was magnificent. That image was inspiring all kinds of poetry in her head. She could write for three days on his profile alone. Too bad she'd given it up.

And the way he said, "Are you coming?", that was another three days for sure of nonstop erotic poetry— each poem a different way to say yes.

See what happens, she thought to herself. You're gone for a month and the whole world changes—or at least the world of work.

Kyra chuckled and thought to herself, wouldn't it be funny if the man in the bathroom was this new guy Race...

"We meet again," he said.

Kyra thought she was hot a moment ago. But now

she understood what it meant to go up in smoke. Coming face-to-face with the man from the bathroom made her feel as though her clothes had just caught fire and melted off of her.

Be cool, she chanted. Getting canned for humping the new CFO would not be good.

She knew there was no way to regain her composure, so she faked it.

"I'm sorry to have walked in on you like that."

"You didn't look sorry," he said, wearing a serious expression that held the distinct undertone of a smile. He was poking fun at her.

Well she could poke right back. "And *you* didn't seem to mind."

First silence, then the room filled with their laughter. Their hearty chuckles sounded good together, blended like a raucous jazz song.

"I'm Race Jennings," he said, and stuck out his hand.

Kyra glanced down at his hand then up into his eyes. "Did you wash your hands?" she asked.

"I always wash my hands."

"Kyra Douglas," she said and shook his hand in response.

His grip was strong and confident. She liked the feel of it and could have held it for a few moments more.

"So, what can you tell me about this computer problem I've been having?" he asked.

He took his seat behind his desk and indicated that she take the seat across from him.

Chantel's office had nothing on this one. More like a hotel suite, Race's office came with rich mahogany wood paneling, mahogany furniture, a lush carpet and windows on two walls. The view of downtown Savannah, Georgia, went on for days.

"Not much," she admitted. "I just returned from sabbatical this morning and found a stack of trouble-tickets from you. I hope you know that's unacceptable. My team's customer service scores are the highest in the company and we want to keep it that way."

"All I need is a computer that works. Believe me, I'm tired of working from home and going to the training lab when I want to read e-mail."

"You can always come down to our area as well."

"What I want is my own computer. One that works here…in this office. I don't get why that's not possible. Is it the wall outlet? After four computers, I can't believe it's the PCs unless they've all come from the same defective batch."

Kyra's mind raced through a catalog of strange circumstances—examples she kept in her brain for times when computers stopped working for no apparent reason. Sometimes, it was a bad motherboard or a virus. Most of the time the error was between the keyboard and the chair—it was just a matter of figuring out what the person was doing wrong.

"And no, it is *not* operator error."

"Are you sure?" Kyra asked. This guy—with his thousand-dollar suit—looked like he could take the truth no matter what. Take it and appreciate it.

"Because all I do is turn it on in the mornings and turn it off before I leave."

"What about Web sites? Viruses? Do you download from the Web?"

"No."

"Do you drink coffee? Maybe you spilled something and it somehow got into the CPU."

"Yes, I drink coffee, but I didn't spill any."

Kyra glanced at her checklist. "What about—"

"Look, Kyra, three techies have already been in here asking all those questions. I didn't accidentally pull the plug out. I didn't install software. I didn't pick it up and drop it."

"All right—sorry," she said, all the while thinking how sexy he looked when he was mad.

"Look, I've got a brand-new computer for you," she continued. "Never been out of the box. I'm going to unpack it and plug it in in my office. I'll use it for two days, maybe three, just to make sure it's running properly. When I'm satisfied, I'll bring it and set it up myself. All right?"

"I guess I don't have a choice."

"In the meantime, you'll have to continue using the computers in the other areas."

He nodded. "Thank you," he said, finally.

Kyra got up. She wished she didn't have to leave. She wanted to talk. To spend more time in the presence of the man whose image was becoming permanently etched in her mind. But she couldn't think of a single reason to stay.

"I know this is late, but welcome to the company."

"Thanks," he said. The smile she'd seen earlier—the one hiding just beneath the serious mask—broke through and warmed the entire office.

"My extension is 7305 if you need to reach me for anything."

"Or we could skip the formality and meet in the men's room again," he teased.

"I'm sure that comment falls under the anti-harassment policy," Kyra said, trying without success to rein in her smile.

"It does?" he asked, all at once concerned.

"Not really, but I was trying to think of something clever to say and that's all that came to mind."

They laughed together again.

"Good to meet you, Kyra."

"You, too, Race."

She turned and headed back toward the elevators.

"Two days," she heard him say behind her.

"Two days," she answered without turning. She hoped to God she could wait two days without striding into his office and ripping his clothes off. Since their run-in earlier that morning, she'd had the nearly uncontrolled urge to do so and now—now that she'd spent time in the man's presence—she got the distinct impression that he felt the same about her.

In two days, when she would be forced to keep her promise and set up his computer herself, she only hoped that her arms and hands would obey and not grope his body the way they wanted to.

I can behave myself. I can behave myself, she told herself. But that was only partially true. Race had an overpowering animal attraction. It was almost paralyzing. If he had said, "Strip, right now," she would have done it. No problem.

God give me strength, she thought, and got on to the elevator. Even a cold shower wouldn't have cooled her lust. Maybe a deep plunge in a cold swimming pool. Maybe an ice bath.

She shook her head, grateful to be the only one on

the elevator. As it descended, Kyra was overcome by the truth. The only thing that would free her from the grip of the most intense sense of lust she'd ever felt, was a morning, afternoon and evening in the arms of that man, riding him until she rode the lust out of her soul, until she was wrung out and couldn't move.

Kyra stepped off the elevator lost in thought and sweating lightly. A nagging suspicion in the back of her mind told her that what she'd imagined as the satiation of the lust, might backfire and be the beginning of an even stronger desire for more.

Where would she be then, she wondered.

She entered her cubicle and sat down at her desk. Quickly she logged her conversation with Race and her plan to test the new computer.

And then in her mind she logged her visions of them making wild love and noted her plan to make her visions real.

What was that? Race Jennings wondered as he turned his chair around. Behind his desk was the most spectacular view of the city. He stared over the tops of buildings and out into the countryside. The summer's rays and temperature had turned the grass and tree leaves green-green.

Could the summer also affect his libido? he wondered.

At first, when he'd seen the woman staring at him in the men's room, he'd wondered what her problem was. Then he'd had to wonder what his problem was. The longer she stood there, the more he wanted to go over, push her against the wall, yank her Dockers down and enter her fast and hard.

He hadn't been able to get that crazy thought out of his head until she walked into his office. Then all he wanted to do was shove all the items off of his desk and onto the floor. Then pull her down and...and...

Shut it down! he admonished himself. You get yourself all worked up and then you'll be—he glanced down where the area below his abdomen tightened with need—all worked up.

Concentrate, he told himself.

He took one more look at the landscape in the distance, and turned his chair back around to his desk.

His computer was coming in two days. Then he could get some things done around here.

He picked up a legal-sized notepad and made a list of the week's priorities.

> Meet with department heads.
> Send out re-accounting memo.
> Schedule next week's staff meeting.
> Plunge into Kyra's slick, wet—

Damn! he thought and slammed the pen down. He had to get up. Move around. Get the blood flowing someplace else besides his groin area.

He couldn't believe his reaction to that woman. He'd just met her and yet his reaction to her was chemical, like they had just stepped into a kind of physiological, organic, biological aphrodisiac. He didn't have that kind of reaction to Chantel and he had a date with her tonight, their second in as many days. She'd agreed to go to dinner with him last night. His suggestion. Then afterward, he'd agreed to go to the club. Her suggestion.

He'd noticed Chantel on his first day at ComTel. She stood out among the ultraconservative suit-wearing women at the company. She dressed as if she'd been styled by a fashion designer. Avant-garde. Nuevo funk. Runway soul. And she walked it well. The woman definitely had a presence about her. Race couldn't help but cast his net just to see what he'd catch. To his surprise, she stepped right in and accepted his dinner offer. In his mind, he was biding his time to the bedroom. Then after that, who knew? Maybe a relationship. Maybe. It depended on how he felt about the sex.

But this thing that happened with Kyra knocked him straight over. Bam! And he was certain she could feel it, too. It was as if she couldn't get out of his office fast enough. Otherwise she might start stripping right then and there, and God help him, he would have let her. They would have both been fired, but who cared about a job when you had that kind of chemistry going on?

Okay, that's it, he told himself. He was now thinking crazy. He'd just gotten this job. The type of position he'd planned on for some years now. He wasn't about to blow it on a ridiculous physical attraction.

He decided to remind himself about the date he'd been looking forward to until thirty minutes ago.

Summoning his composure, he headed straight for Chantel's office. He could say he stopped by to confirm their date. It would get his mind off of fantasy and on to something more realistic.

But as he walked to Chantel's office, he wished to heaven on high he'd met Kyra first.

"She in?" Race asked Chantel's assistant.

"Yes," she said.

"Thanks," he responded and poked his head into her office.

"Hey," he said.

Chantel looked up from her computer and smiled. Whenever she was in her office, which was most of the time from what he could tell, she was always engrossed in something on her computer. Once or twice, he'd wondered what it was.

"Hey, you," she said back. "Have a seat."

He sat down across from her and felt some of the intensity of the past few moments fade.

She was upscale chic and so was her office, with flower arrangements, an abstract collage and a delicate Fabergé egg on her desk.

"I don't mean to interrupt, I just wanted to confirm tonight."

"Yeah," she said, smiling. She had a million-dollar smile. Capped teeth. Lipstick that probably cost half a day's pay. Hours in front of a mirror to get the correct balance of "I like you; I want you; I'm beautiful" in the lips.

He had to admit, he was a lips man. Chantel had designer lips. Kyra, on the other hand, had natural woman, brown pillow lips. The kind of lips he could kiss all day.

Two hours ago, he thought Chantel was one of the sexiest women he'd ever met and now, she was barely on the radar. His scope was occupied with Kyra Douglas.

"Where'd you go?"

"Nowhere," he lied. Actually, he'd gone all over Kyra's body and back again in about three seconds.

"You sure, because you look—"

Chantel's phone rang and he was grateful. He didn't want to talk about what was on his mind. That's exactly what he'd come here to push aside.

His eyes cast a downward glance. He was almost ashamed of his thoughts. Almost.

When the poem on her desk caught his eye, he nearly forgot all about his recent ruminations. The poem didn't look like anything she'd photocopied out of a book. It looked handwritten. It was upside down, but if he read the date correctly, he was sure it was dated yesterday.

Could it be that this corporate vixen was also a poet. His heart stirred at the thought. There was a time he found poems and the women who wrote them the most sensual things on the planet.

"Yes," Chantel said. "I'll e-mail you a copy of last year's budget. I'll do it right now," she said.

When she hung up the phone, he was already on his feet. "I've got a meeting in about twenty minutes, but I'll pick you up at eight."

"How about nine? You know the party doesn't get started until late."

"Nine o'clock it is," he said, feeling the eagerness for a distraction creep in and excite him. And there arose an eagerness for something else as well.

"Did you write that?" he asked, pausing at her door.

"What?" she responded.

"The poem. I noticed it on your desk."

"You like poetry?" she asked him.

"Very much. I haven't had much time for it recently, but back in the day, I was a poetry junky. I belonged to a theater and to a writer's workshop. I always thought my poetry was passable. Every blue moon, I can come up with a good piece. There's nothing like a good poem to put life in balance."

"Yeah," she said. "I know what you mean."

"May I?" he asked, indicating the poem on Chantel's desk.

"Uh, sure," she said. There was hesitation in her eyes. He understood it. Letting someone read your poetry can be like standing in a public place naked. The fact that she would do it meant that he'd earned a level of trust with her.

He read the poem. It was about forced goodbyes and painful regrets. It was good. Real good.

"I'm impressed," he said, handing her back the paper. "Are you published?"

"No," she said, looking sheepish.

"Well you should be. I've never read a poem like that by someone who wasn't."

"Really?" she asked.

"Seriously." He headed back toward the door. "Bring some poems with you tonight. I'd love to read more of your work."

"I will," she said.

At least that's what it sounded like she said. Her voice sounded a little shaky. Maybe she wasn't ready to share herself that way. If so, he would understand. He would leave the decision to her.

He left without another word. He felt much better. He would go back to his office and prepare for his meeting. He would attend that meeting with his lust in check. After all, he had better things to think about now: his date and the fact that Chantel was a poet who writes wonderful poetry. He was looking forward to reading more.

Race pressed the call button for the elevator thinking that today had been a strange twist of resolve and that his reaction to Kyra was a fluke—the result of too much time as a single man and not enough time recently in the arms of a woman.

Well, he was about to put all of that behind him and do what he could to make sure he didn't lose his composure around Kyra Douglas ever again.

Chapter 3

Kyra walked out of her shoes as soon as she got in the door, strode directly to her Sharper Image stereo and turned on Miles Davis. She needed some good trumpet tonight. Kyra always kept *Kind of Blue* in her five-disc upright changer for times when she felt out of sorts. And she definitely felt out of sorts this evening.

She always felt this way right after having mind-blowing sex—which, if she were honest, she'd only had twice in her entire life. Once with a man she was so madly in love with, she couldn't see straight, and the other time with a guy who had plowed so much wine into her she couldn't walk straight.

Both times she'd been reeling from the experience as if she'd just discovered what her body was designed for. Each time, the experience left her feeling confused and frightened. She knew how easy it would be for her to become addicted, or at least accustomed, to a feeling like that. She also knew that she didn't want to experience that kind of lavish fulfillment with someone who didn't love her. Someone who couldn't be committed to her. Because that is what she would become, if she allowed to herself to be propelled to the furthermost edges of bliss. She would become attached and expectant.

It's almost what happened in her last relationship. Turk. She had fallen for the guy, hard. So hard that she hadn't realized that she was the only committed one between them. When they found that they wanted two different things, they'd agreed to go their separate ways.

Only it hadn't been that simple. They'd ended their romantic relationship, and a full and wonderful friendship had blossomed in its place.

Miles's trumpet took up her emotions like a painter taking acrylic cobalt on his brush. His canvas was her soul and he painted rainy afternoons in New York, long solemn walks over bridges, dark and smoky club nights. And she loved it.

She hadn't even turned on the television or any lights. She just let the mood of the song wash over her. A perfect way to unwind before she went to bed after a successful night of teaching. If it weren't for the message light blinking on her phone, everything around her would be calm and serene.

Kyra grunted with exertion as she got up to check her messages.

Too tired to even hold the phone, she pressed the speakerphone button and dialed the numbers to her voice messaging system. She had three messages, all from Chantel. All the same.

Kyra I need some of your poetry. Call me as soon as possible.

Kyra glanced at the clock. It was already nine thirty. In her book, that was late. Nine o'clock was her usual bedtime. That way she could get up at 5:00 a.m. and have a full eight hours of sleep.

As Miles played with cool dexterity, Kyra's mind cleared and all she wanted was sleep. Her first day back from sabbatical had been full. First she arrives to a stack of trouble-tickets from the new guy. Then she sees the new guy in the men's room—manhood in hand. Then she finds that the guy in the bathroom *is* the new guy. And not only that, but there is the strongest sexual attraction to him that she'd ever had before. She finishes work, only to visit her grandmother, read an hour's worth of poetry and then off to teach an Internet class.

She tracked off to her bedroom unbuttoning her blouse as she went. Surely what Chantel wanted could wait. Certainly, the world as she knew it would not come to an end within the next twenty-four hours.

As Miles Davis's golden trumpet played on from her living room, Kyra fell back against her queen-sized bed. It was 3:00 a.m. before she awoke and realized that she had fallen asleep fully clothed.

The next morning, when Kyra arrived in the office there was a big note left in her chair.

I need to talk to you. ASAP!
Chantel

A ribbon of shock twisted through her when she realized that the note was handwritten. That meant that late-sleeper Chantel had actually beaten her there.

Something must be terribly wrong.

Kyra placed her briefcase on the floor beside her chair and dashed off to see what could have brought her friend to work and caused her to write such a cryptic note.

When she walked into Chantel's office, she was struck by how "unassembled" she looked. With a plain label crème suit, she looked barely put together.

Chantel looked up. "I don't know how you get here so early. I feel like I'm still asleep and just pretending to be awake."

"You look like it, too, sister friend. Now, what's up?"

Kyra was too antsy to sit. Chantel's note and the fact that she was here so early in the morning had unnerved her.

"Don't you answer your messages? I called you all evening."

"Sorry. I turned my cell phone off when I went to my grandmother's, and by the time I got home from the Silver Foxx Club, I was too tired to do anything except fall into bed, which I actually did. Now, stop stalling and tell me what's up."

"Okay. Sit down first."

"Chantel!" Kyra said in protest, but took a seat anyway.

"I know we're long friends and tell each other everything, but there's something that I haven't told you."

"Okay…"

"I'm seeing someone," Chantel said, barely looking her friend in the eye.

Kyra's stomach dropped as if she were on an amusement-park thrill ride. "What?" she said.

"I know, see, that reaction is why I didn't tell you."

"Chantel, you just broke up with Nick, what, three weeks ago?"

"Two. But that's not important."

"It *is* important. You were so torn up behind him, I had to get a mop and bucket to keep the floors dry from your tears. You do this every time—jump from one man to another. And I can't believe we are having this conversation again and at work. But since you took it there, I told you *two* weeks ago, I would not go through this another time with you."

Kyra folded her arms in disgust. She cared for Chantel, but her heart, her heart she could choke. "That's it, Chantel. If you need me to clean up the mess this time, I'm not available. Get one of your Prada friends to help you. I'm tapped out."

Kyra and Chantel had a long-standing disagreement that Chantel had friends who helped her shop but never helped her pick up the pieces of her broken life after she got used up by all the men with whom she seemed to get involved. Chantel claimed it wasn't true, but Kyra knew better.

She loved Chantel, really loved her like a sister. She wanted to see Chantel happy and content. After everything she'd been through, she deserved as much. But if she didn't quit hooking up with the wrong guys...

"So I told him I wrote the poems," she said.

The word *poems* coaxed Kyra from her thoughts. "What about poems?"

"He thinks I wrote them."

"Who?"

"Race."

Even the man's name sent strong sexual ripples through her.

"Race Jennings?" she asked and thought, damn, it feels even better when I say his name.

"Yes! That's why I had to catch you first thing this morning, in case you ran into him or something. I mean, maybe you could even put in a good word for me or something. You know, tell him what a good poet I am."

Slowly the gears in Chantel's story clinked into place in Kyra's mind.

"Chantel, what happened to the poetry I left on your desk yesterday?"

Chantel looked as though that question just reduced her to an eight-year-old girl pleading for the return of her favorite toy that had been taken away because she'd been bad.

"I just told you. Race took it. And guess what, Kyra, he really likes it. It was all he could talk about on our date last night. He—"

"Date!" The blood in Kyra's veins turned to ice and then shattered.

"See, there you go again. I know you think I'm making a mistake going out this soon after Nick, but Race is different. And the only mistake I've made so far is not telling him that someone else wrote the poetry. So in a sense, I didn't lie. The only mistake would be if I had to go back and tell him the truth now."

"Hold it, Chantel. I thought you stopped seeing Nick."

"I did. I mean, he comes over sometimes for a quickie, but let's get back to Race."

Chantel clasped her hands together as if she were begging. It was disturbing.

"Please, please, Ky. I really like this man. In the month you were gone, we had time to get to know each other and—"

"Chantel! This is how it always starts. Some *small* lie and then when the guy finds out, it blows up in your face."

"But this time, it won't be a lie. You can teach me how to write poetry. Hell, I'll take a class. Plus, I've been reading your stuff for all these years now, I must have learned something."

No, Chantel, after all these years, you haven't learned anything at all.

Inside her head, Kyra beat herself up for helping Chantel for far too long. Well, she wasn't about to do it again.

"No," Kyra said.

Chantel fell silent. That was a good thing, because if she'd said another word, Kyra would have told her their friendship was in jeopardy.

Without another word, Kyra got up and left her friend's office. She headed to the elevator hoping that she and Chantel would never have a discussion like that again.

"Is he in?" Kyra asked Leslie.

"Yes," the woman said, not missing a stroke in what Kyra guessed was her eighty-words-per-minute keyboard stride.

"He's on the phone, though," she said. The woman didn't look up, didn't blink. She simply kept her head down and kept typing.

Race must have something big going on that his admin felt she had to be antisocial, Kyra thought.

"Thanks," Kyra said, deciding to take her chances and poke her head into his office. If he waved her off, she would wait outside.

He didn't wave her off. Instead, he motioned for her to come in and take a seat. She did so, but not before closing the door behind her.

The moment she found herself in a closed room with Race, her pulse quickened. Today he wore a charcoal gray suit. Obviously designer. Is it possible, she wondered as she shifted in the seat, that he could look even sexier than yesterday?

When he glanced up at her and held her gaze for several hot seconds, she had her answer. He definitely could.

Kyra wrung her hands in her lap. She didn't want to appear nervous, and the fact was she wasn't. She was just so, so—

"Thanks for waiting. I don't know how your department is adjusting to the new project planning process, but my area isn't adjusting well at all. Frustrating," he said.

He'd turned his head away, as if he were hesitant to look at her. But slowly, his gaze claimed hers and they sat in a silence so charged with sexuality that if it went on for much longer, she was sure it would give off its own musky aroma.

"So," he said, finally breaking the silence between them. "I'd ask you if you were here about my computer, but I don't think it would take a closed door for that."

"No. And so far so good, by the way. The computer's been running fine for a full day now. Just one more to go."

He nodded, steepled his fingers and leaned in. "So then, how can I help you?"

You can start with undoing that tie, and then—

"I'm here about Chantel Mosley."

Kyra watched as his eyebrows arched with concern and his jaw clenched as if he'd just stopped chewing a large piece of gum.

"What about her?"

"She and I are close."

"Close?" he repeated and sat back in his chair.

Kyra took a deep breath. "Best friends."

Race groaned with displeasure. He got up from his desk and strode to the large window behind his chair.

It was crazy, but Kyra felt compelled to walk up behind him, push herself against that fine backside of his, wrap her arms around his waist and console him.

When he finally turned around, some of the milk-chocolate color had drained from his face.

She thought about it for a moment then decided that if she kept thinking about it, she would never say what was on her mind. But first things first.

"When I was here in your office yesterday, did something happen?"

"Yeah," he said, keeping his distance.

"You…you…felt…"

"Like I had two options while you were here: take you or die."

He kept his distance and did everything except shove his hands into his pockets. They were treading on dangerous ground now. Either one of them could accuse the other of harassment. And since they were in a closed room together…

"I think I'll open the door," Race said.

Kyra released the breath she'd been holding. "That's a good idea."

When he came back to his desk and sat down across from her, Kyra allowed herself to feel relieved, but just for a moment. In her mind, there were still more questions than answers.

She leaned in and lowered her voice. "Okay, so, what was that yesterday?"

Race leaned forward himself. "I don't know, but I've been taught not to question a gift horse."

"I thought I was going crazy."

"I think it's safe to say we both went a little nuts."

"Speak for yourself!" she said, trying to keep her words quiet but her offense obvious. "I didn't say a thing about how I was feeling."

"You didn't have to."

"What does that mean?"

He leaned in closer. Kyra could see the dark shadow of a beard on his chin. Sexy. Sexy. And the way he smelled just showered, like a manly soap. Woo!

"It means that you were glowing like a candle."

"Oh, and you weren't? Even now, you look like you could pull me up on this desk and—"

"Mr. Jennings," Leslie said, interrupting.

"Yes," he answered, sitting back in his chair and adjusting his suit jacket.

"I've finished the planning reports," she said.

"Thank you," he said. "Please leave them in my inbox."

She did as he asked and made a quick exit. Or did Kyra just think it was quick because she felt guilty?

"Wow, that was close," she said.

"I'll say. Look, Kyra, I don't think this is the place to discuss our *feelings*. Do you?"

"Actually, I didn't come here to talk about that. It just…came up."

Race's eyebrow rose with amusement. Kyra decided she would have to watch her words around him forever.

"I came to find out what your intentions are toward my friend."

His eyes narrowed. "I see. Well, that depends on what your intentions are toward me."

"Do you ever say anything flat-out or do you like speaking in circles?"

"What I *like* is your friend."

Race's honesty sliced through Kyra like Ginsu knives. What had she expected him to say? "After a month of seeing Chantel and one hour spent with you, I choose you over her." Of course he would choose Chantel. After all, what was coursing between them was plain old-fashioned lust. Dirty, funky, sweaty lust.

"Kyra?"

"I care about Chantel and I don't want her to be hurt. So I came here to say that if you're not serious about her, don't string her along. She doesn't need that. No one does."

"What are you? Her guardian angel?"

Kyra stood up. "Yes. I am. And she's mine, too. So, now that you know why this is my business, I need to know what your intentions are. Are you serious or is this just some lust thing with her, too?"

He didn't respond at first. Only gazed at her with eyes that burned her flesh from head to toe.

Hmmm. Spontaneous human combustion. It's not a myth, she thought. Because if he continues to look at me like that, I'm just going to ignite and blow up into a thousand flaming and incredibly horny pieces.

"Believe me, my interest in her, and what I feel right here right now for you, are two vastly different things."

"So, it's not just lust."

"It's not just lust," he said.

His eyes remained steady on hers as he answered. They never wavered.

And she believed him.

Now, if she could believe the lie she had just that second started telling herself. She didn't care if this man dated her best friend. It was only lust she felt for him anyway. And if he were as honorable as he said he was, then it wouldn't hurt her to give up three stinky little poems. She had at least one hundred others. Good ones. Poems she could claim at any time.

She would give Chantel those three. If Mr. Race Jennings really liked poetry, maybe she would share some of hers and tell him that both she and Chantel were poets. There would be no harm in that, would there?

Kyra left Race's office with the sinking suspicion that it might not be that easy.

It didn't take long for her to find out that her suspicions were correct. It wouldn't be easy at all.

Chapter 4

Kyra stared at her friend and had to mentally restrain her hand, because she surely wanted to slap her silly.

This was a strange end to a weird day. But when she thought of it, the part of her day that hadn't involved either Chantel or Race had progressed just fine. No viruses in the system. No security breaches. No one using the company Internet system to access forbidden sites.

And now this.

"What happened to the world while I was away? Did everyone lose their minds?"

"No," Chantel said. "Just me. But in a good way."

"Chantel, I'm not going to write poetry *for* you. Write your own like everybody else does."

"Kyra, you know I'm only good at three things: cooking, looking fabulous and sexing men. After that, forget it."

"Well, until today, you were good at being my friend."

"And you are so good at being mine. You're always there for me. You always come through for me."

"I don't understand how this is going to help you."

"Race loves my poetry—I mean, your poetry. Our poetry? If I can put a poem under his nose every now and then, you know, like *bam*, then you know, it will help to keep him interested. And by the time he falls in love with me, he won't care if I wrote the poems or not."

Kyra thought about that for a moment. Race didn't seem like the kind of man who would easily forgive deceit like that. As a matter of fact, she was sure that if he found out that Chantel had been deceiving him, he would probably break all ties with both of them. The way he demanded excellence in his equipment, she could only imagine what he demanded out of his relationships with people.

But maybe that was the key. Maybe what Chantel needed was a clear reminder that her manipulations wouldn't work and that if she wanted a relationship with a man, it had to come from what's inside *her*.

Tough love, Kyra thought. Sometimes you have to allow people to burn themselves instead of straining your own voice warning them about the fire.

"All right," Kyra said. "I'll be your ghostwriter."

Chantel breathed a huge sigh of relief and held her head in her hands.

"But you owe me, big!"

"Don't worry. I'll pay up," she said.

You bet you will, Kyra thought. When she admits to Race that she hasn't written these poems and he pushes her away, she would get Chantel to agree to sign off of men for at least six months and do some soul-searching.

Chantel needed to find herself, her whole self, not the person she is when she's with someone to make her feel complete.

"If you're leaving, I'll walk out with you."

Kyra left ComTel with Chantel, amazed at how her life had changed in less than twenty-four hours. She had admitted her lust and signed on to be a stand-in poet.

As they headed to the garage, Chantel said, "We may have invented a new profession."

"What's that?"

"Poet double. You know like body double and stunt double, only with poetry?"

"I get it."

"What do you think?"

"I think we're both crazy," Kyra admitted.

"But still friends, right?"

No matter how good her friend looked—today Chantel wore a beautiful warm orange short-sleeve blouse with coordinating tapered pants... Donna Karan all the way—beneath the flawless makeup and million-dollar wardrobe was a sensitive heart.

The closer Kyra got to her car and the more she thought about it, the more she decided it might not be as bad as she'd originally envisioned. Sharing her poetry with Race would be a way of sharing herself. So, if they weren't going to do it physically, maybe she could give him a taste of herself spiritually.

"See you tomorrow," Chantel said. "And, Kyra—?"

"Yes?"

"Thank you."

"You're welcome," she said and actually meant it.

She would help her friend get the tough love that she needed and give a little piece of herself to Race in the process. Maybe this "poetry double" stuff wasn't such a bad idea.

Kyra got into her sedan thinking that she couldn't wait to get started, and she knew the exact kind of poems to write for Chantel.

The inside of Jean Louise was just as elegant as Race remembered. He hadn't been in the restaurant in years, and when he was coming here on the regular, he was a man on a mission. A mission to impress as many women as he could.

He and his oldest friend, Brax, had spent their entire undergraduate and graduate years studying and romancing. They weren't able to balance the two well. There was always much more romancing than studying, but somehow they had both managed to graduate.

Race came out with a masters in finance accounting and Brax came out an MBA. Race made a beeline to corporate America and Brax had hit the road.

Race always thought that song "Papa Was a Rollin' Stone" should have been called "Brax is a Rollin' Stone," because that's what he was. He'd spent all of those years in college only to follow his passion for road-tripping and his need to never let grass grow under his feet, and had become a truck driver. While Race had argued with him to start his own trucking company and make some real money, Brax argued back that that's not where his heart was. His heart was behind the wheel. And his MBA allowed him to operate as an indepen-

dent contractor. He'd been doing that successfully for
fifteen years.

Race poured himself another glass of wine and
thought that they both had done well for themselves.
And no matter how many miles Brax traveled, he and
Race were as close as ever. Race only wished that Brax
were in town now. He could use reinforcements.
Someone who could give him a clear perspective on the
situation at work. Or more importantly, the situation
wreaking havoc in his loins every time he even thought
about Kyra Douglas.

"Sorry I'm late," a woman's sultry voice said. "Traffic."

Race turned around on the bar stool to see Torrena
Kellog-McBride slide into the seat beside him.

She smelled good. And she looked good, too.

"Hey, sweetie," she said, then leaned over to kiss his
cheek.

"You look good," he said, then kissed her on the
forehead.

"Don't I always?"

"No, there was that time right after—"

"Never mind!" she said.

Race took the glass that was waiting for her and
poured her some of their favorite wine.

She swirled the liquid around in the glass, inhaled the
aroma, took a sip and waited. He knew she was waiting
for him to say something. But he had no idea how to
describe the day he had or the dilemma in his life. So
he just sat and soaked up the pleasure of her company.

"Why'd you pick this place? We haven't been here
in years."

"I know. I just needed something familiar."

"You mean something old and comfortable."

"Like you?" he joked.

Torrena held on to her glass and stared straight ahead. "I'm going to pretend like you didn't say that. Now, you wanna tell me what's going on? I left Jeff at home to finish dinner."

"Call the fire department," Race teased.

"O-*kay*!" she said.

"How is Brodie?

"Fine. Recovering from a severe sunburn, but other than that fine."

"I sure hope your children get enough of your melanin to give them some natural sunscreen."

"Me, too, sweetie."

Torrena's husband was full-blooded Irish and as pale as Race had ever seen. The man could burn on a cloudy day.

"So, is it your new job?"

"No. Get serious. I'm the best thing that's happened to that company in a decade. I'm going to save them millions."

"All-*righty* then. That means two things. A, you are still as arrogant as ever. And B, it's a woman."

"How about C—two women?" he said and drained his glass.

Torrena whistled and everyone in the bar turned to look at her for a second. "Two? You've always liked a lot of women, but you usually take them one at a time. These ladies must be something."

"One of them is something. The other is something *else*."

Torrena helped herself to the rest of the wine in the bottle. "I'm going to need another drink and all the details."

Race wasted no more time and filled her in on everything.

"In my younger days, I would have said, 'Be honest, up-front and juggle.' But unless they're in their early twenties, they're too old for juggling. What they want is real and a ring."

This time Race whistled.

"Of course, I'm just making assumptions here, but when women get my age, we've already done the dating/partying/boyfriend thing. We want a man. A man we can stand still with."

"That's why I wanted to come here. Lately, I've been wondering whatever happened to the good old days."

"They settled down," she said.

Well, Race sure hadn't. And he didn't think he would ever want to. He'd always imagined himself as one of those old men people point at and talk about. "Look at that old geezer. He's got a revolving door of women at his place." Whereas Brax never let the grass grow under his own feet, Race had never let the grass grow under any woman's feet.

"So what are you going to do?"

"I don't know. But what I do know is everything would be fine if my brain didn't go into sexual overload whenever I'm within fifteen feet of Kyra. She's like a sensual power plant and when she's near, she lights me up something fierce."

"Wow. But not more than me, right?"

Race laughed and blew out a hot breath before he

could think better of it. Then it was too late, so he just let it all out.

"Woo! Torrena. I'm telling you. This woman, I mean. Good God!"

Torrena's smirk of disapproval was unmistakable. "Really?"

"I can't even *explain* it to you."

She studied him carefully and then said, "Are you sweating?"

He nodded. "And that's not all."

Torrena glanced down at him. Her eyes traveled beside her and beneath their table.

"All-*righty*, then," she said and looked away. "See…that's just way too much information."

"I need help," he said honestly. He had to free himself from this woman whom he barely knew. The one who'd taken his drive into the stratosphere and he hadn't even been inside her.

And then he heard his mind say something that made him groan.

Yet.

"Well, I guess it had to happen sometime."

Race nodded but didn't say anything. He didn't have to. They both knew the deal. Torrena was the one that got away. She was the one who would have made him settle down and forget his penchant for looking at women. But they had been too much alike. She was looking for diversity in men when they were together and so their timing had been off. Way off.

But the part that knocked him over every time he thought about it was right after they had ended their re-lationship, she had started one with Jeff and just like that, they were engaged and then married. It had taken him years to come to terms with the fact that he just wasn't the one.

He'd had many relationships since then, but Torrena still held a special place in his heart. He believed she always would. No one could replace her.

"This is different, T. This is just animalistic, carnal, insane, don't make no damn sense, I don't know you from Wilda on the wall, but I've got to have you right now!"

"Then you just have a decision to make. Either you're going to pursue it and be a dog to Chantel by banging her best friend or you're going to ignore it."

He finished off the last of the second bottle. "People think I'm a dog anyway."

"Yes, but up until now, you haven't been."

"So what are you saying?"

"I'm saying make up your own mind."

"But you definitely have an opinion."

"Yes."

"Well, that's what I invited you here to get."

"Forget about the lust."

"Stay with Chantel?"

"Yes. Of course the honorable thing would be to leave both of them alone."

"Is this your jealousy talking?"

"Yes."

"Umm. Nice to know you still think that way about me sometimes."

"When it comes to you, I'll always be possessive. But I love you, so I want what's best for you. If you think Chantel will make you happy, go for it."

Race nodded. He was sweating again. Another flash

of Kyra, naked on his bed, blazed up in his mind. Pursuing Chantel he could do. He'd planned to do that anyway. But ignoring the Kyra effect, that was completely different. It would take willpower that he wasn't sure he had.

Yet, his mind asked again. *Why did they have to be friends?*

Chapter 5

Her two days were up.

Kyra rolled the mouse and clicked the button, and typed across the keyboard as if she were angry with the computer. She opened Microsoft Word, created a short memo, then closed the software program. She opened the company's e-mail system, sent an e-mail and closed the program. She played Free Cell, played a music CD and calculated her bills for the week. Everything on this new computer worked perfectly.

She shut down the machine and placed the tower on a cart to transport to Race's office. Sam Rubio, her manager, had been on her case both days, popping into her office to remind her of how important it was to get the new CFO a computer that worked properly. He sounded as though he were blaming her team, but the truth was Sam had been in management for so long, he'd forgotten that most computer problems were trace-able to operator error. And as soon as the person says, "I don't know what happened," that's a sure sign that they know exactly what happened. They just don't want to admit that they clicked on something they shouldn't have and now their computer won't work.

Kyra believed that instead of being cooped up in her office running prediagnostics on a brand-new computer, she should be in Race's office working with him to recreate what he did that made each of his four new computers go kaput.

She sighed. Technical observation. "T.O." she'd called it in a proposal she'd written and given to her boss. She believed that if technicians spent at least one third of their time observing how their in-house customers used their computers, they'd know a lot more about what kind of software to buy, how to educate customers so that they didn't have the problems they often encountered and how to prevent problems before they started. The projections on her proposal would save the company hundreds of thousands of dollars in time and money.

But her proposal was rejected. Sam worked his way up to management so that he could get away from having to interact with customers so closely. And it was obvious, he didn't want to do anything that might in any way change that.

"Knock, knock."

Kyra heard the voice, but didn't like it. It was Chantel. She was probably coming around to find out where her poems were. The truth was, she hadn't written any. Deep down inside, the idea of fronting poetry for Chantel didn't sit right with her. And to come up with something, under pressure, within twenty-four hours, wasn't the way she typically wrote poetry. The other truth was, her mind had been so preoccupied with thoughts and images of she and Race, all she could do was be still and let them wash over her in hot waves.

Kyra looked at the clock on her credenza. Two fifteen. Chantel had waited all morning and most of the afternoon before coming to find out where her poems were. For a woman who has the patience of a jackhammer, that was commendable.

"Hey, Chantel," Kyra said, turning around.

Chantel stood at the corner of Kyra's cube dressed in red Dior.

"I just stopped by to pick up a poem. Or two?"

Kyra gathered the computer cords together and placed them on the cart next to the tower.

"I didn't write any poetry, Chantel."

"What? Why? You said you would help me." Chantel's voice sounded as if there were tears in it. Kyra hated when she sounded like that. She was a pushover for crying folks.

"I just didn't feel the inspiration last night." At least, not for poetry. My body was inspired to do something altogether different, Kyra thought.

"Ky, I can't wait for inspiration to strike. I need the poetry now—today. Race and I plan on going to Forsyth Park this evening for a picnic. The highlight of the picnic is the poem I promised him."

"Well, you'll just have to unpromise," Kyra said, making sure she had the owner's manual on the cart.

"Are you reneging?" Chantel asked.

Now, instead of sounding sad, her voice was cross, accusatory. And rightly so. Kyra was reneging on her agreement. She couldn't get inspired about writing poetry so that her best friend could get in good with the man Kyra herself wanted to strip naked and ride wild.

"Maybe," Kyra said.

"Ky!"

"Look, Chantel, I'm sorry. I don't have time to discuss this. I have to install a computer. Afterward, I'll come to your office, explain things." Kyra pushed the cart toward the door. "I promise."

"Your promises don't hold much weight with me right now."

"I know," Kyra said.

The two friends looked at each other for a long moment. Kyra wondered if Chantel could see Race in her eyes, the fire he'd stirred inside her, and her jealousy that he'd chosen someone else. Maybe she wouldn't have to have a conversation after all. Just give Chantel a few minutes to look into her eyes and right into her soul. Because that's where the truth was. That's where Race was. Waiting. Simmering. Burning.

Kyra hadn't been the same since she'd walked in on him in the men's room. Something about Race flipped on a switch inside her and released a heat that could make her sweat in a blizzard. Sadly, she realized something else.

Chantel deserved to know the truth.

"I have a three o'clock, but I'm free after four," Chantel said.

Kyra nodded. "Sounds good. See you at four."

Kyra headed off to Race's office. Chantel didn't accompany her to the elevators or follow behind her. Kyra imagined that she was still standing at her cubicle, wondering what in the heck they were going to discuss at four. Or maybe she had seen everything there was to tell in Kyra's eyes and knew exactly what she was going to say.

In either case, Kyra dreaded the conversation, but knew it was inevitable.

"Okay, try creating a spreadsheet," Kyra said.

Race rolled his chair closer to his desk and clicked away until he'd created a small table. Then he turned around and slid her a sly glance.

"Satisfied?" he asked.

Kyra said yes, but felt no. How could any woman be satisfied to be in a room with Race Jennings unless he was inside her?

"Well, *I'm* not. The computer always works when you techies come in to install it. But a few hours after you leave, the computer conks out. Completely. By this time tomorrow, this computer won't work."

"Just so you know, I ran every diagnostic known to man on this machine. It's working perfectly."

"Well, then you need to stick around for the rest of today, come back here first thing tomorrow and stay until the end of the day. Somebody needs to see everything that happens so that you know the problem is *not between the keyboard and the chair*."

Kyra's eyebrow rose.

"I have friends who are techies, so I know how you all think."

Kyra laughed. Sexy *and* a sense of humor. It was getting harder and harder to keep her clothes on by the minute.

"As I was saying, if you're right here, you'll see the computer go out and if you see it go out, it will give you a better idea of how to correct the problem so that it doesn't happen again."

When Race finished his sentence, he got up from his seat and walked to the window. He'd been doing that since she rolled the cart into his office. And if he wasn't moving away from her, she was moving away from him. The longer they stayed close to each other, the less willpower they seemed to have. Five minutes seemed to be all they could tolerate. After that, it was move away or be humped.

Chapter 6

Think about something constructive, besides ripping this man's clothes off, she ordered herself.

"It's funny you mentioned staying here and watching you work. Eight months ago I turned in a proposal to my boss recommending something similar to that."

"Really?"

"Yes," she said, heading to the other side of the room. When they were as far away from each other as they could get, she continued.

"I think us techies, as you call us, should spend one third of our time 'in the field' studying how our customers use the technology we provide and maintain for them. I had some financial-savings projections that you bean counters would love."

He arched an eyebrow. "Touché," he said. And then he looked as though he were deep in thought.

"You know," he said peeling himself off the wall, "I think you're on to something. I'm going to call Sam and request that you spend some field time with me in my office tomorrow."

A quick bolt of fear shot through her. "You can't do that!"

"Sure I can. It's no problem. I'll just call him and make a special request." He headed toward his desk. "It'll take all of fifteen seconds."

"Not that! You must have lost your marbles. I've been here less than an hour, and already we're trying to stay far enough away from each other so that we don't—"

"Point taken. But I'm an accountant with no immediate access to spreadsheet software. So, if getting you in here on a 'field study' will get me a working computer, I'm willing to risk it."

"I'll assign one of my team members."

"I've had my fill of your team members. I've had a month of them in your absence. Now, I assume you're the lead for a reason."

He was already at his desk, hand on the receiver. Kyra groaned.

"Sam is such a brownnoser, he'll probably agree," she said, looking away. She couldn't look at him now. Not with the potential of eight hours of proximity ahead of her. She had to go home and pray, light candles, say some Hail Mary's, throw salt over her shoulder, or seriously contemplate calling in sick.

The queasiness in her abdomen told her that if Sam agreed to Race's request, she wouldn't have to pretend to be sick, she would be.

"Race—"

He held up a hand and picked up the phone. Kyra turned away and paced. It was the only thing she could think to do beside covering her ears and chanting, "La, La, La."

Race hung up the phone after a few minutes. Kyra groaned again. Since Sam didn't hardly do any work, she knew he was in his office. She didn't bother to turn around. If she had, she would have seen Race eyeing her backside favorably for the fleetest of moments.

"What did he say?" she said, trepidation lacing her words.

"He said you'd be happy to."

She closed her eyes. *Where is my willpower?* The inside of Kyra's mouth suddenly tasted desert-dry. She had to get out of Race's office, away from the proximity of his influence, plod her way to the nearest water fountain and drink to calm her nerves.

"Look, Kyra, what I told you yesterday still stands. I'm on the up-and-up with Chantel, which makes you and I impossible."

Chantel—she'd have to go talk to her right now, before she lost her nerve. Chantel was a good friend. She owed it to her.

"Chantel is a good woman, Race."

"Yes," he said.

She was headed toward his office door when she heard him say something else.

"And a damn good poet."

She swung around and for the first time in about fifteen minutes, she looked him dead in the eye, her heart doing a quick beat in her chest. "You liked m— Her poetry?"

"Liked it? It's some of the best poetry I've ever read.

She said she's not published. I can't believe that. It's better than some of the stuff I've read in the journals."

"You read literary journals?" she asked, taking a step forward. She was taking a terrible risk moving closer into his atmosphere, but his appreciation of her work drew her to him against her better judgment. "The only folks who read lit mags are English majors and writers."

His eyes sparkled with that comment and Kyra's soul melted.

"I useta write a little something back in the day."

Kyra nodded to herself. Now, his hair made sense. It wasn't quite dreds, but it wasn't one hundred percent corporate. With dark brown sections of hair clumped together, he straddled the line of those two worlds beautifully.

He looked slightly confused. "Don't you think she's good?"

Kyra felt the blood rush to her face. "Well, yeah, I mean, sure."

Kyra couldn't leave well enough alone. She had to know. "So, what about it, exactly, do you like?" She took another tentative step closer and held her breath.

"Well, I've only read three of her poems, but each one of them got to me. On the most basic level they got in."

His eyes hardened just a bit and he had a faraway look. "I like it because it's easy to understand, and because when I read it, it's like I'm reading the truth. The truth about her, the truth about me…the truth about us all."

The truth, Kyra thought. Now there's irony for you.

"Well, I'm sure that you've got at least a dozen spreadsheets to create. And I've got other customers to service, so I will get out of your office."

"Okay, techie," he said. "See you first thing tomorrow morning, bright and early."

She nodded and her stomach did a lazy somersault. Tomorrow.

Kyra headed down the hallway with Race's full-bodied cologne still filling her nostrils. She could breathe in that fragrance forever and never get tired of it.

Tomorrow, she thought again. She had a lot to do between now and then. She had to resurrect her proposal. This opportunity with Race would give her a great pilot program to document. She had to document their discussion and action today for the activity log, and she had to contact Chantel and let her know she would have to reschedule their "discussion." Just that quickly, her plate was full.

In addition to all of the things she had to do, at the top of her list was writing. From the beautiful echo of Race's compliments in her head, Kyra could write one hundred poems. But for the time being, she only needed to write three.

And she couldn't wait to get started!

Sine Qua Non

> wrung out
> your silky scent
> doin' the funky chicken in my nose
> wanting you now
> only pain sings this song
> YOU created this
> definition of a woman
> how come

and how come
oh how come
the chords you play keep
feeding my melancholy full
of lust and lies
say WHAT?, don't
you hear me askin?

"Brodie! Turn those pork chops over!"

"Torrena, are you listening to me?" Race crossed one leg over the other. He was propped up in his bed, wearing maroon-and-gold-flecked silk pajamas. After the crazy day he had at work, he thought he was going to go home, shower and lounge around to give his brain a rest from number crunching. But the words in Chantel's poetry haunted him in bizarre, consuming ways. In a million years, he would never have pegged her for a poet. But yet he held in his hands the three poems she'd given him, poems he couldn't stop reading. He'd plugged his department projections into his spreadsheet that afternoon and the numbers were off...way off. He couldn't trust himself to start running financials for the entire company if he couldn't even get his own department numbers to add up.

"Okay, I'm hanging up now."

"No, Torrena, wait."

"I'm trying to, sweetie, but you're not making any sense."

"That's because God has a sense of humor and now that my professional life is in order, he has seen fit to turn my personal life into a joke."

"Don't blame this on God. You're the one that got

caught up with two best friends. He didn't tell you to do that."

"You sound like this is something that I can control." He thought about how being in the same room with Kyra set every nerve ending in his body ablaze. If there was a way to control that, he hadn't thought of it yet.

"Look, you're a numbers guy. Certainly you can 'figure' a way to get your over-the-top lust to shut down."

"Everybody wants to be a comedian. And there's nothing funny about feeling out of control. Now I called you to get a woman's perspective on this."

"*This* woman has got to go save her kitchen from burning down. Brodie is char-frying the food again!"

"Torrena—"

"You want my advice? It's the same as it was before. Leave them both alone. Just do you for a while."

He groaned. That was not the answer he wanted to hear.

"Gotta go, sweetie."

"Later," he said, and hung up the phone.

Immediately, images of Kyra flooded his brain. They turned over like pages in a Playboy layout. He could see her. Smell her. With another groan and a glance down at the area tightening just below his abdomen, he realized he could feel her as well.

He placed the receiver on his nightstand knowing that his friend was right. He slipped off the pajama bottoms, closed his eyes and prepared for a long evening of "doing him."

Kyra wasn't sure if it was the heat on the page or the heat in her soul that was causing her to sweat. It sure wasn't the temperature. Even though it was a warm July in Savannah, her air-conditioning was blasting in an attempt to keep her sweat at bay.

And she actually was sweating. She felt the tiny beads pop out on her top lip and a thin film of perspiration on her arms and hips. She'd never known herself to sweat so much when simply writing poetry, but here she was at just a few minutes past midnight wringing yet another poem from her soul.

Ne Plus Ul·Tra

> it was instinct
> even before
> you read me like a poem
> i felt your harmony traveling in my soul
> check my glow: thirsty and piping
> only your songs can quench and cool
> i shine
> like midnight on the ocean and you...
> you are my truth, my promise of new light
> let me lay next to your fire!

When she'd gotten home, she had every intention of taking a long bath, putting on a robe and sitting down to write. After the quick snack she'd made out of a Granny Smith apple, she'd gone straight to her writing desk. No television, no radio, no stereo. No dinner. After writing two poems, her verse had taken a sharp turn to the right—right sensual that is.

She couldn't help it. It was as though someone else were steering the pen.

Black ink darkened the tips of her thumb, forefinger and middle finger. Kyra used a dip pen and an ink bottle to compose her poetry. She enjoyed the way in which using that process improved her poetry and made the words she wrote so much more elegant.

It had taken her nearly nine months of practice to get her handwriting to the point where it was more calligraphy than just regular writing.

When the phone rang, she hesitated to answer it. She didn't need anything breaking her concentration or disrupting the flow of letters on the page. Then she realized how late it was and figured anyone calling this late must have something important to say.

This better not be Chantel pestering her about *her* poetry, she thought. That would put her in the mind to just keep the poems to herself and forget about sending them to Chantel.

Quickly, she replaced the pen, wiped the ink from her fingers and picked up the cordless on a nearby table.

"Hello?"

"Hello to you."

"Turk, what's wrong?"

"Nothing. I called to find out what's wrong with you."

"Nothing's wrong with me," she lied. I can't think beyond Race Jennings's intense gaze, but other than that, I'm perfectly fine.

"What makes you think there's something wrong?" she asked. She walked back to her desk and held up her handiwork. It looked good, if she did say so herself.

"I just drove past your place. I saw a light on. Being that you are in bed by eight—"

"Nine."

"Same difference. I had to call and check on you. Everything all right?"

"Yeah. Fine. I just got the poetry-writing bug. I haven't been able to put my pen down for any length of time since I walked in the door."

"Is it that Race joker?"

"He's not a joker."

"Didn't he have a date with Channy?"

"Yeah."

"Then he's a joker."

"I will not allow you to talk about my best friend in that manner. Besides, she's your sister. Now apologize."

Silence.

"Apologize."

"Okay, all right. So, forgive me already. And read me something. I've had a bad day that ended in an even worse night."

"Bad first date?"

"Yeah."

Kyra smirked. A bad first date for Turk meant that he didn't get any.

"No worries, mate. I've got something for ya right here." Because Turk was the king of rubbing friendly salt into a wound, Kyra chose the most sensual poem she'd written that evening and began to read.

"What are you trying to do—make me have an accident? I am still driving."

"So it was good?"

"Good? I'm ready to turn this puppy around and use

your spare key to let myself in. You sure you don't need a back rub or something?"

"I'm positive, Turk, but thanks for the offer."

"Something tells me that Race is going to be a handful. If you ever need to practice—"

"Turk!"

"Right. Okay, then. Go to bed. Rest up now, while you can. In the meantime, I'm pulling in to my garage right now. I got a woman waiting for me inside."

"You're kidding?"

"Not at all. Her name is Wendy and as soon as I blow her up, she and I are going to have the time of our lives!"

"You're kidding, right?"

"Yeah. But just barely. But I am serious about one thing. Get some sleep, kiddo. You're spending way too much brain time on this guy."

"You're right. Hey thanks for listening and calling to check on me."

"Anytime and anytime, baby. Good night."

"Good night."

Kyra hung up the phone and pushed the image of a brown plastic doll inflating far from her mind.

She gazed appreciatively at her work. She'd done well tonight. Very productive. She chose her poem called "If You Have to Get Out Fast," and moved over to her computer.

After she accessed her e-mail account, she typed the poem into an e-mail message and sent it to Chantel at work. Satisfied.

Her friend would see first thing in the morning that Kyra had agreed to write the poems for her and, not only that, she had created some of her highest quality verse.

Chantel would be ecstatic. She could just imagine the look on her face.

The next morning, after the sweetest dreams Kyra had ever had in her life, she rolled into work at her usual time. Surprisingly, she didn't wake up exhausted from going to bed four hours later than usual. On the contrary, she arose exhilarated and ready to get to the office.

When she rounded the corner to her cube she saw her overhead light turned on. Concern furrowed her brow. *What the heck?* she said to herself and stepped into her cube, where a very happy Chantel sat in a flamboyant yellow pants suit with her feet up and a big sloppy grin widening her cheeks.

"Miss Thing, care to get your feet off of my desk?"

"Anything you say, Poetess," Chantel said, smiling her face off and swinging her long brown legs to the floor. Kyra would choke a goose for legs like Chantel's. Kyra knew her legs were no joke, but Chantel worked on her legs daily doing the kind of exercises Kyra thought only masochists do.

Kyra loved herself too much to put her body through that much torture. Instead, she made it a point to walk at least three hours per week. Walking kept her body in the kind of shape she loved.

"You were in the zone last night, Ky. This poem was off the hook."

Kyra took her seat behind her desk. "Tell me something I don't know."

"Well, well, the doubting Tomasina finally comes

around. How long have I been telling you you're
good?"

"Long enough to know it's the truth," Kyra said. She
unpacked her business bag and pulled out the work
she'd taken home but didn't get to.

Kyra allowed herself a small smile. "It just took the
message a while to sink in." Or the right messenger, a
voice in her head told her.

Chantel stood and moved so Kyra could get to her
desk. "I owe you. Big."

Kyra turned on her computer. "This, I know."

"Let me get you a gift certificate for that company
you like. What's the name of it, DAK? You can buy
some of those gadgets you love so much."

DAK. Kyra hadn't thought of that company in
months. For years, she considered herself somewhat of
a gadgeteer. But recently, when she put all of her spare
time and energy into getting published, she'd put aside
her interest, nearly forgotten it. She wondered if she
could pick up where she left off?

"Chantel, I haven't worked on that kind of stuff in
months. Almost a year. Just take me to lunch at Olive
Garden."

"You got it, poetry girl." Chantel turned to leave.
"Well, I'd better go. I have a date to get asked out on.
One walk-by should do the trick."

"Are you going to give him the poem now?" Kyra
asked eagerly.

"No. I'll wait until our next date, but I'll keep you
on speed dial."

"You do that," Kyra said, feeling confident and a
little cocky. Her confidence level had risen exponen-

tially in the last twenty-four hours. Kyra hadn't felt this good about her writing in way too long.

"What are you doing here?" Her boss poked his bowling ball head into her cubicle, wearing a sour frown.

Kyra frowned. "I'm getting situated. You know, that thing you do before you start work."

Chantel's eyes widened in surprise. Sam's narrowed with frustration.

"Jennings expects you in his office today. All day."

Suddenly, Chantel's expression changed to one of high curiosity.

Kyra shook her head, not wanting to discuss the whole spending-the-day-in-Jennings's-office thing. She couldn't quite look her friend square in the face.

"Don't ask," Kyra said.

"You know I will," Chantel said, maneuvering past the man whose big head was still in the entryway.

"Get on it, Douglas!" Sam ordered and stepped away.

Get on it, indeed, Kyra thought. That's something she would be fighting all day not to do.

Kyra answered a few e-mails, reviewed the current project log book and finished clearing her schedule for the day, prolonging the inevitable as long as she could.

When there was nothing left for her to do, she grabbed a notepad and an observation form she had developed when she put her proposal together. Before leaving her office, she checked her reflection in her computer monitor. She looked better than she felt. She felt like a lousy friend.

God, please give me strength today, she prayed then

walked out of her office determined to push her attraction to Race as far away as possible. The trouble was, even as she created mental resistance to her lust, just thinking about Race brought on such longing, she knew the only thing that could keep her hands off of Race Jennings today was if they were tied behind her back.

Chapter 7

Race paced in his office, calling himself a crazy, insane, and sexually frustrated lunatic. Since the moment he arrived at his office, he'd come close to calling Kyra and leaving her a message that he'd changed his mind. He didn't need watching. He'd make do. And if this computer took a nosedive also, he'd just try again with another one.

But the truth was, a modern accountant without a computer was as ridiculous as a rocket scientist without the rockets. He was hired to create a financial plan to get ComTel America back on track, and he couldn't do that without his tools.

He'd just have to put the fact that he couldn't wait to see Kyra, to be near her, for his body to thrum with her nearness, out of his mind. The fact that he hadn't been able to do that since he first saw her didn't seem to assuage him. Today he was determined. He would be successful, just the way he had been successful in nearly every other area of his life.

When Kyra walked into his office, he knew he was in trouble.

Was she more sexy today than he'd seen her all week? Yes. He thought she was. Her blouse and pants just a bit tighter. Hair curly and wild, more makeup? Yes. He could smell her perfume from where he stood at the window behind his desk. Devastatingly alluring. And her lips...lethal.

Just tear my clothes off, why don't you? he thought, but instead said, "Maybe this was a bad idea."

"I tried to tell you that yesterday, but you wouldn't have it. So, now you're stuck with me. I've decided to get a practical example for my proposal. If this day with you pans out, it might give me the leverage I need to be granted a study of the process or at least a pilot of the program. You're my guinea pig."

He nodded and noticed that she hadn't moved an inch since she came through the doorway. Well, if she meant what she said, then she would have to get closer than that.

Apparently, she wasn't going to make it easy on him, with her extra attention to the details of her appearance and her determination to get data for her proposal. So, he decided not to make it easy on her.

"Well, I guess we should get started then."

"Yes," she said.

Race's heart pounded and his mouth watered. He could already taste her sweet skin in his mouth. In his mind, she tasted as good as she smelled. And her skin was soft and yielding to his, wherever he touched it. And...

"Are you sweating?" he asked, noticing the way her skin glistened even in the harsh light of his office.

"No," she said a little too quickly, "but can you make it cooler in here? It's kind of stuffy."

At that, Kyra slid off the light jacket she wore and exposed the most exquisite arms. Feminine and strong at once and the same russet brown complexion her face had. The erotic attraction coursed slowly through his veins.

Damn, it was hot.

"The thermostat is to the right of you on the wall," he said, knowing that if he came anywhere near her now, he'd pull her into his arms and kiss her until they were both breathless and lust-driven.

Her smile didn't match the ardor in her eyes. She turned, adjusted the gauge and faced him again. The only nervous moves missing were him rocking on his heels and her twiddling her thumbs.

"You know this is ridiculous," he said finally.

"It's stupid," she agreed, but still didn't move.

"We're adults," he said, feeling cooler air disturbing the atmosphere, tempering the tension between them.

"And we're at work," she said.

"There's that," he responded.

"All right then. If you won't move, I guess I will. And just remember, you brought this on yourself."

The nerve of this woman, he thought, and all the while his nerve endings sparked and ignited with each step she took.

Look at those hips, his mind said. Don't you want to touch them?

"Yes, but not here," he said out loud.

"Pardon me?" Kyra said, sliding one of his guest chairs around to face his computer.

"I mean you're awfully sure of yourself."

She stopped fiddling with the chair and gave him a cocksure smile. "I know you want me."

Admiration flooded his soul. He loved a woman who didn't hesitate to speak her mind.

"Ms. Douglas, before we violate any more office etiquette guidelines and ethical behavior standards, we'd better get on with it."

Race had one of the largest offices in the company, but right then it felt about as big as a pillbox. When he sat down at his chair, it was as though he and Kyra were bunched up and practically on top of one another. And in actuality they were still several feet apart.

Race took a deep breath. "So, how does your field observation process work?"

"As unobtrusively as possible. The name speaks for itself. I watch you work and I fill out my form documenting what software you use, how you use it, how often. I'll write down what you don't use as well and be here to answer any questions you have about the way any software works, fixing little pesky glitches you've just been putting up with, and show you ways to use the software to work smarter."

"Like my own personal IT coach," he said, warming to the idea.

"Yes. At least until I collect enough information to summarize your work habits."

"What about e-mail? I'm not sold on the idea of you reading my e-mails over my shoulder."

"Then I won't. Entering passwords and observing e-mails are excluded from the field observation."

Race stroked his chin. Her theories seemed not only sound, but advantageous. Instantly, numbers and dollar figures added and subtracted themselves in his mind. What her project would cost in time, it would far make up in monetary savings for the company.

"And you say your proposal was rejected?" he asked, settling behind his computer, getting ready to work.

"Sam didn't like it," she admitted. He saw the disappointment drive the light out of her eyes. It made him uncomfortable. Pained him to see her pain.

"I've got all my spreadsheets on CD. I'll transfer them to my computer and set up my work folders."

Kyra nodded. "I'll watch," she said.

And boy, was she watching. Every move he made she committed to memory. For twenty minutes, she forgot that she was supposed to be observing for a purpose. She didn't have one note written on her form.

"Are you getting all this," Race asked. He'd been quietly working. She vaguely remembered seeing him add tables in an Excel spreadsheet and update a database MS Access. Beyond that, her attention had been on what wonderful-looking hands he had. Strong, sturdy, clean, neat. She even found the veins visible on the backs of his hands attractive.

God help me.

"Yes," she said finally, "I'm getting it. I'm getting it all."

Race laughed. "Well, I'll say one thing. You haven't tried to touch me yet."

"What?" she said, feigning offense.

"Don't deny it. Your hands have been twitching since you sat down."

Now she knew her hands hadn't actually been shaking, as he suggested, but touching him, finding out if his body was as solid and muscled under his clothes as it looked, had occupied a portion of her thoughts, yes.

"Don't hate on me 'cause you don't know what to do with your eyes. You've been side-looking over here for the past fifteen minutes. You've spent more time with your eyes on me than with your eyes on the screen. I mean, honestly, do you even know what you're typing?"

"Of course I do!" he said, brushing off her comment. He clicked the "calculate formula" button on the spreadsheet and groaned.

"What's wrong?"

"Nothing," he said through clenched teeth.

"Don't lie. There's too much between us for you to lie." As soon as she said those words, she clamped her mouth shut. He gave her a look that said he knew what she'd said was true, but he wasn't ready to admit that kind of truth yet. *She* was lying. Not being honest about the poetry was the same as lying.

"My numbers are off. Way off. I must have used the wrong formula. And I never do that."

He turned toward her. Held her gaze. Ignited her passion. Reluctantly, Kyra looked away.

I'm a good friend, I'm a good friend, she repeated silently. And she reminded herself of how hard Chantel's life had been recently. She deserved a relationship with a good man. And besides, Chantel did see him first. More important than that, Kyra was good about reading people. Her read of Race told her that he was a good man, a really good man. A man who could make just about any woman, especially Chantel, content and happy.

What kind of friend would she be to try to intercept Chantel's man?

"If you and Chantel don't work out…" Kyra began.

Race's eyebrow rose. "Yes?"

After feeling on the verge of admitting something forbidden, Kyra came to her senses. "I can't help you. I don't believe in sloppy seconds."

"Nor do I," he said, but didn't stop looking at her. His eyes took in her face and shoulders, then traveled down the length of her arm to one of the hands he said was twitching.

His brow furrowed. "What's that?"

His gaze was training on the tips of her right fingers. So much so, she could feel her hand warming to his rapt attention.

Kyra ran her thumb across the places on her forefinger and index finger still stained with the ink and emotion of her poetry. Nervousness twisted her stomach into a small knot.

"Ink," she answered honestly, then added her lie. "A pen I was using yesterday exploded in my hands. It stained my fingers."

He nodded and continued looking at her fingers. Then he looked up. "I'm not sure why, but that black ink at the tips of your fingers looks like it belongs there. And it reminds me of something."

Intrigued, Kyra turned a little in his direction. "What does it remind you of?"

"I don't know. Just something I've seen before."

Kyra shrugged. "Well, let me know when you think of it." Her voice had gone tissue-paper thin. The moment was warming up just a little too much. She decided to get up and stretch.

"Up so soon?" Race asked, returning to his work.

"Yeah."

She kept herself from pacing by walking to the window and pretending to look out. She felt him…watching…wondering. She wrapped her arms around herself as if they were his. She surely wished they were, had fantasized enough times about—

"Hey," Race's deep voice said.

Kyra stiffened and melted at the same time. He was behind her. Directly behind her. The warmth of his body wrapped itself around her as sure as if it had been his hands, his arms, caressing her. Holding her.

She imagined turning slowly and her head tilting up and up until she was face-to-face with him. And just when he was about to utter another word, she would stand on her tiptoes and take his mouth slowly at first, until the fierce nature of her passion turned a tender kiss into a storm of desire on his mouth.

"Race," she responded. Her voice came out thick. Deep. Husky.

"Knock, knock!" a woman's voice said from behind them.

They both turned to see Chantel standing in the doorway, file folder in hand.

"Hey, you guys," she said. Kyra would have sworn

she was still wearing that enormous smile from earlier that morning.

"I'm not going to interrupt. I just had something to drop off for Race." Chantel placed the file folder on top of his desk. She bent over just enough for him to get an eyeful of cleavage.

"I know my e-mail said I would give it to you tonight, but I couldn't wait." Chantel practically skipped back to the door. "You two get back to what you were doing."

The moment Chantel left, Kyra and Race moved away from each other like two magnets slowly repelling. She felt guilty for what she'd just been thinking and even more for what she was about to do. Her intuition told her that Race felt some of the same.

"Let's take a break, shall we?" he said.

"Good idea," Kyra said.

She picked up her notepad and form. They were both still very empty. Not a word on either.

She exited his office knowing that unlike Chantel's suggestion, there would be no "getting back to what they were doing."

Kyra's mind was made up. No matter how much intestinal fortitude it took, she was going to overcome this attraction she felt for Race. She would work like a madwoman to get him out of her system. Even if it meant taking Turk up on one of his outrageous and numerous offers.

Chapter 8

can't look at you
without seeing the shame
in my own eyes
or tasting cold dry
remorse
for all the things i want
to do to you
that require fingers
and hands
lapping tongues
two hips.
but you are
untouchable—
super bad daddy mack
untouchable
like Shaft.

No matter how
you talk that talk
my arms will never be long enough
to answer you

Race struggled with the truth. Even if he were in a stadium with Kyra, he could feel her, want her. There was no space large enough to contain his lust and he would always feel as though they were on top of each other. Groping. Stroking.

But he believed that he may have found a cure for his acute fascination with Kyra Douglas. He picked up the poem again and reread it.

The words had the same effect. Deep, wrenching jolts. They stirred him, moved through him like a swift and rushing current. They imbedded in him. Created visions he would never be able to erase, nor would he want to. They were bold, vivid and made him feel alive in a way he hadn't in far too long.

In moments like these, he seconded-guessed his decision to work in corporate America. He'd envied the paths of his friends who had gone the way of their passions. Painters, writers, sculptors, social activists. Of course not. After all these years, some of them were still just scraping by. But they were all happy and wouldn't change places with him and his six-figure salary for any reason.

The woman who wrote that poem didn't need a cushy job to be happy. She had the soul of an artist who needed to focus on her craft rather than events planning for a corporation.

Her true talents were being wasted.

He smiled. For the first time in two days he'd spent more than two minutes of concentrated thought on something other than Kyra and the way her eyes sparkled when she thought she'd got him on a point.

"Jennings?"

"Yes?" he said, surprised that the CEO was in his office. He hadn't heard him come in.

"Sorry to disturb. You look deep in thought."

"It's all right, Ken. What can I do for you?"

"I just stopped by to see if you're all set for the planning meeting on Friday."

Planning meeting. "Yeah, Ken. I'm doing a Power-Point on last quarter's financials and projections for the next quarter."

"Will those projections be based on process changes or our current budget system?"

"Current. It's too soon to report on any other numbers yet."

"Sounds like a plan. How soon do you think you'll have projections on the new numbers?"

"Two months, three tops."

"I'd like to see them as soon as possible. Sooner than that if you can do it."

Race smiled. "Understood."

Ken moved toward the door. "Carry on," he said, then stopped just before he stepped completely out of the office.

"Oh, and Jennings, if you have to think that hard, the answer is 'no.'"

The tall man slapped the office wall with the palm of his hand and then disappeared down the corridor.

Race placed the poem back into the file folder. If only his dilemma were that simple, he thought.

Kyra let the phone on her desk ring four times before she picked up. If it was Chantel, she wasn't in the mood for her gratitude about the poem or her enthusiasm about Race. If it was Race, she wasn't in the mood for the question she'd been avoiding in her head—"When is she coming back to his office?" If it was her boss, she had no tolerance for his need for continuous updates whenever she worked on a major project.

And her work with Race was major. It could mean a promotion for her if she got great examples from it. She'd move from lead tech to consultant.

Kyra didn't have to wonder what it would be like to make more money. She'd thought about it enough times. Speculated about the 100-year-old Ross rolltop desk she'd had her eye on at Mike's Antiques. As if she didn't have enough subscriptions to lit mags, she would love to add *Conjunctions* and *Chicken Bones* to her growing monthlies. And most of all, she'd like to take her parents on a trip east. They had a pair of twin cousins living near Nicodemus, Kansas, who must have been in their eighties now and whom they hadn't seen in thirteen years.

But most of all, she would take that trip to New York, go to the Nuyorikan Café, and do something she hadn't been able to do in all her years of writing poetry—read her work out loud to an audience.

For that, she had to get control of her emotions and longings. She had to rein in everything inside her that craved to reach out and stroke Race Jennings.

After thinking it through, Kyra believed that if she

kept her focus on her goals, her determination to get them would keep her mind right as well as her body and her soul, no matter how desperately they ached for the handsome new CFO.

By the clock on her computer, it was just after lunchtime. She had gone up to the company cafeteria and purchased a turkey sandwich, a bag of chips and grape juice. She'd made quick work of the chips and juice. The sandwich seemed too heavy to tackle right now. There was too much on her brain. Kyra wrapped the sandwich in the box that it came in, wrote her name across the top and headed toward the floor's refrigerator.

"I'll have you know, I don't appreciate all the extra work."

Kyra jumped and whirled around. "Bless it, Orlando. You scared the microchips out of me!"

"Sorry. I thought you saw me come up."

"Well, I didn't," she said, passing by the water fountain and considering splashing Orlando with the water.

"Jennings got you hoppin'?" he asked.

He had no idea. "Not at all."

"Then why is Sam giving me all of your work tickets today?"

"Because he's the biggest brownnoser in the company and whatever the CFO wants, the CFO gets."

"So, it's true. Jennings has his own private data tech."

"Techie!"

When they reached the break room, Kyra put her sandwich in the fridge. "That seems to be his favorite word."

Orlando looked unimpressed. "So, you going back to his office this afternoon?"

"Yeah. I'm going to do some observations. See if I can get to the bottom of his computer problems."

"I think he's sabotaging them somehow. Trying to get out of work."

Kyra checked the man's thin face to see if he were serious. The hard expression told her that he was. Orlando, the purveyor of conspiracy theories. Everything was a mystery to be solved with him.

Kyra knew better than to respond to his off-the-wall beliefs. When he got hold of one, he never let it go. Even when he was proven wrong, he used it as further proof that he was right and that someone was covering up the real truth.

"Well you better get back there. If you've been gone for a while, chances are that he's already downloaded whatever virus he's infecting his computer with."

Kyra pursed her lips to keep from laughing. When she'd regained her composure she said, "Okay, Orlando. You let me know if you have any questions on those tickets."

"Will do," he said and went back toward the sea of cubicles where they both worked.

As she approached Race's office, she went over her goals again. More money. Antiques. Lit mags. Office. Nicodemus. Keep your eyes on the prize. Keep your eyes on the prize.

Keep your eyes...

"Hey, techie. You came back."

God, but the man has a beautiful smile, she thought. A smile that will not derail me. I shall not be moved. And his eyes...

"Had to. We've got a computer to keep alive, right?" she asked, walking right up to his desk. "So, are you ready for me?"

The silence between them was thick with innuendo. Race smiled again, broader this time. Within seconds, his hearty laughter broke the tension. Kyra tried to remain aboveboard, but lost the fight with herself. She set the laughter free and their rising chuckles mingled delightfully in the air.

Kyra sat down before she fell down. "I didn't mean that the way it sounded," she managed to say between chops of laughter.

"I know," he said, shaking his head as if to say, "I give up."

He was still smiling. Something he hadn't done all morning. She liked his smile. Just the brightness of it bolstered her spirit and her resolve. She could do it. She could keep her mind focused.

"The answer to your question is no. I'm not ready for you." In the back of Race's mind he asked, 'Is any man?' "But I'm ready for a computer that continues to work past the first one or two days that I have it. So, shall we resume?"

"I think so," she said.

Kyra moved Race's furniture one more time, taking the chair she sat in from the opposite side of his desk and moving it beside his chair. She sat down, got out her form and prepared to fill it out completely this afternoon.

"What have you done since I've been gone?" she asked.

"Not much really? Answered a few e-mails. Played Minesweeper."

"Minesweeper?"

"Yeah. It clears my head. Besides, I like the challenge. It's almost like a mystery."

"You and Orlando with your mysteries."

"Who's Orlando?" Race asked, the playfulness draining from his face.

"We work together. It doesn't matter. Let's focus on your work. Why don't you just do like you did this morning? Pretend that I'm not here."

"Hmm," he said, then turned away from her with a skeptical look on his face. He opened his Web browser and typed a site address.

"That…is impossible," she heard him say under his breath.

Against all the sense she had in her head, she touched his shoulder. When the lightning shot from his body to hers, she jerked her hand away. The expression on his face said, "Silly girl, didn't you know that was going to happen?"

Surprisingly, her determination held. Even against the flip-flops her stomach was doing as a result of just touching him.

"Race, I've come to a conclusion that I'm not going to let this—whatever this is between us—affect me. As of just a few minutes before I walked in here, I've put on the brakes against it. And it will help me if you don't mention it. Don't make jokes about it. Don't allude to it." *Don't give in to it,* she wanted to add. "Because from now on, I'm not. As far as I'm concerned, it doesn't exist."

The fire in his eyes that she'd grown so fond of, in a matter of hours, diminished to almost nothing. His face held a blank expression. She didn't think anyone else could have noticed the change in him. But she did.

Had their attraction meant that much to him, she wondered? It couldn't have or he wouldn't have chosen Chantel, right? For once there was no voice in her head. Nothing to give her a clue as to what this man was thinking. While Race and Orlando enjoyed a good mystery, she was the one with the puzzle to be solved.

Another time, maybe. Right now, she had work to do.

"You're right. We've been aboveboard, but out of control at the same time. And if there's one thing I know, it's how much it costs when employees misuse company time."

"I agree," Kyra said, relieved.

For the rest of the afternoon, she and Race didn't say much. He truly worked as if she weren't there. Periodically, he asked her to move away when he opened and responded to confidential e-mail. Most of the time, she was right there, watching.

And he amazed her.

He was nearly a genius when it came to numbers. He did things with a spreadsheet program Kyra would never be able to do with a million years of training. And his dexterity with the database software was equally impressive.

Kyra had more notes than she knew what to do with. With every note she took, she came closer and closer to an idea on ways to help managers work smarter and faster. It was a combination of her knowledge of the possibilities of the software and Race's actual use of the software.

With the examples she had documented, she might just get her promotion after all.

"Well, madam techie, you must be my good luck charm. It's the end of the workday, and my computer is still working."

"What can I tell you? I'm good," Kyra said, then regretted the words as soon as they left her mouth. After laying out her expectations, she couldn't get away from his office without another accidental innuendo.

"Let's get something straight," he said, gazing at her dead on. His darkened eyes bore straight through her and held her fast in her chair.

"I've come to a conclusion that I'm not going to let this—whatever this is between us—affect me. As of just a few minutes before you walked in here, I've put on the brakes against it. And it will help me if you don't mention it. Don't make jokes about it. Don't allude to it."

Kyra smiled. Damn him. "I apologize."

"Accepted."

As soon as the word left his mouth, some of the light returned to his eyes. It warmed her in all the right places, despite her wall of determination. But she hadn't given up yet.

"I think we've gotten you—" she stopped short.

"Over the hump?"

This time, Kyra laughed first. There was just no changing it. No matter what they did, everything carried extra meaning. But the fact that she'd spent the afternoon focused on her work, and not the man, gave her hope. If she did it once, she could do it again. And with dedication, she'd get better and better until finally, he would be out of her system.

"Well at least we finished the afternoon the way we started," she said.

"Mm-hmm," he said, still laughing. "I actually enjoyed having you here. I spent so much time trying to impress you with my spreadsheet skills, I finished two projects way ahead of schedule."

Kyra wanted to touch him again. Show him how endearing she found his comment. But she wasn't ready to be "shocked" again. Instead, she gathered her form and her legal pad, got up and moved the chair back into place. "Oh, really? Well imagine what you'll finish tomorrow."

At her remark, the light faded in his eyes again. "I don't think it's necessary for you to come back tomorrow. This computer made it past the danger zone. Looks like I won't need your *services* anymore."

The pit of Kyra's stomach dropped so fast, it made her dizzy. Why did his remark trouble her so? Because, you know you want any excuse to be near him, that's why, she thought.

Suddenly the voice in her head was back with a vengeance and saying things she didn't want to hear.

"Well, if anything happens, you have my extension."

He nodded. "Thanks, Kyra."

Now the voice was purring at the sound of her name on his lips.

"Have a good evening," she said and made a quick retreat before the voice took over.

She couldn't get away fast enough. When she got to her cubicle, Sam was hovering, obviously waiting for her to return.

"How'd it go?" he asked.

"Fine. His computer's fine."

"Good," Sam said.

She thought he'd at least want to hear about her afternoon. He didn't. He turned and headed toward his office. Kyra entered her cube wondering how Sam ever became a manager.

She plopped down in her desk chair and exhaled loudly. Suddenly, it felt as though it had been a long day. Kyra checked her e-mail and realized she had way too many messages than her brain could handle right then. The light on her phone flashed red. Voice mail. She realized that she hadn't picked up the message from earlier that day. Suddenly, it was way too overwhelming for her. She just wanted to be home with her incense, Miles Davis and Langston Hughes. She shut down her computer, packed up her briefcase and headed out.

Despite all her efforts, the last thought in her mind before she left the building was, "I hope Race's computer breaks down."

Damn that voice.

Chapter 9

Talk about bad timing, Race thought. Just when he'd decided that maybe he could live with being labeled a dog. He had it in his mind to break it off with Chantel so he could get his freak on with Kyra.

His common sense and better judgment were gone. Flown the coop as soon as she smiled with those big juicy lips of hers. And then she came back for her observation and the Gap Band started singing, "You dropped a bomb on me...baby."

She'd played the P card: platonic. He couldn't imagine being in the same room with Kyra and that word. If he ever tried to say that word in reference to anything about her, his mouth would shrivel up and his tongue would fall out.

Platonic!

The only reason he hadn't had his way with her was because they were at work. If they had been in a club, at her place, or his, he would have pushed her up against a corner and given her a kiss her body couldn't refuse.

A car horn blared behind him. He wondered how long the stop light had been green and pressed the gas pedal on his Infinity.

The drive home was a blur filled with images of Kyra and words from Chantel's poetry fighting for dominance. Why can't I be a "dog" like some of my friends, he wondered. Then I could have them both and not think twice about it. But Race had lived his live one formula at a time, one objective at a time, one woman at a time. And his laserlike focus had served him well.

Until now.

Now his thoughts were scrambled like eggs at IHOP. He entered his apartment and headed straight for his bedroom. Suddenly, he couldn't get into the shower fast enough. He yanked his clothes off and made his way to the tub. He didn't wait for the water to warm up, and stepped into it full blast and cold. "Arrrgh!" he said in the small enclosed space. His growl bounced off the glass and came back at him as if to taunt him.

"If she can turn it off, so can I," he said, the water cascading against him, the soap sliding against his skin.

Race knew himself well and one thing was certain—he was competitive and didn't take losing well at all. She would not get the best of him by flicking off her desire. Race would train his mind to cool the fire raging in his body for her.

"Like ice," he hissed as cold water continued to pound down on his body.

"Like ice."

* * *

During dinner with Chantel, Race actually managed to have a good time. He only thought about Kyra twice—once when Chantel smiled and he thought, "Those sure aren't Kyra's lips," and again when she winked seductively at him. It touched his ego but the gesture didn't bring it like Kyra.

"Do you have more poetry?" he asked when they were nearly finished with their meal. He'd taken her to Garibaldi's, where the food was exquisite and the view of the city was spectacular. They'd both ordered a pasta dish and were right in the middle of their meals.

"Now, Race," Chantel said, straightening and pushing her chest out just a bit, "I'm beginning to think you only want me for my...poetry."

He thought about that before he responded. Was she right? No, she couldn't be. He had been interested in her way before the poetry. Hadn't he?

"That's not true, Chantel."

"Good," she said. Then she leaned in. "And it just so happens that I do have more poetry."

"Really?" he said, feeling the quickening of his heart.

"Yes. Why don't I share it with you when we finish eating?"

"Sounds good," he said. He really wanted to hear the words now. Be fed by them instead of this salty pasta. Since he'd been taking out Chantel, they had been to more Italian restaurants than he knew existed in the city. She must be the carb queen. One more lasagna, seafood fettuccini, or spaghetti and meatballs dish and he would swear off pasta for the rest of his life. Even the steak came with a side of spaghetti.

"How's your veal?" she asked.

"Good. What about your manicotti?"

She licked her lips. Not so much overtly as leisurely. "Heavenly," she purred.

Now, that's a sign if he ever saw one, he thought. It was the thing all single men looked for. The signal from a woman that said, you can have me now. I won't put up any resistance.

Her eyes said it. Her body whispered it. "It's yours if you want it." But did he want it? That had been his original intention. And in twenty-first-century standards, he'd waited quite a while to get it. Over a month was a long time these days.

The vision he saw between he and Chantel wasn't a table with food on it, it was a line. He struggled for a moment with whether or not he would cross it. Then he wondered why he was struggling. He was a single man with a healthy sex drive.

He leaned forward a bit. "Why don't we read the poetry in my apartment?"

Her smile was triumphant, sexy as hell, and he liked it.

Hmmm. Could there be a dog in me after all?

Turks's lips were all over her. And so were his hands.

"Ky," he said. "I knew," kiss, kiss, "you'd," kiss, lick, "come around again," lick, lick, suck, kiss, lick, "one day."

She was on her stomach. She squeezed her eyes shut and gritted her teeth, while Turk grabbed her flesh and slathered her with his tongue. What on earth had she been thinking? That *this* would get Race out of her mind. How could she ever believe that Turk's inept bedroom skills could purge her memory of Race's chameleon eyes, his dark chocolate voice, or the current of electricity that passed between them when they touched.

"Oh, baby," Turk said, rubbing himself against her. He rocked back and forth like a kid on a mechanical horse that someone had just dropped a quarter in. He always liked to do it from behind. She thought maybe a fling would clear her head.

But it was just comical.

And then the worst thing she could possibly imagine happened.

She laughed.

And Turk stopped rocking.

"Are you laughing?" he asked.

"No," she lied. Unfortunately, it was the snort that gave her away. Then she couldn't stop laughing.

He rolled away and stared at her. Hurt feelings made his eyes look liquid and vulnerable.

She got herself under control and reached out for him.

"No!" he said. "I can't believe you're laughing at me."

He stood up. They hadn't even gotten their clothes off fully. He was still in his boxer briefs. She in her bra and khaki pants.

"I'm not laughing at you. I'm laughing at us."

He pretended not to listen. Instead, he yanked on his clothes and refused to look at her.

"Turk...Turk, stop," Kyra said.

He paused with one leg in his pants and one leg out. She didn't laugh again, but she wanted to.

"This isn't us. Not anymore."

"Then why did you get me all worked up?"

"Because, I thought, I mean, I wanted…"

Turk finished putting on his pants and buttoned his shirt. "Oh, this dude must be somethin' else if he's got you this open."

"What are you talking about?" she asked. But she knew good and well what he was talking about.

When he wouldn't answer, she fessed up.

"All right. I'm sorry. I was using you. I thought you could help me get Race off of my mind."

He finished dressing and then said, "Next time, just tell me you need a diversion. We'll go to the movies or something."

She got up from the place on her bed where Turk's body had repeatedly smashed hers into the mattress.

She put on her coy face, clasped her hands behind her back and twisted from side to side. "Still love me?"

"Of course, you little geek. Come here."

He stretched out his arms and Kyra walked right into them. They hugged for a long time. Kyra inhaled deeply. Turk smelled just like he always did. Woodsy. Spicy. Friendly. She'd known that aroma for years. It was comforting. Sturdy. Reliable. Even if Turk was a bit crazy.

"Okay, okay," he said, pulling back. "I need to go home right now."

Kyra nodded and noted the bulge straining against his trousers.

She walked him to the door. He turned and smiled.

"No chance I could get a hand job?"

"Out!" Kyra shouted and shook her head. "Go home to your doll."

"Don't think I'm not," he said, almost running down her stairs.

Before he got into his car, she called out to him.

"Turk, you don't really have a doll, do you?"

He didn't respond. Just smiled, blew her a kiss and got in his ride.

Kyra watched as he sped down the street. Something told her he would break every speed limit in the city getting home.

"Is this your place?" Chantel asked. Her eyes lit up the moment Race pulled into the driveway.

"Yeah," he said not moving.

"Impressive," she said and raked her eyes up and down him, as though she were appraising him all over again.

"Shall we go in?" she asked, reaching for the door handle.

He heard the eagerness in her voice. Before she could open the car door to get out, he locked it.

He rubbed a hand down the center of his face. His hand paused briefly at his mouth as if to prevent the words he knew were surely coming from leaving his mouth.

"Chantel…" Race began. "This is not going to happen."

"Why not?" she said, shifting her body toward him.

Because while they were in the car, he could say no, he thought. If he got her upstairs…

The honesty he'd been wrestling with during the entire drive to his home took over.

"I like you. A lot, actually. I see so much potential in you that ComTel has yet to tap into, but I have to tell you—I like your poetry more."

Chantel blinked once, twice, three times, then pursed her lips into a thin line.

"I'm sorry, but it's the truth. And before we go too far with this thing, I had to tell you what was up with me."

He waited a beat to feel out her reaction. So far, so good. No freaking out. No tears. No screaming. Just silence. He figured it was safe to continue and lay it all on the line.

"If you want to be friends, I'm all for that. We have good conversation. And we like some of the same things." Although pasta is not one of them.

"I would love to keep reading your poetry and—"

"Fine," she said, tucking a stray hair behind her ear. Her face had turned still and unreadable.

Unease slid inside him like an eel of guilt. "Are you sure?"

"Yes," she said.

Her face relaxed then. She rubbed her hands against her legs, stared down at them and smiled weakly.

He wanted to comfort her in some way, but didn't know how.

"Guess you'd better take me home."

"Yeah, I'll take you home."

Race put the car in gear and let out a long silent breath of guilt. It was mixed with relief, though. He knew he'd done the right thing. Too bad the right thing was sometimes the most painful thing.

Like this issue between he and Kyra. He knew letting it go was the right thing. And he knew it would hurt. But not like tonight. No. Leaving Kyra alone, which he'd already made up his mind to do, would hurt much, much worse.

Chapter 10

She'd done it. Kyra Douglas had gone cold turkey on her Race Jennings addiction and had kicked the habit. She'd come to work for the past few days sunny side up, with her poetry the only superflous thoughts in her head.

Kyra felt good about herself. Better than she had in two weeks. And then she turned on her computer and accessed her assignment log.

The first item was highlighted in red on her list.

Computer Malfunction—Jennings Ext 7669—27th Floor

She leaned back in her seat and smiled. Her heart pounded as if she'd just run a marathon.

Damn.

"Something wrong, Douglas?" Orlando asked.

"Yes," she said.

"Jennings?"

For a split second, she thought she'd been found out. She imagined that someone had discovered the lust beyond lust that had her so tightly wound no cold shower would lower her temperature.

"Yes," she said.

He grinned. "I saw that trouble-ticket. Since you were the last one on it, I thought I'd let you take it."

"Thanks," she said. The sarcasm in her voice was truly fake. Truth was, a tiny part of her couldn't wait to get back into Race's office. And if she ever fixed the problem with his computer, she couldn't trust that tiny scandalous part of herself not to sabotage it so that it would break down again.

"When you figure out what he's doing to kill his computers, let us all know," Orlando said.

"Will do," Kyra said, with anticipation pulling the corners of her mouth into a girlish grin.

She barely scanned her e-mail, answered a few voice mails, and then gathered her notes and headed out to the 27th floor and the man whose very presence made her feel as though she were naked and orgasmic. She decided to stop at the cafeteria first and get a cup of ice water. Heavy on the ice.

That morning, she decided not to let on that she had been feening for him, for the dark inferno of his eyes, the lush flesh of his lips.

Have mercy, she thought, wondering how on earth a feeling this fierce could be controlled.

Fake it till you make it, she thought and went up to Leslie's desk.

"Is he in?"

"In and expecting you."

"Thanks," she said, held her breath, and went inside.

Race stood at the window with his back to her. "What took you so long?" he asked.

"What are you talking about? It's six forty-five."

"Don't you get here at six-thirty?"

"Yes," she admitted, wondering how he knew that.

"Then by my calculations, you could have been here ten minutes ago."

He turned around and presented her with that strikingly handsome face of his.

Damn. Damn. Damn.

"Look, I got here as fast as I could. You're my first call."

"I'm your only call until I get a computer that works."

His words came out with sharp edges. No chance she would fall off the wagon.

She walked over, calmly focusing on her task.

"So what happened?" she asked, boldly sitting in his chair. The soft leather felt good against her backside. Soothing. Comforting.

"Nothing. That's the problem," he said, standing over her. Kyra's temperature rose about two degrees.

She licked her lips. "You're going to have to be more specific," she said. Her voice was strangely deeper.

"I did this," he said, reaching around her and pressing the on button.

She took a deep slow breath of his cologne. It was just as she remembered it. Just as potent and just as arousing. She squeezed her legs together and prayed.

They waited in silence. She listened for the fan and the sounds of the operating system booting up. Nothing. She placed a hand against the CPU, wishing the company had gone to laptops and docking stations like she'd recommended years ago. But no. They still purchased towers for their employees. As per her boss's boss.

She eyed the motion pendulum and the photograph of a little girl he'd placed on top of the tower.

"Cute girl," she said, letting her curiosity get the best of her and hoping that he would take the bait.

"My sister," he said.

She started at his response. "Your sister? How old is she?"

"Eight," he said.

She turned around. He was still standing behind her. Still close. And still handsome. "How old are you?"

"Old enough," he said.

Kyra got up. Checked the connections. Checked the cables. Made sure that everything was plugged up and plugged in. She'd even brought an outlet tester and a voltage probe to test the outlet and wires. She disconnected the computer, checked the current.

It was fine.

She rebooted the computer back up.

Still nothing. No matter how many times she pressed the on button. She checked to make sure the monitor was on. It was. Kyra rapidly became frustrated by the noncompliant computer. She had no clue what could be wrong.

Glancing at Race's coffee mug beside his keyboard, the thought entered her head that he was a klutz and always spilling his coffee into the keyboard.

"Tell me exactly what you did this morning."

Race took in an exasperated breath. "I came in, turned on the light, unpacked my briefcase, turned my computer on—or so I thought—and answered voice mail messages."

"What about yesterday?" she asked.

"Yesterday, the damned thing was working. All day. When I was ready to go home, I packed up, turned my computer off and left."

"I wonder if the cleaning crew has anything to do with sabotaging your computer," she said. That was the only explanation she could muster.

"I thought about that myself. But why my computer? Has this been happening to anyone else?"

"No," she admitted.

"I can't see them doing it to just one computer."

"Me, either. Unless you have an enemy."

"No enemies," he said.

She paced back and forth. She would not let this mystery get the best of her. She was one of the best systems engineers in the area, if she did say so herself. She would get to the bottom of this if she had to spend the next six months with Race to figure it out.

"Think again," she said. "Did you do anything else this morning?"

Race paused. A look of sheer frustration crumpled his handsome features into a frown. "I told you everything," he said.

He was barely keeping his anger in check. She could hear it in the strained tones of his normally sultry voice.

She was about to suggest that they try yet another

computer when the expression on his beautiful face changed. Softened. And then looked questioningly.

"What?" Kyra asked.

"I got my balls started," he said.

"I beg your pardon?" she said.

"This," he said, pointing to the swinging pendulum on top of his computer.

"When I couldn't get my computer to work, I stopped it from swinging, so I could concentrate."

Kyra went over to the contraption, an idea already forming in her mind.

"Do you always put this on top of your tower?"

"Yes, it's part of my morning ritual. I have one at home and when I got this new job, I thought it would be nice to have one at work. The sound keeps my thoughts in order, except when I'm angry. Then it just frustrates me. Why?"

Kyra picked up the apparatus. "Because sometimes these things are magnetized."

"You mean to tell me—"

"That you've probably been short circuiting your own computers? Yep. That's exactly what I mean to tell you."

Kyra didn't want to. Lord knows she didn't want to, but she couldn't help herself. The first chuckle escaped her lips, nice and low. Almost undetectable. And then, a blast of laughter rose up from her belly. She knew she couldn't contain it, so she just let it rip. And she also couldn't resist putting Race in his place a little between spasms of laughter.

"All this time…you've been reaming my team like they're incompetent…when all the while…it's been… you!"

Kyra held her stomach, took the pendulum and sat down in a chair across from Race's desk.

He was incredulous. There was not even the hint of humor on his stony face.

"I'm...sorry," Kyra said, pulling herself together. She knew that was totally unprofessional. But she and Race had a different kind of vibe going on. No matter what they did. They knew each other in a way that belied office formality. She knew she could be herself, say anything, do anything when she was with him, and he would accept it. She knew it, like she knew her own name.

"Laugh, laugh," Race said. "Smoke in your amusement settles like a fine dust on chaos. Sweet ignorance make me smile."

"What?" she said, her compulsion to laugh halted by his words—words she recognized as her own.

"It's from a poem. One of my favorites. Chantel wrote it."

Kyra nodded, pulled her lips in and stopped herself from saying, "No, I wrote it! I wrote that poem!"

"You really like her poetry, don't you?" Kyra asked quietly. Timidly. Afraid of how she would feel if he said, "No."

"Yes. She's gifted in a way I don't believe she even realizes. She could be famous. I don't know why she's working here."

"Really?" Kyra asked, delight pulsing brightly through her veins like orange light.

"No doubt. I assume she's shared her work with you. Don't you think she's talented?"

Kyra lowered her head a bit, stared at the pendulum. "I guess I never thought about it."

"So what do we do now?" Race asked.

Caught up in the moment, Kyra responded, "Maybe we could read her poetry together sometime."

Race frowned. "I mean what do we do about the computer?"

"Oh," she said, embarrassed. "Well, if this thing is magnetized, which I'm almost certain that it is, it means that this computer is shot. I'll order you a new one, install it when it comes in and watch you work for a day or two—without the pendulum. Make sure you're all set."

"Sounds like a plan," he said.

Kyra got up and headed toward the door. Sadness gripped her as she realized that she'd solved the problem. She should be relieved, but she wasn't. The thought of not spending time with Race emptied her. Made her feel hollow and vacant.

"Thank you," Race said before she reached the door.

"You're welcome. I'll send a tech by with a cart to take your computer."

He nodded.

When she reached the door, he called to her once more.

"Kyra," he said.

She turned. "Yes?"

"About the poetry…I'd like to read it with you some-time."

Hope warmed the place in her belly that had grown cool. She was missing him already.

"I'd like that," she said and exited his office before she said anything crazy like, "Especially since all the poems I've written lately are about you."

She headed back to her office wondering just how much longer she would be able to keep that fact to herself.

Chapter 11

He'd already splashed on his favorite cologne. He was about to put on just a dash more when he heard a familiar honk. Glancing out the window, he saw Chantel in her little red Corvette. He grabbed a folder containing her latest three poems and headed out.

"Where are we going?" he asked.

"Someplace special," she said, grinning wildly.

The hot August wind whipped through her straight hair and tossed it around her head like fingers grabbing at the air. The car motor whirred around them.

Race let his enthusiasm for fast cars take over for a moment. He hoped the place where they were going was miles away. He didn't want to get there too soon and spoil the ride.

He looked over at Chantel and marveled at how she was unlike any other poet he knew. She seemed happy right now. Sometimes he saw a deep sadness in her eyes. He often wondered if that was where her poetic sensibilities came from. He always hoped that he wasn't the cause of that sadness. Right now, the sadness was gone. In its place was a bright and shining smile.

Why did that smile make him uncomfortable? he wondered.

They drove to the edge of the city. The day had not even cooled off. Even though the top was down, the heat still brought beads of sweat to the surface of Race's skin.

The cluttered signs of the city eased as businesses fell away to open spaces and sprawling homes.

"Road trip?" Race asked the farther they drove.

Chantel threw her head back and laughed in response. "Hold on!" she said, shifting gears and speeding down the roadway.

Race decided to stop wondering and just let Chantel take control. It wasn't that he hated surprises, just disliked them. He preferred to know what was going on in his world. Especially if he was speeding along in a sports car. The final destination sure would be a nice piece of information to have.

Chantel pulled up in front of a small row of storefronts in a retail area of the suburbs. The shops looked like throwbacks from the turn of the century and gave the retail area a distinct retro feel.

"We're here," she said, pulling up to one of the shops. A goodly number of cars filled the lot near the shop named The Griot.

"Ready?" she asked, already sliding one of her long brown legs out of the car.

"Sure," Race said and got out with her.

When they entered, Race had the distinct sense of déjà vu. It snatched his breath and made him stop short.

Instead of one shop, they'd walked into two. The owner must have knocked a wall out to expand the place. It was filled with intimate tables and chairs alongside big, comfortable-looking chairs, couches and love seats. Members of a band were on stage tuning up.

"Coffee, jazz and poetry. What more can a neo soul ask for?" Chantel said.

Race's heart melted. Years ago, he practically lived in places like this. He was always there reading, writing, listening. He and his circle of friends were going to conquer the world with their poetry and art. But somehow most of them had allowed the realities of the world take away their literary dreams. Most of them found themselves in corporate jobs or on the road, like his friend Brax. Ernest was the only one who kept his soul engaged in "the word." The poetic word, that is. He started his own literary magazine called *Truth to Power*.

It was time to change that, Race decided.

"Well, what do you think?" Chantel asked.

"I think I'm going to owe you big for this."

"I think you're right," she said. "Now, come on, let's grab a seat."

Although Chantel moved toward a love seat, Race steered her clear of that and over to a table and chairs near the stage. When a server came to take their order, they each ordered a cappuccino—Chantel's with whipped cream.

"How'd you know I'd like it?" Race said.

"You seemed like the type. I've been trying to get a

friend of mine to come here ever since it opened a couple months ago. She won't do it. She's kinda the poetry type, too."

"Really? I'd like to meet her."

"Oh, she's really shy. She probably won't."

Race nodded and paid for their coffees.

"There's a slam tonight. That's a contest, right?"

"I haven't been to a poetry slam since I lived in Philly. And yeah, it is a contest. Judges are selected randomly in the audience and they rate the poets on a scale of one to ten. There's usually a cover charge and the slam winner splits the money from the cover with the establishment or gets all of the money."

"Should be fun," Chantel said and took a sip of her cappuccino.

"It should be really fun, especially if you enter."

"Me!" she said, nearly choking on her coffee.

"Yeah, you. I don't know anything about the competition, but I don't see how you could lose. Your work is amazing."

Chantel looked as though she'd been caught cheating on her taxes. "I don't. I mean, I can't. I—Race, that's silly. We came here to listen. Besides, I don't have any of my poems with me."

"I do," he said, raising the manila folder in the air. "Right here."

All of the color and vibrancy drained from Chantel's face. "Oh," she said.

Suddenly he understood. "Are you one of those writers who is too shy to read her own stuff?"

"Yes," she responded, perking up. "That's it. I'm too shy."

"Nonsense. I'm right here to support you. You have a friendly face in the audience. Just focus on me and you'll do fine. Put a little oomph in your performance and you'll win this puppy hands down."

She looked as though she were considering his words, Weighing each one with the utmost care.

He placed a finger on her chin and lifted her head a bit. "What do you say?"

She stared at him with those big fake lashes of hers. "All right," she said and let out a big sigh.

Race drank from the coffee cup. The liquid went down hot and sweet. "Don't worry. Everything will be fine."

But everything wasn't fine. Chantel signed up to read and selected a poem without incident. The band played. They were actually pretty good. And the poets read. Some were much better than others. Some were too obscure to even try to decipher. So far there weren't any that Race thought were better than Chantel.

When Chantel's name was called, the color drained from her face again. Her hands started shaking and she looked as though she might faint.

"Are you all right?" Race asked, suddenly concerned that his prodding and pushing may have been a bad idea.

"Yes," she said and drained her coffee cup.

Chantel reached for her poem and Race pulled it back. "You have to read from memory," he said.

"Oh, God," she said.

"Don't worry. You'll be fine. Remember, you wrote it, so even if you don't get the words exactly right, you'll get the sentiment right."

She nodded. Sweat glistened across her brow and she hadn't even read yet.

Race crossed a finger or two thinking that perhaps he shouldn't have been so insistent.

Chantel stepped on the stage. Race had never seen anyone's eyes get that big except maybe in a cartoon.

"You want anything special, Miss Lady?" the bandleader asked her. She shook her head and stared out into the crowd.

The band played a soft mellow tune. Kinda sexy like her, Race thought, and just as he was about to rescue her from what was obviously her growing fear, she spoke.

"This is called, LS Movement."

Then she closed her eyes and began to recite. "Some funk we got, here between your skin and my mind, where you sweat and press, I lean and sigh…movement."

It was going well. She didn't sound as into it as Race thought she should. But the important thing was she was getting through it. His prize prediction was a bit premature, but she was getting her feet wet.

Maybe next time, he thought.

Then the verse broke down, or rather she did. Chantel stumbled through the next stanza and completely botched the next. When she opened her eyes, a few members of the audience were booing and laughing.

Race cast a hot glare toward the folks at that table. They obviously hadn't come to support the poets. Only to help them fall flat on their faces.

When they quieted down, he went up to the stage

where Chantel stood looking shell-shocked and embar-rassed.

He wrapped his arm around her shoulders. "I'm sorry, Chantel. You wanna get out of here?"

"Yeah," she said.

He didn't know what made him do it, but he took her back to his place. Chantel seemed to need a big shoulder to lean on and he needed to make a big apology.

Chantel glanced around. "Sweet place."

"Thanks," he said, checking his cupboard for tea and hot chocolate.

"Maybe we should have gone to dinner first. I'm starving."

"We can still go out. Or, we could order in. Which would you prefer?"

Chantel stretched out like a cat on his sofa. She really was trying to get him caught up. But he just wasn't feelin' her.

He could hear some of his friends now. "Man, if she's tossin' it up and servin' it on a platter, you have no choice but to get your grub on!"

And why wasn't he? That question plagued his mind. Made him think he was losing it.

That Kyra had done something to him. Mixed up his typically well-ordered logical mind. But she would barely give him the time of day. Well, he could say one thing about her...she was loyal.

"What do you think?" Chantel said.

"About what?" he asked.

She smiled. He knew it appeared as though he'd been staring at her long, bare legs.

"About preparing a meal ourselves?"

A stone of unease dropped in Race's stomach. Cooking was not something he was even remotely good at. And as far as food in his refrigerator, the pickin's were slim.

Chantel rose and headed into his kitchen. "There must be something in here that we could whip into a meal."

"I doubt it," he said, but that didn't stop her. He hadn't had a home-cooked meal in longer than he could remember. If she wanted to cook, he wasn't about to stop her.

"I have to warn you. My culinary skills are nonexistent. So, if you want to cook, you're on your own."

"Not a problem. As a matter of fact, I prefer it that way."

And that was the last word he heard from her in a while. What he did hear was cabinets swinging on hinges, drawers being opened and closed, hands rummaging through utensils. Soon enough, those sounds gave way to smells. Potent, full-bodied smells. For a while Race had been content to create the atmosphere by turning on the stereo, setting the dining room table and lighting candles. He had to go into the kitchen to find out what she had found to cook that had his stomach growling so loudly it sounded as if it were talking.

"What on earth did you find to cook?"

"Oh, this and that," she said, sounding like the bashful woman he knew she wasn't.

"It smells good," he said, standing over her shoulder.

Rice and gravy. One smothered pork cutlet, one smothered chicken breast. Carrots that smelled sweet and buttery.

"If there's one thing I can do, it's cook," she said.

"And write poetry," he added, lifting the lid on a small pot.

"Oh, yeah. That, too," she said. "I'll be ready to serve this in a few minutes. Why don't you open that bottle of wine I saw in the fridge?"

"Will do," he said.

As he retrieved the bottle and located the bottle opener he heard his mother's words—"Find a woman who can cook. A woman who can take good care of a kitchen can take good care of a man."

He wasn't sure where she'd gotten her logic, but in the back of his mind, he'd always held the criteria of cooking skills as something he'd look for in a woman by his side.

Maybe I should reconsider Chantel, he thought.

Race took the chardonnay and two wineglasses into the dining room. He poured the wine to let it breathe. Moments later, Chantel came into the room with two plates of something that made his mouth water.

She placed a plate in front of him, sat down across from him and put her plate down in front of her. The presentation looked like something one would find on the Food Network.

He was about to speak, but Chantel cut him off before he could start.

"I'm going to call it, Chantel's surprise," she said.

He picked up his wineglass. His stomach growled. "To Chantel's surprise," he said.

Her eyes sparkled suggestively. "To my surprise," she said, raising her own glass.

They both took long sips of the wine and dug into their food with vigor.

After several forkfuls, Race smiled. "I'm impressed,"

"Thank you. I love to cook, and I'm always experimenting with new things. This was a challenge, but I enjoyed trying to come up with a coherent meal with the selections you had in your kitchen."

"Thank you for being polite," he said. He knew he lived a stark bachelor's life. He wouldn't know how to put a meal together if his life depended on it. That meant his kitchen was far from stocked. If it weren't for housewarming gifts from friends, he doubted that he'd have pots or pans to cook with.

"You whip up a good meal like you whip up a good poem," he said.

She smiled and kept eating.

"Are you working on anything special right now?"

"No," she said, then took a sip of wine.

Race felt that same wall of unease fall between them. She was always quick to show him her poetry, but she never wanted to talk about it. He enjoyed her work so immensely; he couldn't resist asking her about it.

"Have you thought about putting your existing work into an anthology?"

She looked up at him as if she didn't quite know what an anthology was. "No," she said.

"Why not?" He took a bite of chicken. When he finished chewing, he said, "It's obvious you've got a theme running through it. Desires…just out of reach. It would be perfect for a chapbook."

Chantel looked afraid, as if he'd asked her to commit a felony or something. She opened her mouth to answer, when her cell phone rang.

"Gotta get that," she said.

She got up quickly and rushed to her purse, which she'd left on the couch.

He watched her, wondering why the subject of her own poetry made her so tentative.

"Hey, girl," she said, answering. "Oh, lord. I forgot. Race and I decided to have dinner at his place. Yes, Race. No, no." Then she lowered her voice. "I think I might be here for a while, so I'll need a rain check on the movie. Uh-huh. How about tomorrow? Okay, call you then. Bye."

Chantel closed her cell phone and put it back in her purse.

"I'm not keeping you from anything, am I?" Race asked when she returned to the table.

"No. I just missed a movie date with Kyra."

Kyra. There was a name he was trying to keep out of his thoughts all evening.

He hadn't been successful at all. Sitting next to Chantel at the club, he'd been looking at her but felt Kyra's presence. Sitting across from Chantel now, he was looking right at her, but seeing Kyra's face. And when he thought of the words to Chantel's poetry, it was Kyra's voice that he heard saying them.

Suddenly, his appetite was gone.

"What's wrong?" Chantel asked. She had finished her food and was nearly finished with her glass of wine.

"Nothing. Uh, I'm sorry, Chantel. I just thought of something that I was supposed to do and forgot. Please forgive me, but I'm going to ask you if you don't mind eating and running."

Her disappointment was obvious. Palpable.

"No, I guess not."

"Good. I apologize for this."

Race's frustration made it so that he couldn't get her out of the door fast enough.

"All right then. See you tomorrow?"

"Sure."

Whoosh. The door closed shut behind her.

He hadn't had a turmoil of emotions this bad in many, many years. Back in the day, when he thought he was some kind of poet, feeling like this would drive him to pen and paper.

And then without thinking, he headed to his office, grabbed a pad and wrote down everything he was feeling. He wrote until his entire arm grew tired and the sun was nearly due to come up.

It was like a dam bursting onto page after page. Emotions he'd held back rushed forth and came out through the ink, and filled every page.

Dots of perspiration broke out on his face and neck. For hours and hours, he couldn't stop.

When all his emotions were spent and written out on the pages in front of him, Race got up and finished off the wine, drinking straight from the bottle.

Something had turned him inside out. He couldn't wait to turn that something into the poetry he'd been longing to write for so many days.

Surprisingly, the person he wanted to share his words with wasn't Chantel. It was Kyra. They had promised to get together to read poetry. He would call her first thing in the morning and set a date.

Race went to bed then and wrote poetry in his sleep, dreaming of the moment when he could share his words—indeed his very soul—with the woman who had reawakened the poet in him.

Even the very next moment was not soon enough.

Chapter 12

Well, this is it, Kyra thought. The last legitimate excuse that she had for going into Race Jennings's office for any length of time. And because he'd been through so much drama, her boss ordered Race a top-of-the-line computer, with more bells and whistles than he could possibly use at work. DVD burner. Pentium 4. Hyper memory. His computer shouldn't break down before retirement. Unless something so drastic and unpredictable happened—like the computer imploding—and he needing her services again, she'd have to be satisfied with the occasional passing him in the hall, and of course seeing him the times he was with Chantel.

She tried to convince herself that this was a good thing, but felt like a deflated balloon nonetheless.

When she arrived at his floor, she ran into him as he

walked back to his office. As usual he looked the epitome of style, even on a casual day.

"I hope that's for me," he said.

"It is. And this time, I'm sure you won't have any problems."

They entered his office. There was no sign of the swinging balls.

"You're going to stay to make sure, right?"

Kyra thought of the wonderful time she would have just being in Race's presence. But her workload was backed up something awful. Her observations had already put her way behind. And the sooner she weaned herself from the powerful feeling Race brought over her, the better.

"I'm confident that we've solved the problem. I checked the pendulum. It was magnetic."

"I see," he said.

He said nothing more, simply watched as she hooked up his computer, turned it on and checked the system to make sure it was running properly.

With each minute that passed, Kyra's spirit sunk deeper and deeper.

"Log into your e-mail for me," she said, moving out of his chair. In a very short time, she'd become accustomed to the soft leather, the sense of being pampered that the chair provided. And the fact that it was where Race spent most of his time didn't hurt, either.

He sat down and did as she asked. He was able to log on and check his e-mail messages. He had several.

"Well, I guess that's it. I'll wait until Monday before I leave to close out your ticket…just in case you have any trouble. But I'm sure you won't."

"You're sure?" he said. His voice was ultraprofessional, but the expression in his eyes suggested he was talking about more than just his computer.

"I'm positive."

She headed toward the door. She was walking a lot slower than her normal brisk pace. Before she could step outside his office, she stopped and turned. She couldn't resist making one more comment to him.

"Let me know if you need anything."

She didn't wait for him to respond. Instead she picked up the pace and made it quickly back to her cubicle. A thin veil of perspiration covered her face and neck. She knew it had nothing to do with walking fast and everything to do with Race Jennings. The man was a biohazard and she was becoming radioactive.

Good God almighty! she thought. That man sure did something to her. She didn't have to have sex with him—although she realized that would be nice. Just being around him was ultimate satisfaction.

Kyra picked up her latest issue of *Wired* magazine and fanned with it. She had to get the man and his mysterious mesmerizing method off her mind.

There has got to be some meeting scheduled for today, she thought. At ComTel there was always a last-minute meeting scheduled at some time during the day. She would check her e-mail in hope that a notice was there and she would have to immerse herself in preparation for the meeting, the kind of preparation that would take her mind off of lust at the office.

When she opened her e-mail, she realized with hot exhilaration that she may never be free of him and that just maybe he was struggling with her absence as much as she was struggling with his.

The most recent e-mail was from Race. He must have sent it the moment she left his office. The subject line read, Dinner and a poem?

She opened the e-mail and her heart sounded almost as loud as his pendulum—clanging, banging and beating in her chest.

Don't think logically. Just react spontaneously.

Let me take you to dinner tonight. We can have a great meal—anywhere you want. And we can read poetry. Maybe Chantel's. Maybe not. Since you're not that familiar, I can expose you to words that will get in your soul and caress it...the way I want to sometimes, but can't because we're at work.

Don't think logically. React spontaneously. Act emotionally. See me tonight.

Race

Kyra didn't know whether to be flattered or offended. She believed she was a little of both. Was this man a straight-up dog or had something happened between he and Chantel?

The systems engineer in her wouldn't let her do anything other than think logically at that moment. She couldn't accept. Unless...

She didn't even bother engaging her security screensaver, which she always did. Instead, she hurried to Chantel's office and hoped that she was in.

Just like Race, Kyra met Chantel in the hallway.

"Hey, Ky!" Chantel beamed. She was stunning in a

vibrant purple suit and purple pumps to match. "I was just about to call you. I need some more poetry quick. This thing between Race and I is really heating up. He's such a wonderful man."

As they approached her office, Chantel lowered her voice. "Can you write me some 'I'm really diggin' on you, we were meant to be together with your fine ass' poetry?"

Kyra almost laughed. That was the only kind of poetry she was able to write lately. She had an entire notepad full of it.

"Sure," she said. Her voice came out a little sadder than she would have liked.

"What's wrong?" Chantel asked and took a seat behind her massive cherry desk.

"Nothing," Kyra said, sitting across from her. She remained still as the sad truth washed over her. She had her answer, without any probing of any kind. Chantel and Race were going strong. Perfect. So good in fact, Chantel wanted poetry to attest to that fact.

What a sour pickle, Kyra thought. She was writing poetry so that her best friend can hold on to the man she would give up all her computer skills to lie on top of.

"Life is funny," she said out loud without realizing it.

"You said it!" Chantel said. "I've been outbid on a Fendi bag ten times on eBay. It's crazy what people will pay for fashion."

Kyra took a good look at the woman who she knew had her back no matter what, and thought that it was crazy what people will do for love.

"So, what were you coming to see me about?"

"Huh? What? Oh…I just wanted to see if you needed any more poetry."

"Yeah, girl. As much as you can write. And while you're here," Chantel began then pulled out a drawer and drew out a package. "I was going to wait until later, but I can't. You're my girl and what you're doing for me, well, I can't thank you enough, Ky. So, I bought you something."

Chantel handed over the package. It was a flat box about the size of a paperback book. It was wrapped in white paper with gold brushstrokes. The bow was bright gold and so was the card. It read, For your creativity. Love, Chantel.

"Chantel—"

"Open it," she said.

Kyra did as she was instructed and her mouth dropped open in awe. It was a writing set. But not just any writing set. It was a Levenger pen-and-ink set with three different-sized nibs and a small pot of India ink. Kyra had promised herself a set like this whenever she got a poem published in a major magazine or literary journal.

"I know it's early, but I also know that you deserve it now. And not just for helping me, but for being the best-kept poetry secret in America. Your time is coming, Ky. I can feel it."

Fresh tears sprang to Kyra's eyes. She couldn't believe her thoughts and behavior over the past week. It was as if she'd forgotten how to respect a friendship like the one she had with Chantel. She got up and went to hug her friend. They shared a long embrace and then stared at each other with tearful smiles.

"You've never given up on me," Chantel said. "With all my flaws and every mistake I've made with men, you've been there. And I promise, this time with Race, I'm going to prove to you that I've made a good decision. I've picked a decent man. You'll see. This time, I got it right."

"Okay, okay," Kyra said, not wanting to think about the e-mail she received only minutes earlier. "Let's get ourselves together, before we start Niagara Falls up in here."

The two friends chuckled and wiped tears.

Tell her! Kyra's mind screamed. *Tell her her man is a dog!* But Kyra couldn't hurt her friend that way. As much as she wanted Chantel to learn a tough lesson about men and the way she deals with them, in the back of Kyra's mind, despite her crazy attraction, she hoped this time things would be different for Chantel.

"I'd better get back to my office," Kyra said. "I haven't done a lick of good work all week," she admitted.

"All right, girl. I'm going to get back to this Fendi. I'll be darned if I'll be outbid again."

Kyra laughed. "You sure have it good."

"Don't I?" Chantel admitted.

Kyra stopped before walking out of her office. "Thank you," she said, feeling humble and unworthy.

"You're welcome," Chantel said.

Kyra exited her friend's office knowing that she wouldn't allow herself to feel unworthy for too much longer. As soon as she returned to her office, she replied to Race's e-mail accepting his offer for dinner. Only she had no intentions of sharing a meal with him. Her goal was to clear the air between them once and for all. To make her position clear and to make sure Race knew that no matter what hot feelings passed between them, she

was off-limits. Period. End of story. Clarifying her
position off-site was only logical. She smiled at her
present knowing that nothing Race Jennings could say
or do would make her betray her friendship with
Chantel.

Nothing.

Chapter 13

ComTel was at a crossroads. Race realized this with a mixture of excitement and trepidation. He was excited because if he could veer the company away from the financial disaster it seemed to be headed for, it would be the biggest boon for his career. After that, he could write his own ticket. And he was up for the challenge. With the projects he'd worked on in previous companies—Strategic Cost Marketing, Balanced Score Card, Pyramid Budget Reduction—he'd been preparing for this undertaking his entire career.

His trepidation came because of the critical monetary juncture of the company. This was it: the make-or-break point. The place where companies either reinvented themselves and continued, or faltered and went the way of the dinosaur. Outdated and extinct.

The state of the company would not forgive, or

survive, a false move. His cost-justification plan had to work, or else. He would have been hired in vain. He would have failed to save the company he was brought in to rescue. Not only would that signal an end to his position as CFO, but a serious injury to his career. One he may never be able to recover from.

Race sat back in his chair and reviewed his plan one more time. Before he was hired, employees at ComTel were accustomed to spending any amount of money on anything they wanted. All they had to do was put in a requisition for it, and it was theirs. The telecommunications industry had seen a boon in the late eighties and through the nineties. Some years the industry had seen triple-digit growth.

But not anymore.

Nine-eleven brought a dip in the economy that some businesses were having trouble recovering from. ComTel was one of them. Race believed that ComTel needed a complete financial planning overhaul. But to kick off the process, simply instituting a plan that would put a purchasing process in place—requiring purchases to be evaluated and justified—would save the company upwards of one million dollars in the first year alone. His five-year plan included a phased-in process to cut costs, share resources, strengthen investments and solicit employee participation in creating money-saving opportunities in the company.

He realized as he prepared for his presentation that there was no middle ground with the plan. It would either work or it wouldn't. The success of ComTel was literally in his hands.

The board of directors had been in session all

morning. After getting preliminary schmoozing and catching up out of the way, they were going to listen to Race's presentation right after lunch. He'd prepared an upbeat slide show presentation. It would be quick and to the point. What he anticipated taking the most time was the question-and-answer portion. But after reviewing his notes and figures all morning, he knew he was ready for that, too.

He hadn't eaten lunch. He wanted to be fresh and ready for his presentation, not on the verge of sleep brought on by an after-lunch lull in energy. He would grab a bite from the cafeteria afterward.

He checked his watch. One-fifteen. He was due in the multimedia conference room at one-thirty. Wanting to be prompt, Race picked up his portfolio, planner and handouts, and headed toward the elevator lobby.

When an elevator stopped on his floor, a woman rushed off. "Enter at your own risk!" she said.

Race got on the car not knowing exactly what the woman meant, but hoping that she hadn't just passed gas or something.

He pushed ten and watched the floor numbers change on a large LCD screen above the door. Until the elevator stopped on the twentieth floor and Kyra got on, Race had been rehearsing his presentation in his mind. When the doors closed, all he could think about was the very thing he'd been trying not to think about for days.

"How's it going, techie?" he said, belying the familiarity he felt and the marvelous way in which her very presence did his body good.

"What's up, bean counter?"

Race was about to respond, when the car hiccupped.

"Whoa," Kyra said.

No sooner had she uttered her reaction, the car hiccupped again, lurched, then came to a slow stop on the fifteenth floor.

Race frowned and waited for the doors to open. They didn't.

Frustrated, he pushed the open button. Nothing happened.

"Well, I'll be…" Kyra said, looking displeased.

Even more frustrated, Race pressed more buttons. Buttons for floors above and below them.

"No!" Kyra protested. "Don't press anymore buttons. It's not…Stop!" she said and moved between Race and the floor panel.

"I'm trying to get this thing moving," he said.

"I know. But you aren't helping if you overload the circuit boards with commands. You're probably making it worse instead of better."

"So, what do you suggest?"

"I suggest we use the phone and call the maintenance department."

Race stepped forward. He was so close, he could smell the soap she showered with that morning. He reached around her to open the little door and pull out the phone.

This can't be happening. This can't be happening, he repeated in his mind. He had a presentation to make and of all people, he couldn't get trapped and shut up in an elevator with Kyra Douglas. *No. No. No.*

As soon as he put the phone to his ear, it called out to the maintenance department. The line rang and rang and rang. When no one picked up, he hung up the phone.

"What happened?" Kyra asked.

"No answer," he said and picked the phone up again. This time the line rang twice before someone answered. "Yes?"

"Hello. This is Race Jennings. I'm inside an elevator with another employee and the elevator has stopped on the fifteenth floor."

"Okay…"

"Actually, it's not okay. We'd like to get out, if that's not too much trouble."

"Okay…hold on."

"What's going on?" Kyra asked.

"They must have some numbskull working today. She doesn't seem to know her a—"

"Hello?" a person on the other end of the line said. This voice sounded different, but just as vacant as the first in an exasperating kind of way.

"How long will it take to get us?" Race asked.

"Where are you?"

"In an elevator."

"Okay. Which one?"

"The one that's stuck!" Race shouted. Then he scanned the panel and saw the number.

"Number six. We're in car number six."

"We?" the voice said.

"I'm here with another person," Race said.

"Okay, who?"

"What does it matter?"

"Because I have to fill out a report."

"Just get us out of here!"

"Um, Jill and I just fill out the reports. My manager works the equipment."

"Then put your manager on the phone!"

"I can't. He's at lunch."

"You have got to be kidding me."

"Uh, no. He'll be back in about half an hour. Call back then, okay?"

"Race!" Kyra said, taking the phone from him. He didn't know what she'd seen in his eyes, but it must have been violent. She snatched the phone away and stood back as if he were a bomb about to go off.

"Hello?" Kyra said into the phone. "Hello?"

She held the phone away from her and stared at it. "They hung up," she said.

"Yes," Race said, calmer than he felt. "We have to call back in half an hour."

"What?" Kyra asked, still holding on to the phone.

"Yeah. The guy who 'works the equipment' is at lunch. He should be back at two."

"Long lunch," Kyra said. "How can I get down?"

"How is it that you have jokes and we're stuck in an elevator?"

"Relax," she said, hanging up the phone. "It could be worse."

"How?"

A white-hot moment passed between them. Kyra waited too long to answer his question. In the time she took, he stared at her lips, imagined kissing them, heard sweet moans coming from her mouth. Pushed her chin up with his thumb, caressed her neck, played with the soft flesh he found there.

"I don't know," she said.

Race patted his pockets on the off chance he brought his cell phone with him. Of course he hadn't. But maybe…

"You don't happen to have a cell phone on you, do you?"

"Sorry. Fresh out."

Race blew out a hot breath. "This is ridiculous."

Kyra sat down on the floor. "Maybe it's fate."

"What do you mean?" he asked.

"I mean we've been doing a real good job of avoiding each other lately. This will force us to be close and disregard the weird—"

"Powerful—" he said, sitting beside her.

"Potent—"

"Incredible—"

"Mystifying—

"Attraction," Kyra finished. "But no matter what, Chantel is my girl. I wouldn't be her friend if I didn't hold her down. And I'm reminding you, I'm holdin' her down. You get what I'm saying?"

"Unfortunately, I do," he said.

"What 'unfortunately'? How can you say that? What kind of man are you?"

"The kind that knows when and how to stay out of trouble."

He turned to Kyra then. Looked at her dead on. "I'll behave, Kyra. You have my word."

"Good," she said, although she didn't quite sound as happy as that word implied.

"So, were you on your way to a meeting?" he asked.

"Isn't everyone around here?"

"Yes," he said, thinking of himself. "I suppose they are."

"I spend more time in meetings than I do actually at my desk working."

Race considered that and wondered how many other people in the company that was true for.

"Well, Mr. Money Man…any statistics on how much money this company spends in meetings?"

He chuckled. "No," he said. Then he got a feeling in his gut as if he'd just been struck in the stomach by a rogue bolt of lightning.

"What a great thing to analyze, though. If we could calculate that dollar amount and compare it to our ROI from those meetings, I'll bet people would be a lot less inclined to call meetings on whims the way they do."

"You've got a point," Kyra said.

Race sat up straighter. "We would really know if our employees are spending time in meetings or investing time in meetings." He smiled. "Kyra, you're a genius!"

"I know," she said, returning his smile, "but don't tell anybody."

They shared a laugh and glanced at each other playfully.

By the time a half an hour had passed, both Race and Kyra were late for their respective meetings and there was no sign of the car moving on its own.

"Ring the alarm again," Race said.

"What good would that do except scare whoever happened to be walking by and annoy the hell out of me?"

"You've got a point," he conceded.

When he took off his suit jacket, he noticed Kyra's

glance was on him. All on him, as if her eyes were taking the precise measurements of his muscles.

She could fight it all she wanted, but her eyes told the truth. She was into him. More than a little bit.

Damn female loyalty.

Men don't have nearly this much trouble going behind each other's backs. It was sad but true. And then Race realized how much he admired her for sticking to what she believed in and honoring her friendship.

"What do we do now?" she asked.

Race never realized how thin the elevator carpet was until his backside was against it, or how cheap the imitation wood paneling looked. He stared up from his position on the floor, grateful for the reminder that it's good to get a different perspective on things.

"Got any work?" he asked.

They had both gotten as comfortable as possible, sitting against the back of the car and stretching their legs out.

"Not unless you want to talk about your computer."

"No. It's fine. Better than fine. That machine hums like a sports car. I have no complaints."

"What did you do with your balls?" she asked.

"My pendulum is in a box in my apartment where it's safe."

"You don't have to keep it boxed up. You can have it out as long as it's away from your computer," she said. Her voice sounded so seductive, even when she wasn't trying.

Race loosened his tie and collar. Suddenly they felt just a bit too small. Choking. Cutting off his air. Out of the corner of his eye, he saw Kyra fidgeting as well.

She blew out a quick breath of exasperation. "Is it hot in here?"

Of course it is, Kyra, he thought. The only thing he'd been able to concentrate on since she stepped in this car was her legs, how long they are and what they could possibly taste like, the way they would shake after some really good lovin'. The heat radiating from his body because of those thoughts alone could ignite a series of small bonfires.

Kyra usually wore pants. Today was no different. She was the queen of pant suits, the kind that were sexy as hell because they hugged her body in all the places that curved and made a man want what was beneath that fabric.

The woman wore business casual suits almost every day and every day he saw her, he wanted to take them off. He knew in his soul that the woman could put on a potato sack and make it look sexy.

"Hmm," she said. "I guess not."

He'd seen her work, so he knew she wasn't that naive. "Of course you're hot. I'm hot, too."

She put her head in her hands, and shook it as if she still couldn't believe the way their bodies reacted to each other. "Do you think it would help if we moved away from each other."

"No."

"Me, either," she said.

He took a deep breath and released it, nearly angry. She was the one who placed them in the predicament they were in. He'd have taken her days ago if she'd let him. Sated this crazy urge drilling down in him like a railroad tie. Then it would be over and done with. This need. This burning inferno of—

"What are you wearing? It smells, so, so—"

"I was just about to ask you the same thing."

"Okay. We have got to get out of here. This is just plain nuts. I can't stand to be next to you if my hands aren't—"

"Shut up!" he said. "If you aren't going to do it, don't speak it."

"You're right. Of course. I should just chill. Just sit over here, keep my hands to myself and chill."

"That's right," he said.

"And what are you going to do?"

"Pray."

They looked at each other and couldn't keep straight faces. Soon their laughter filled the car and put them both at ease.

He closed his eyes for a moment and realized that hell couldn't burn as hot as his skin that very moment. He felt as though he'd turned into Johnny, the Human Torch from the Fantastic Four. Only Race didn't have to say, "Flame on!" His skin ignited every time he saw Kyra.

"What are you thinking?" she asked.

"I'm thinking somebody better hurry up and open these doors before I roll over and—"

"Never mind! Oh, this is terrible. What are we going to do?"

"Stay away from each other."

"We're doing that now."

"Oh, that's right. How's it working for us?"

"Not good," she admitted. "Well, okay…what usually takes your mind off of sex?"

"Having it," he answered honestly.

"I beg your pardon?"

"After I have sex, it frees my mind to think about other things...for a while anyway."

"Men. You are all alike."

"What was your first clue?"

"Hey? Aren't you even going to deny it?"

"What good would it do me?"

"None."

"Just like I thought."

"Wow. I never pegged you for a man that gives up easily."

He turned to look at her then. Really look at her. Did she really want him to go there?

"I know how to pick my battles. Sometimes it's best to save your energy, for—" he let his eyes travel the length of her body "—other things, better things."

She moaned in protest. "You're wrong. You're wrong. Stop talking like that, *please*."

"All right. I'll change the subject," he said. And not a moment too soon. His jones for the woman sitting next to him in the elevator was about to reach an all-time high. And after that, who knows what would come out of his mouth.

God, why would you create an intensity like this and not allow people to control it the way they need to. I'm at work, he went on pleading with God, and I want this job. I can't afford to do something boneheaded and stupid to lose it! Okay, God. Okay? Do you hear me up there?

"Wow, you really are praying."

"I sure am, Kyra," he said.

"Is it hot in here to you?" she asked, shifting next to him. It looked as though she were trying to move away.

He wanted to answer, "I'm always hot and burning, whenever I'm near you." He didn't though. He respected her choice to ignore their attraction and said, "It's a little warm, yes."

"That's what I thought."

She used a folder she'd been carrying to fan herself. It didn't do anything but circulate the fragrance she wore and make him even hotter than he was before she started fanning.

"Okay, I'm going to try again," Race said.

He got up and pulled the phone from its place inside the small compartment. The line rang and rang and rang.

Frustrated beyond reason, he began pushing the alarm button. It was annoyingly loud.

"Hey!" he called. "If there's anyone out there, we're stuck in here and need help!"

"Race!" Kyra said. "Calm down! Are you claustrophobic?"

"Hell, no!" he said and slammed the phone into its slot behind the door. He stopped ringing the alarm and paced in the small space.

Until then his concern was that the thirty-story building wasn't big enough for the two of them. And now, to be in a confined space with a woman his body craved, was too much.

It was making him crazy.

"I'm going nuts!" he said. "I need to get away from you."

Kyra looked him up and down. "Well, that's pleasant."

He stared at her. He tried looking in her eyes, but

every time he did, he ended up staring at her mouth. "You know what I mean."

"Yeah," she said, softly.

At her admission, he sat back down on the floor of the elevator.

"Can I just ask you a question?"

"I guess," she said.

"Has anything like this ever happened to you before? This kind of crazy, over-the-top—"

"Wild out, attraction?"

"Yeah," he said.

"No."

"Hmm. My first time, too."

They stayed silent for a while. And the world was silent around them. No ringing phones. No copy machines, fax machines, or coffee machines.

No interruptions.

Just the two of them. Being together in a way so deeply right, it angered Race that he couldn't have that feeling in his life all the time.

Finally, Kyra spoke up. "What *is* it?"

"I think it's chemical," he admitted.

"Chemical?" she asked.

"I did an Internet search on instant attraction and—"

"You did a Web search about us?"

"Just listen," he said, annoyed. "This kind of thing happens all the time. It's well documented."

"And?" she asked. Now she seemed intrigued. Sitting up straighter. Leaning a bit more toward him. Less tense. Interested.

"And scientists think that it has to do with the electricity in our bodies. Some folks have more than others.

Some folks emit it in different ways. And the output of some seems to be a perfect match to the output of others. The energy fits together like puzzle pieces. It's like the energy is constantly seeking out complementary energy. It's equal. It's opposite."

Kyra smiled. "And it reaches out, when it gets near it. It's pulled and drawn. Like magnets. Only since it's electricity, it's more powerful than a magnet."

"I see you've been on the same Web sites I've been on."

"Guilty," she admitted.

Funny, he thought. Nothing he did, no matter how he tried to put it out of his mind, nothing so far deterred his thoughts or his attraction to Kyra.

Obviously, he needed to try harder.

"Tell me about your name. It's not one I've heard before."

"It's not as uncommon as you think. I've met two other Kyras in my life. They told me that they've met other Kyras."

"Interesting," he said.

"Actually, it is." She did the right thing by keeping her face straight ahead. Not looking at him. Looking at him could mean disaster for them both. "I was named after my aunts—Keisha, Yvette, Robin and Ava."

"You're kidding?"

"Not at all. My mother loves her sisters very much. Now, what about you? I've *never* met anyone named Race. Is that short for something?"

"No. My parents were a force in the sixties. Sit-ins, marches, protests. You name it, they did it. They were arrested, hosed down, tear-gassed and shot at."

"Whoa. Where did you grow up?"

"Alabama. Montgomery. They said they named me Race because race is so important in this country. They wanted me to have the utmost pride in being African-American and to conduct myself in a manner that uplifts the race. And to never, ever forget what it means to be a person of color in the country. And what it has meant to be a person of color in this country."

"You have brothers and sisters?"

"I have a sister. Afrika. And a brother, Blaque."

"Your parents were hardcore."

"Still are. They still live in Montgomery because there's much work to be done."

"You're not serious," she said.

"Don't think I'm not. Sixty-year-old couple with picket signs and black fists marching in predominately white neighborhoods talkin' 'bout, 'We shall come over! We shall come over!'"

"You're making that up!" Kyra said, laughing.

Now, he'd done it. He'd made her smile and laugh. Her happiness stirred his soul. Made him even warmer.

"Well, I may be exaggerating a little bit, but not much. I usually tell people that so when they meet my parents, they aren't so alarmed at how militant they are, still, at their age."

"So are you like them? Are you...militant?"

"I used to be," Race admitted. "I followed right along in my parents' footsteps as an activist and cultural worker. When I got arrested the first time for protesting a mill working company for discrimination against black men, my parents said, 'Right on!' and called all their friends and told them how proud they were that I was in jail."

"No, no, no!"

"I'm telling you the truth here."

"I don't believe that," she said, laughing again.

"I couldn't lie to you," Race admitted.

"No," she said, then turned and looked at him strangely. "I don't suppose you could."

Distraction, distraction, his mind called. Otherwise, he wouldn't care if they ever got out of there. They would just jump each other's bones and get it over with.

"What do you think of this?" he said, and pulled a piece of paper out of his pocket.

He'd been carrying that paper around in his pocket all day. It was something that popped into his head last week.

"I know you said you don't know much about poetry, but I wrote something for Chantel. I thought since you're her friend, you could tell me if she'll like it."

Kyra smiled weakly. "I'll try," she said.

"Ink" he began, "like blood flowing, connects letters, words, people, friends like us who conjugate like verbs, diagram each other like sentences, the sweetest syntax is shared."

Race's blood coursed through his veins unchecked. It had been years, years, since he'd read a poem out loud to anyone. It was like unzipping his body and letting Kyra see exactly what was inside him.

He knew his poem was a rough, but with some polish, it might be good. That was until he saw the look on Kyra's face.

"What?" he asked.

"Well…"

"Don't toy around. I'm a big boy. I can handle the truth."

"You sure?" she asked.

"Of course," he said. He knew he'd been away from poetry, but he remembered the important things.

"It needs work," she said.

He nodded. "I know. It's just my first draft. I'll tweak it to—"

"A lot of work."

"What?" he asked, not sure he heard her correctly. She couldn't have been speaking about the lyric he'd spent several days working on.

"Like what?" he asked, not sure if he wanted her to go on.

"Like dismantle it and start again," she said, staring at him with timid eyes.

"Maybe you just didn't understand it," he said.

"Then what good is it?" she said.

"Some poets and their poetry are deep. It's not superficial. Not everyone can get to where some poets go with their words. Besides, you said you don't know much about—"

"Again, I say, what for? If you write a poem that only you and a handful of people on the planet can relate to, you're doing a disservice to the art."

"Sometimes it's art because not everyone can relate to it."

"Who said that?" Kyra said.

"I think I just did," he said, feeling defensive.

Kyra sighed. The intensity of her gaze told him that there was passion behind her words. He wondered where that passion came from. At the same time he was intrigued and wanted to see all the passion she was willing to show him.

"Well, you're not alone. There are plenty of people

who believe that. But I believe poetry is a service. Poets have the privilege of transcribing, interpreting and recording the human experience."

"I agree," Race said.

"Then do you agree that it makes no sense to build an apartment building that you have no intentions of allowing people to move into. You can do it, but it's an affront to the materials you used to build it and the people who need shelter that you won't allow to come in."

Race laughed.

"My parents have furniture that no one can sit on. It's their furniture. It's their prerogative. But all my life I've always wondered, why?"

He sighed. "You have a point."

"It's your work. You can write it anyway you want. But why not write it in a way in which people can connect, directly, and that doesn't alienate people because they don't feel 'smart enough' to 'get it'?"

"For someone who claims not to know much about poetry, you sure have a strong opinion about it."

"Maybe I don't know much, but I do know that the primary reason people give for not reading poetry is that they don't understand it."

Forget passion. She was downright indignant about this poetry thing. Race was starting to believe she knew more about poetry than she admitted to. It made him wonder.

"How do you know that?" he asked.

"I, uh, Chantel told me."

"Umm," he said. But he was not convinced. The expression on her face and the feeling in his gut told him something was amiss. If there was anything to that chemical attraction theory, then he knew to trust his instincts.

Maybe Kyra believed that computer techies had to keep their poetry appreciation a secret. Curiosity churned inside him. He wondered what else she knew.

"Any suggestions on how I can make my poem more understandable?"

"It sounded like what you were doing was relaying a feeling. That's fine, but try telling a story instead. Sometimes feelings are best understood when they are brought out in the lessons of a story."

"Great suggestion," he said, thinking that was a powerful idea. All the books he'd read about writing poetry in the past and he'd never gotten a piece of advice he connected with more so than what he'd just gotten from Kyra.

"You fix computers, you fix poetry. What else can you do?"

Kyra stared into his eyes. He liked the way she looked at him. He swallowed dryly. They were getting too cozy.

She got up and walked toward the elevator panel. "I'm calling again," she said. But she didn't have to. No sooner had she picked up the phone, than a voice came over an intercom system that Race didn't even know existed.

"Sorry about the delay. I understand you are stuck between floors."

"Actually," Race said, standing, "it looks like we've stopped on the fifteenth floor." He felt awkward speaking to an invisible voice in the sky.

"According to the computer, you're between fifteen

and sixteen. But whatever the case, we're gonna manually lower you to the first floor. We'll get the doors open there and take the elevator out of service. We've been getting calls on this car all morning."

"Thank goodness," Kyra said. She combed her fingers through the thick twists of her hair.

She's nervous, he thought. Heck, he had to admit, he'd been affected, too. Being caught with Kyra in a small space, it was enough to make him forget to be a gentleman and go for what he knew both their bodies wanted.

He'd been good. Very good. He was going to reward himself by taking Kyra's advice and reworking the poem to tell a story. The story of his love affair with words. Maybe that would get Kyra and her luscious lips and her rich, dark want-to-immerse-himself-in skin off his mind for five minutes.

They waited. For three minutes there was nothing, just his and Kyra's breathing and impatience. Then a jerk, a creak, and the car started moving down.

He and Kyra looked up to see the numbers on the LCD panel flicker, dim and finally come back to life.

Race picked up his papers and jacket. He inhaled deeply of the air that had become concentrated with Kyra's perfume. He shrugged. He'd missed the meeting. He'd missed the first opportunity to show the powers that be his financial plan for the company. Under any other circumstance he would have been irate, angered that all his hard work had gone for naught. But an unusual calm possessed him. Made him believe that he would have another chance and reminded him that all things happened for a reason. He would put his time with Kyra to good use even if it became nothing more than a memory he kept close, an inspiration he grabbed in the middle of the night when his house was silent and his bed was empty.

Right before the doors opened, Race took a deep breath and one more look at Kyra. Surprisingly, she smiled.

"It's been fun," she said.

The sarcasm in her voice told him she was far from serious. "Really?"

"No. Let's not ever do this again."

"Agreed," he said. But he didn't mean it. What man wouldn't want to be stuck in a confined space with a beautiful woman? He couldn't think of one.

He stretched a bit. Being on the hard floor of the elevator, no matter how brief, was enough to make him feel stiff. *Note to self: get a massage. Full-body. ASAP.* All this chemical attraction business between him and Kyra was making him tense.

At the ding, the doors whooshed open. Cool air met Race and Kyra as they hurriedly stepped out into the bright lights of the lobby.

A man in a maintenance uniform passed them as they stepped out of the car. He pressed the "all stop" button in the elevator and used a set of keys to open the control panel.

"Are you going to take an elevator back up?" Kyra asked.

"No," Race said. Frankly, he didn't know exactly what he was going to do. But one thing was certain; he needed to recover from being in Kyra's close proximity.

"I think I'm going to sit in the rec area and read my proposal."

"Is there someone upstairs who might wonder where you are?"

Race glanced around. The lobby looked the same. Gray marble flooring, cherry wood paneling, high lighted ceilings. And all the people with their business suits, ties and briefcases went along as though the world hadn't just changed.

"I guess," Race said, stroking his chin pensively. "Will you do me a favor and tell Sally what happened and where I am."

"Sure," Kyra said.

She headed off toward another elevator that had just come down. How he wanted to watch her walk away. But that would just be torture. Instead, he kept his eyes on the outside doors and the employee sitting area just to the side of those doors.

"Race?" Kyra's voice caressed him from behind.

"Yes," he said, barely turning, barely looking at her.

"Good luck with your poem," she said and stepped on to the elevator. The doors closed before he could respond.

"Thanks," he said anyway.

Chapter 14

Turk looked hungry. "So enough about your personal life, how's your work life?"

Kyra shrugged. "Same ol', same ol'. Nothing to jump off a cliff over."

"What about your boy and his computer? You get it fixed?"

"Yeah," she said, remembering the problem. Just the visual image of the pendulum swinging and short-circuiting Race's computer made her smile.

"What's funny?" Turk asked.

"Race. He broke every last one of those computers by putting a magnetic toy on it."

"What kind of toy?"

"You know those Newton's Cradles that swing back and forth. His was magnetized."

When the chuckle broke free, Kyra had no intentions

of laughing, but then she got caught in a wave and couldn't stop. "He...he wrote these nasty...nasty e-mails about my team...and how they didn't have a clue how to fix a computer, when all the time..."

"Sounds like an idiot to me," Turk said.

"Hey!" she shouted. "He's far, far from an idiot."

Suddenly, her giddiness evaporated in a cloud of protection that she felt she had to provide.

"Darn, woman. Calm down."

"Sorry," she said, embarrassed that her back had risen so high with his offhand comment.

"Don't be sorry. Just realize that you're sprung."

She sank into a chair. That one word had pulled the energy straight out of her. "No, Turk. I can't be sprung."

"Why not? Most people experience it once in their lives. Go with it while the feeling is still fresh and wet in your drawers."

"You are so nasty!" she said, turning up her nose.

"And truthful. Every time you mention *Race*, I can tell he got you changin' your panties two or three times a day."

Kyra smacked Turk this time. No playing. She hit him dead upside the head.

"Ow! Don't punish me 'cause the truth hurts. Besides, if you'd give him some, you wouldn't have all this frustration or embarrassment because of the way he makes you feel."

She turned her head. She didn't want to hear the words that were coming out of his mouth.

"You know I'm right. If you were gettin' it on the regular, you'd be braggin' about it. Maybe not a lot, but you'd be braggin'. Admit it."

"I don't care what you say, Turk. When it comes to

the men I select, I have some rules, like, I don't date married men, bi-men, men with girlfriends, or broke-down men. And I especially don't date my friends' men, current or ex. Several of those categories fit this situation. They are overlapping. And you don't get it. Race has a girlfriend who just happens to be my best friend and your sister. Even if they broke up today, he'd still be off-limits. I don't date my friend's ex's. Never have. Never will."

"Humph. With my sister, that means half the eligible bachelors in town."

"You are *wrong*, and you know I'm going to tell her!"

"Tell her. She knows it's true."

Kyra shook her head in disbelief. It was true; Chantel had had her share of men. She'd gone through them like sand through the hourglass. Most of them had dogged her. And she hadn't learned her lesson.

But Kyra was hopeful. Race didn't seem like the typical player, dog or hound who was just out for a piece. But then again her opinion could be tainted by her attraction to the man and the fact that she hadn't been able to get over the image of discovering him in such a vulnerable position since she'd run into him in the men's room.

Since then, she'd written ten poems. Most of them good, if she did think so herself.

"Kyra has just left the building," Turk said.

"Sorry," she said, looking up. "I was just thinking about words."

"Whose?"

"Mine," she admitted.

"Lay some on me," Turk said. "My soul could use a good poem."

Kyra was hesitant. When they were together, Kyra would read her poetry as a prelude to sex.

"It's okay. I won't try to jump your bones or anything."

"Better not," Kyra said.

She thought about getting up, but she didn't need to. She had a poem in her mind. She'd been working on it all day. It was about impressions. The first kind. It seemed to her that Race had made an impression on her. The kind that deserved and probably required deep reflection and study. And the best way she knew to do that was to set her reflection to verse, to set it free.

She closed her eyes and spoke the words floating and simmering and dancing and reeling in her mind.

"What do you do when your first impression of a man is so complete, you know him instantly, and you want to spend every minute of the rest of your life proving what you know?"

"Wow, Ky. You're getting better."

"You think so?" she asked.

"Know so. You have to keep your dream alive."

Suddenly Turk started talking like Jesse Jackson. "Keep hope alive! Keep hope alive!" he chanted.

He slid over and kissed her on the forehead. "I gotta go, Maya Sanchez."

"So soon?" Kyra asked. But it wasn't soon. Turk had been at her apartment for nearly three hours.

"Yeah," he said. "I got a date."

"A date?" she asked, thinking this was the first time he'd mentioned dating in a few weeks.

"Yeah. A date. And she's hot." Then he paused. "Jealous?" he asked.

Now, Kyra paused and gave his question serious consideration. He had been her man at one time. Did she mind him seeing other women? She thought and thought and then answered honestly.

"No."

"Damn!" he said and snapped his fingers.

She walked him to the door. He turned inches away and stared down into her face. He used to do that when they were together, right before he would plant a serious kiss on her. She prayed he wasn't going to try anything like that. She would hate to give him a black eye. It would ruin his handsome face and probably hurt her hand, but she would do it.

"God, Ky. You look beautiful. I know I say that all the time, but you really do. You're not even with this guy, what's his name, Race? But it doesn't matter. He's gotten inside you somehow...and it shows. You look...radiant and sexy as hell."

Kyra smiled and blushed. "Thank you, Turk. Now get out of here!"

He didn't say another word, just strutted like a rooster/pimp. He was always complaining about going up and down her long apartment staircase. But not tonight. Tonight he looked as though he could conquer the world.

If only she could purge the desire she had for Race to look at her the way Turk did. For him to say the things that Turk said—even some of the nearly vulgar things.

"God, help me please," she said out loud and then went to her writing desk to put her thoughts to paper. She hoped getting them out would keep them out.

And for the rest of the night, it worked. Getting her feelings on paper helped her to put thoughts of the tall, dark and handsome man out of her mind.

Until the next day at work when she discovered both an e-mail message and a voice mail message from Race.

The man is crazy, she thought. We agreed to stay away from each other and here he is calling me, e-mailing me. She couldn't resist. She played his voice mail message one more time as if the words would change the second time she heard them.

"Kyra, it's Race Jennings. I have something I need to run past you. Please call me when you get a chance. I'll be in meetings all afternoon, but I'm free this morning."

Stunned, she played the message one more time. Compulsively, she was about to play it a third time when Chantel poked her head into her cubicle.

"Knock, knock," she said.

"Hey," Kyra said, hanging up her phone.

"Hey. What's up?"

"Nothing. I mean, you know. Same ol', same ol'."

"Do you have something for me?" Chantel asked.

"Oh, yeah. I do," Kyra said. She would have dropped off the poem sooner, but as she was headed toward Chantel's office, she saw Race headed in that direction, too. So she'd decided to avoid him first thing in the morning and go to her office instead. Little did she know that Race was already there waiting for her...electronically.

"Here you go," Kyra said, handing over the manila folder.

"Thanks!" Chantel said, moving off.

"Aren't you going to read it?" Kyra asked.

"Don't need to. You've been in the zone recently. Everything you write is all the way off the chain. I know what's in here is the bomb."

"Thanks," Kyra said.

"Thank *you!*" Chantel said, and took herself and her orange miniskirt suit back to her office.

Kyra hung her head. She didn't know how much longer she could keep up this charade of ghostwriting poetry for her friend. Even though the poems came fast, turning them over to be claimed by someone else was taking its toll.

"What's wrong?" Orlando asked.

"Nothing telling the truth wouldn't fix," Kyra said, feeling a bad case of the guilts.

"What did you do? Tell Sam he was handsome?"

Kyra laughed, wishing she really could share the details of her deception with someone. "Something like that," she joked.

"Well, just remember, brownnosing may get you ahead, but you still have dookey on your face."

Kyra laughed. "Get out of here, Orlando! Let me get some work done!"

"What for? No one else is working," he said and headed for his cube.

Kyra sat down, grateful for the distraction. No sooner had she let the relief wash over her, than her phone rang. She glanced at the caller ID.

It was Race.

Damn, she thought, and willed her hands not to move. But her right hand had a mind of its own. Completely disregarding her wishes, it picked up the phone and brought it to her ear.

"Systems. This is Kyra," she said, offering her usual greeting in a situation that was far from usual.

"Kyra, I've been trying to get in touch with you all morning. Can you come to my office for a moment?"

"Did your computer break again?"

"No. It's something else."

"Race, my plate is full this morning. I've got—"

"Please," he said. "How about ten a.m.?"

She closed her eyes and swallowed hard. "I'll see you at ten."

"Good," he said, and hung up.

Damn, damn, damn! her mind shouted. Oh well. If he wants anything other than business, she was out. And she would go straight home, to douse herself in ice cold water. And then she would put in her resignation, she thought. Two of us under the same roof is not going to work.

But Kyra had no intentions of resigning. And unfortunately, she'd used up her sabbatical. The only thing left to do was fudge on her sick time. Instead of taking days off for an illness, she could take days off, weeks even, to cool off from the effects of Race Jennings.

"Woo!" she said and picked up a file on her desk and fanned with it. Even over the phone, the man had access to the dials that turned up her heat. Talk about a heat wave. Whew!

For a moment, Kyra wondered what would happen if she came clean. If she just went to Chantel and said, "Girl, I don't know what's wrong with me, but I can't stop thinking about your man," or "Channy, your man has been putting the moves on me and *hon*-ey, it's workin'!" Her mind didn't linger on that absurd thought for too long. Chantel looked pretty and feminine, but she had a touch of street rat in her. For all Kyra knew, Chantel would pull something out of her purse and threaten to do her bodily harm.

Kyra sighed with exhaustion and racked her brain to figure a way out of the curse and spell her aching body was under. She had no idea something so potent could exist in life. It almost made her believe in magic and voodoo.

"I think someone put roots on me!" she remembered a woman saying in an old commercial. And that's just the way Kyra felt.

She glanced at the clock on her computer. Eight-fifteen. She had less than two hours to check the logs and backups, find security updates and check for system patches. She would do it, commit to it, and think no more about her ten o'clock meeting.

Surprisingly, it worked. By the time she headed to Race's office, her libido had calmed down. It was in check and obeying her wishes. Then she stepped into his office and all her hard work unraveled within seconds.

He was wearing a suit. A nice suit. A really, really, really nice suit. He looked too good to work. Just strut and stand and pose. One hundred percent way too sexy for his office.

"Morning," she said.

His eyes sparkled. The way they always did when he looked at her. "Good morning," he said. "Thank you for coming."

"No problem," she said.

She came in, all the way, and took a seat across from him. Breathed slowly.

"What can I do for you?"

He pulled a piece of paper from a leather portfolio on top of his desk. "Let me know what you think of this," he said.

She took the paper as he handed it to her. When she got a good look at it, she realized it was a poem.

"Race, I don't want to take work time to—"

"Then don't. You get a fifteen-minute break in the morning. I'd bet the farm you haven't taken it. I'd bet my soul that you never take breaks. Work straight through, right?"

"Right."

"According to my calculations, the company owes you about ninety days worth of breaks. And I'm the CFO, I can calculate pretty good. So, what's fifteen minutes now?"

Kyra smiled despite herself.

"I just want some feedback. Please," he said.

"All right," she said and read the revision of Race's poem.

"Well?" he said when she'd finished. "What do you think?"

"I think it's better," she said telling the truth. It was better.

"But?"

"I didn't say *but*."

"I know. I heard one, though."

"There's no *but*. What you have is good for a second draft. You took my advice very well. You just need to keep at it. Put some emotions in it. Make the readers feel what you are talking about."

"I thought I did that," he said, scrunching his face and raising his voice.

Kyra was taken aback. "Look, if you can't take criticism, I'm out."

"Sorry," he said. "It's just that I haven't done this in so long, and I'm rusty...at everything. Including taking criticism. Please go on."

Kyra sat back for a moment and thought about how to restate her opinion. "You've heard of Frank Sinatra?"

"Yeah," he said, deepening the frown on his face.

"I heard a story about the first time he went to a voice coach. He sang 'Stormy Weather.' At least he *tried* to sing 'Stormy Weather.' The coach told him that it was obvious he didn't know what he was singing about. He really hadn't experienced that kind of pain and until he did, he should stay away from those kinds of songs. It wasn't until Ava Gardner broke his heart that he could sing those songs and really interpret them. Frank singing 'Stormy Weather' after a breakup with Ava is enough to give a person goose bumps."

Race shook his head. "I'm missing something here," he said.

"I assume this poem is about Chantel?"

"That's right."

"Well, there's no emotion here. Just words. Don't get me wrong, they're good words. But there's nothing underneath them. No emotion. What do you feel, Race? Write about that."

He didn't say a word. Only stared straight ahead. Straight through her.

"You okay?" she asked.

"Fine," he said. "You've given me something to think about...."

"What?" she asked, noticing that he had more to say.

"It's just that I used to be good at this. At least I thought I was good. Hmm…? I think I should have never brought my pen out of retirement."

"No, no. You've got some skills here. I can tell. Don't put your pen down or retire it. Just keep going. You'll get it."

"You think so, huh?"

"I know so."

They smiled at each other freely. Race was clearly grateful for her opinion and her encouragement. She could see it on his face.

When his phone rang, the disappointment they shared was palpable.

He just stared at the ringing machine as if it offended him. He didn't move to answer it. Instead, he looked up at her.

"Well, I guess break is over."

"I guess so," she said and handed him his poem.

"Thank you," he said.

She got up, smoothed her pants and toned down the smile that wanted to take over her face. "Anytime," she said without thinking.

His eyebrows rose and a cool expression took over his entire face. "I'll take you up on that."

Kyra left without another word. She didn't need one. He had said them all.

Chapter 15

Race grunted and crumpled up yet another poem. He'd understood exactly what Kyra said all too well. He had taken her advice and tried to write about his feelings. More specifically, his feelings for Chantel. Trouble was, he didn't have any.

He only had feelings for the poetry she wrote. Could he write about that?

He scribbled across his notepad "Ode to Chantel's Poetry" and started writing. But even that didn't come out right.

Frustrated, he tore the paper from the pad, crumpled it into a ball and tossed it aside with the other attempts he'd made.

Eleven in all.

It was turning into a long evening.

Tired of his poor attempts at poetry, Race realized

he needed something more positive to focus on. No sooner did he have that thought, but his phone rang.

Call from Ernest Maduli. Call from Ernest Maduli.

Race smiled at his audio caller ID and picked up the phone.

"What's up, man?"

"Everything. You ought to know that by now. What's up with you?"

"Other than a new job, not much."

"Well, something's up. Otherwise you wouldn't have sent me that poem. Thought your inkwell was dry, my brother."

Race wondered to himself if that was true. "Well, it was, but lately, I've had my pen in the ink pot just to see if it still loves me."

"And?" his friend asked.

"Time is a B. Unforgiving as hell."

"That's because you've been away from the well for so long, you've forgotten how to drink. But a few sips should clear you right up. I could use a deep and deep brother such as yourself."

"Forget about me," Race said, even though he was flattered by his friend's words. "What about the poem I sent."

"It's the truth, brother. That's why I called. Figure I would tell you in person instead of sending a letter. I'm going to put it in the December/January issue."

"Excellent!" Race said.

He'd taken a chance. A bold chance. He knew Chantel's poetry deserved to be published, so he'd sent Ernest one of his favorites. And his instincts had been correct.

He couldn't wait to tell her the good news!

* * *

Kyra closed her eyes and let the soapy, hot water soothe her. She'd run a bath with her favorite bath salt. She'd turned off the lights, turned on Miles and lit one hydrangea-scented candle to keep her company in the bathroom.

She'd had a long day. After a twelve-hour shift, she'd finally caught up with the work she'd missed while helping Race with his computer. Her daily status reports had piled up. She hadn't turned one in all week. She knew her boss, who didn't have a clue anyway, had no idea what she'd been doing last week, with the exception of working with Race. He was probably oblivious to everything else. Well, she'd e-mailed him everything before she left. She'd done so much work that tomorrow she might actually be able to coast through the day, barring emergencies.

Slowly she moved her legs. Listened to the sound of the water and the sound of notes so pure they almost made her cry. Miles, she thought. A splendid blending of pain and perfection.

Her thoughts of pain and perfection made her remember Race's poem. He was striving for perfection but what'd he'd written was painful to read. There was potential, but mostly it needed a lot of work.

What was he trying to say, she wondered. The poem seemed to be about friendship, which was strange since Kyra believed that he and Chantel were more than friends. And the poem was bereft of emotion. Just bone dry. Surely if he cared anything about Chantel, there would be some emotion there, even if it was clumsy and awkward, and full of rookie writing mistakes, there'd be some trace of feelings.

But there was nothing.

The realization made Kyra sit up in the tub. Did Race care about Chantel at all? And if he didn't, then he was wrong to play games with her.

Kyra leaned back and let the water cover her once more. As soon as she was finished relaxing and bathing, she would call Chantel, see if she had any of her famous peach cobbler, and talk to her about her "relationship." Try to find out if there was any trouble in paradise that Chantel needed to talk about.

"Hey, girl!" Chantel said, opening the door to her apartment. "You're lookin' good. What's his name?"

Kyra stepped past her friend, who was wearing a designer jogging suit more expensive than most of the business suits the ComTel employees wore.

"There's no man," Kyra said.

"Really? 'Cause I've only seen you look like that when a guy was rockin' your world on the real."

"Not this time. I just had a nice long bath with candles and Miles."

"Miles Davis. Girl, you are in love with a dead man."

"He's alive in the most important way possible. In my heart. Through his music. The man is immortal. He'll live forever!" Kyra said. And she meant it. She did feel a little somethin' somethin' for Miles Davis. He was a musical genius and had touched her soul the way no man alive ever had. One day when she was married and had children, Miles would still be her man.

"So, you got some cobbler for me?"

"It's in the oven," Chantel said.

Kyra followed her into the kitchen.

Chantel's apartment was everything one might expect from a woman like her. Pure designer luxury. From her French media cabinet to her Dutch colonial dining table, Chantel's apartment was a testament to taste, elegance, style and expense.

"I thought you said you had one already made?"

"I lied."

"Chantel, you didn't have to make one especially for me. You didn't have to go to that trouble."

"Yes, I did. Look at the trouble you've gone to for me. You've had poetry ready for me every day for two weeks. I can at least make you a cobbler."

"Thanks, girl," Kyra said.

"No problem at all and no trouble at all, either!" Chantel said. "Now, what do you want to drink with your pie?"

"Milk," Kyra said.

"You got it!" Chantel said.

"So, how's your home computer?"

"I haven't had any problems since you got rid of all that spyware."

"Good. Do you remember what I said?"

"Yes. Stop opening attachments."

"Right. What else?"

"Stop downloading so much," Chantel said, pouring the milk.

"And?" Kyra said hoping her friend remembered the most important thing.

"Keep my virus protection software running at all times and scan my hard drive at least once per week."

"Wow. You do remember."

Chantel leaned against the sink. "That's right. She can be taught!"

The two shared a laugh and then Chantel joined Kyra at the kitchen table.

"So, you've never said how it's going. I mean, I'm writing all this poetry. So, does he like it? Or in Dr. Phil-speak, 'How's that workin' for ya?'"

"Sorry, girl. I should have shared all this with you sooner. He loves the poetry. Absolutely loves it. As a matter of fact, it's all he wants to talk about when we're together. I think he's in love."

"Really?" Kyra said, ignoring for the first time the delicious sweet aroma coming from the oven to focus on Race's love for her words.

"What are you saying?" she asked.

"I'm saying, sista girl, keep them coming, okay. He's taken. Completely."

The question nagging in the back of Kyra's mind came limping up to the surface.

"So when are you going to tell him that you haven't been writing the poems? And how? I mean, don't you think it's going to be quite a blow when you tell him the truth?"

Chantel got up and put on two brightly colored oven mitts. The mitts matched the décor of the kitchen. Matched Chantel's carefree and fashion-conscious life-style. Most people would hang those mitts for decoration.

"I've been meaning to talk with you about that," she said, opening the oven.

The heavenly aroma of fresh peach cobbler rushed out and assaulted Kyra in all the right ways.

But something was wrong.

"Especially now," she said, placing the cobbler on a rack to cool.

"What do you mean?" Kyra asked. She sat back in her chair and waited for Chantel to tell her whatever it was that was keeping her from looking Kyra in the face.

Suddenly, her friend spun around with an artificial smile plastered on her face. "Ky, I have a surprise for you. Your poem 'One Mo' Gin,' is going to be published in the *Truth to Power* literary journal."

"What?" Kyra said, taken aback. From her friend's strange behavior, she'd assumed that it was bad news that she needed to relay. But this news…she couldn't believe it!

"What! How!" she said, wanting all the details and wondering why her friend didn't seem to be forthcoming with them.

"Well—"

"Oh, my God!" Kyra said, unable to control herself. She bounded from the chair, rushed over and gave her friend a tremendous hug.

"Careful!" Chantel said, a little out of breath. "This oven is hot."

"Sorry. I'm sorry! I just, I mean, I can't believe you did this for me. How did you arrange it?"

"Actually, it wasn't me. It was Race."

Kyra backed away, not understanding. "Huh?"

"Let's sit down," Chantel said, placing her hand gently on Kyra's shoulder.

Kyra shrugged off the hand just as gently. "I don't want to sit down," she said.

"Suit yourself," came her friend's response. Chantel wasted no time in reclaiming her seat at the table.

"Chantel, what's Race got to do with this?" she asked. Now the feeling that something was amiss returned with a mission. It churned up her stomach like a rototill.

"His friend is the editor of the magazine. So, he took one of the poems that I gave him and—"

"You *gave* him?"

"Well, yeah. He likes them so much, I want him to have them. So, I—"

"Chantel, you have no right to give away my poems."

"Now, listen. You're going to love this. Anyway, Race's friend likes your work and he wants to publish it in the December/January issue of the magazine. So what do you think?"

Kyra made her way back to the table. A feeling in her gut told her to walk cautiously.

"So, then Race already knows you're not writing the poetry, right?"

"Not exactly."

"What do you mean *not exactly?* He has to know. Otherwise—"

"Ernest is publishing the poetry under my name, Ky. That's what I wanted to tell you."

Kyra was standing still. She knew she was. But the room was spinning. Everything in Chantel's kitchen whirred around her as if she were the center of a malicious hurricane. Her stomach soured. She couldn't eat peach cobbler now if someone force fed it to her.

"Chantel, you cannot be serious."

"It's just one poem."

"One poem that I've given birth to like it's my own child. And you *know*, you *know* how badly I want to be published. It's what I've lived for for fifteen years. Do you think I'm going to let one of my poems be published without my name on it? You have lost whatever that is that passes for your mind!"

"Ky, stop. Sit down. Have some cobbler."

"I better get out of here right now, while we're still friends."

Kyra headed for the door, hot tears stinging her eyes. Every time. It happened every time. Chantel lost her mind when it came to men and always, always ended up doing something really stupid in the name of *love*.

And every time, Kyra went along for the ride. Thinking that she had to be there for her friend because that's what friends do. Humph. Another one of her stinking rules. Always have your friend's back.

What a crock if it always ended up hurting her in some way!

Kyra made it to Chantel's front door and swung it open. "You will call Race tonight and tell him about the poetry. If you don't, I'll tell him first thing tomorrow!"

"Kyra, I can't!" she called after her, but Kyra was already crossing the yard and heading toward her car.

"Ky! It's the only thing I've got with Race! We don't have anything else! Please, Ky! He won't love me if I tell him!"

Kyra could hear no more. She couldn't get into her car fast enough. She did everything except peel out. She sped down the street so fast, she had to quickly remind herself that she was in a residential district.

When she slowed down, her heart was racing and her

breathing was ragged. Disappointment flooded her spirit. The opportunity to have her poem published in a respected literary journal should be a joyous occasion. She gritted her teeth and stepped lightly on the gas pedal, wondering if her friendship with Chantel was really worth it.

If she ended her friendship with Chantel, that would solve a problem that had plagued her for weeks. She would be free to date Race without feeling as though she'd violated some sacred rule.

Humph, she thought. Wouldn't that be something?

Chapter 16

He couldn't believe that he was nervous. He checked and rechecked everything.

House neat and tidy. Take-out keeping warm in the oven. Jazz playing on the stereo. Champagne on ice. Paper and pens on the dining room table.

He clapped his hands together and rubbed his palms vigorously.

Everything was in order.

So why couldn't he sit still? Because the thought of doing writing exercises with a poet that he admired sent sparks of inspiration igniting in his body.

He hadn't done anything like this since his writing days with Ernest and Torrena in the writer's workshop. They'd spent weekends sometimes doing exercise after exercise until their fingers went numb, but their tablets and notebooks were filled with some of the best writing the world had ever seen. He was convinced of it. The creativity and inspiration that came out of their sessions had to be unmatched on the planet, or at least Savannah.

He remembered the synergy as though he could touch it. Hold it in his hand. Squeeze it. He hoped he and Chantel could find that synergy. The thought was strange though. So far, they hadn't been able to. Even the friendship he'd hoped they could share felt unnatural to him somehow. But he was hoping that tonight would change all that.

He'd dug into the cardboard filing box where he kept all his old work. All the stutters and stops of a fledgling writer exploring his chops. He'd sifted through misbegotten prose and some pieces he felt were actually good, and found his favorite writing exercises, energizers and activities. He picked out the ones he'd had special success with, the ones that had been the best writing of his short career as a poet.

He hoped Chantel would like them. He hoped that her writing would thrive with them as his had once. And he hoped that the exercises would bring them closer. Perhaps not close in the way that she might prefer, but close like colleagues. He hadn't shared any of his writing with her. Only Kyra. Kyra said that his work wasn't ready yet. He agreed with her. The exercises were just what he needed to step up his skill, bring his A game out. He hoped he had one.

As seasoned a writer as Chantel obviously was, he just hoped that she hadn't already grown tired of the kind of exercises he was about to suggest or, worse, that she'd done them all.

Now, that would be a disappointment. And another thing for him to be nervous about.

He paced back and forth at the door. Nothing he could do about his selection now, because her sports car was pulling up in his driveway. He'd coaxed her over on the pretext of a surprise. He sure hoped she like surprises.

"Right on time," he said, too eager to wait for her to ring the doorbell. Instead, he had the door open and was waiting as soon as she stepped out of her car.

"I believe in being punctual," she said, not so much walking as sashaying up to his door.

Race thought that having Chantel over might be difficult or awkward.

He was wrong.

She looked as beautiful as ever. Her personality was as pleasant as ever. Over the past few days, they'd hung out periodically, sometimes for lunch, sometimes for dinner, always for poetry. Platonic with Chantel made perfect sense.

Race couldn't believe it. After years of numbers in his head, he was pushing his passion away and awakening a new one.

He was obsessed. Chantel's poetry had awakened a sleeping giant and that giant was roaring through their conversations. The giant did most of the talking, most of the remembering, most of the philosophizing about simile, metaphor, lyric verse, blank verse, free verse. It was like discovering a treasure chest you'd forgotten you'd buried right in your own backyard. He was sure he'd talked Chantel's ears off. Strange, she didn't seem to mind it.

She differed with him often when he asked about her favorite poets, her favorite stanzas and poems. When he asked about her form preferences sestina or villanelle, she said, "I like them both. What about you?"

It was as if she wanted him to monopolize the conversation.

Well, tonight he decided to change that. It was his turn to listen and he was determined to take it. Anyone who could write poetry the way she did had to have some important opinions on the art form and the people contributing, or not contributing, to it.

He'd checked his reflection in the mirror just before Chantel arrived. He remembered when his hair was a mass of thumb-thick locks that hung midway down his back. He was fond of nearly buttoned, free-flowing shirts then, and linen fabrics. But that was a time before Palm technology, before corporate agendas and designer suits. He didn't think there was room in his life for both worlds, but recently the black ink of Chantel's poetry blurred those worlds. Blended them together, and in a strange neo-funk cosmopolitan corporate kind of way…he liked it.

She gave him a quick kiss on the cheek as she entered. "Thanks for the invite," she said. Her eyes twinkled with mischief. He'd better clear the air and clear the air fast. She obviously had the wrong idea of a surprise on her mind.

"It's awfully bright in here," she said, entering the living room.

"Let's go in the dining room," he said.

"Sure, but I have to tell you, I already ate."

"That's good," he said, only slightly disappointed

about the dinner he had warming in the oven. He was relieved that he didn't cook it, and said, "Because dinner is not really what I had in mind."

"Me, either," she responded and spun around.

He collided with her and they both toppled over and into the dining room table, sending Race's carefully arranged paper, pens and exercises crashing to the carpet.

"Oh! Ow! Sorry," Chantel said.

"Here, take my hand," Race said, helping her up.

"My bad. I didn't realize you were that close behind me."

"It's all right," he said.

It's a sign, his mind cautioned. Get her out of your home now or else you're going to be sorry.

"Shut up," he whispered.

"I'm sorry?" she said, pulling her miniskirt down as far as it would go, which was only an inch or two below her rear.

"Nothing," he said. "Please have a seat."

She sat down, crossed one long solid leg over the other. He pretended not to notice and proceeded to pick up the papers and pens.

"You said you had a surprise for me...."

"That's right," he said. He had everything off of the carpet now and placed neatly on the dining room table.

"Would you like some champagne first?" he asked.

"Not really," she said. Her eyes and her voice went heavy with lust.

Race had to set her straight now before Chantel was so far gone he'd never get her back into writing mode.

"I thought we could write together," he said and sat down across from her.

"Could what?" she said, blinking as though she had a large eyelash in her eye.

"I dug out a few of my old writing exercises. I thought we could—"

"Write? You want to *write?*"

"Yes," he said, swallowing. Maybe it was too late. Maybe she was already over the edge.

"Since when do you write?"

"Well, I never mentioned it before, but one of the reasons I like your poetry so much is because I used to write poetry myself back in the day. At one point, I thought I was going to make writing my career."

"So, you want to write *poetry?*"

"Well, no. Not poetry, per se. I just thought we could do some exercises to get the creative juices flowing."

She leaned forward a bit. But only a bit. "And then what?"

"And then see what we have. We might have the makings of some good poetry after this."

"Poetry?" she said. She'd turned into a human echo.

"I would love to write with you. We could share what we come up with, and if we feel adventurous, collaborate on something."

Suddenly, she looked panicked, and a little queasy. "I work alone, Race. Kind of in a, uh, vacuum. Now, it might sound unusual to you, but that's how I work."

"That doesn't sound unusual to me at all. Most writers create alone, in their own worlds. In silos. In vacuums, as you put it. But these exercises can get you out of that routine for a while. I've seen some rare and beautiful pieces come out of these exercises. And I would love to share something rare and beautiful with you."

"You would?" she asked.

"Of course. I'd be honored."

He waited for several moments. She seemed to turn the idea over in her mind several hundred times before she spoke.

"Let's do it!" she said.

"Excellent!" he said. He couldn't wait to get started.

But they were only two exercises in and he couldn't wait for it to be over, although Chantel seemed excited by the process.

"Let's do another!" she said. Her voice sounded drunken. Giddy. Childlike. All Race could wonder was where were all of those fabulous words she used to write those brilliant poems with. He hadn't seen a one since they started writing. As a matter of fact, what she'd come up with had been amateurish, juvenile and incredibly bad. Just terrible.

At first he thought she was joking when she read her first exercise. But when she'd glanced at it proudly with dreamy eyes, he realized that she was one hundred percent serious. Every moment since had been painful and he couldn't wait for the pain to stop.

After two more exercises where the best she'd come up with was,

> This girl likes a man
> This girl hopes with a great big hope
> That the man likes her.

He decided it was time to end the evening.

"I'm sorry you're not feeling well, Race. I could stay and make you some chicken soup."

"No thanks," he said, steering her back with his hand. "I just need some aspirin and some rest."

"Well, you call me if you need anything else."

"I will," he said, closing the door softly the moment she stepped out of it.

Something strange was going on with her. He had the distinct feeling he'd spent the evening in the company of a flimflam woman.

This girl likes a man!

He couldn't get to bed to start dreaming about Kyra fast enough.

Chapter 17

"Knock, knock," came the familiar call.

Kyra knew who it was immediately, but with the morning she was having, she was afraid to look up. It was only 8:00 a.m. and already, she'd had enough demands on her time to put all of her projects behind schedule. And the requests were so unusual and far-fetched, that she'd wondered if suddenly the world had gone crazy.

She hoped that Chantel had some good news.

"Hey, Chantel," she said as she finished her morning search for new security patches and warnings about new viruses. "What's up?"

"I have a favor to ask you."

"You and half the world. Sit down."

Chantel took a seat in Kyra's cramped cubicle. Even though Kyra's position meant that she had one of the largest cubicles in the company, a cubicle was still a cubicle. There was never enough room or enough privacy.

"What's on your mind?"

"Funny you should use that phrase. I want what's on my mind to be what's on your mind."

"Meaning?"

"Meaning, I'm thinking about reading at the Griot this week."

All of Kyra's emotions collapsed into a tight ball and crashed in the pit of her stomach.

"You're what?"

"I want to read one of your poems, a long one of course, at the Griot on poetry night."

Kyra grit her teeth. For all the years she'd been writing poetry, writing was still a solitary event for her. And beyond that, an event she shared with precious few people. And as strongly as she felt about her verse, she'd never been able to get up the nerve to read it in front of an audience. Even the thought of that made her sick to her stomach and dizzy.

But never in her wildest dreams had she imagined anyone other than herself reading her poetry to an audience. Certainly the first time out, the one reading her poetry should be her.

Certainly.

"Chantel, I don't think that's a good idea. Isn't it enough that I'm letting you *borrow* my poetry, but to read it in public…"

"There is no doubt in my mind that Race would love it. When we were there last week, he practically pushed me up on stage to read. Of course my tongue tripped over the words and I made a complete ass of myself, but I think I have it all figured out now."

"You were going to read my work without my permission?"

"Yes, sweetie, but I realized that was wrong. I needed to ask your permission. And I needed to ask for your help."

"Help? Help how?"

"You know those gadgets that you are so fond of, the things you're a genius with? Well, couldn't you rig a transmitter that I could put in my ear? Something that you could be on the other end of—wirelessly of course—and you could talk me through the poem. That way, I could convey all of your emotion and conviction and read the poem just the way you would. I mean if you think about it, this could be your rehearsal for the time when you actually get up there yourself and read."

Kyra eyed her friend, who was all decked out in a Donna Karan suit that looked as though it had jumped straight off the pages of *Cosmo*.

"And this will do what for you exactly?"

"It will make Race appreciate me even more."

Chantel smiled broadly and tossed her head skyward. "I'm telling you, Ky, with every poem I bring him, he falls deeper and deeper. I could never be as eloquent as you are, but you put my thoughts and feelings into words so precisely, it's like you're seeing inside me to the way I feel about Race. You express love and ardor and attraction so well. And he connects with it each and every time."

"Really?" Kyra thought she felt the ball in her stomach shrink a bit.

Chantel leveled her gaze at Kyra. "Really?"

Kyra was on the verge of saying yes. If she herself couldn't connect with Race directly, at least she could help her best friend to do so. And getting her words in front of a live audience—well, she'd had plenty of opportunity to do that hadn't she? That jazz club wasn't that new. She could have done what Chantel was offering to do a while ago. But she hadn't. She hadn't taken the chance. So why should she mind when someone was willing to take the step that she herself was too reluctant to take. Oh, her mind was spinning.

"Is there a way for me to see the audience's reaction?"

Chantel smiled and looked twenty pounds lighter. "We'll make a way."

"O-kay," Kyra said, nodding her head. "But only one time. You're taking the poetry *borrowing* thing much further than is probably necessary."

"Thanks, Ky!" Chantel said, jumping up. She grabbed Kyra quickly and gave her a tight hug. "You are better than the best!"

Kyra waved off her friend's comment. "Whatever."

"Poetry night is Thursday. Can we be ready by then?"

"Yeah," Kyra responded, her mind already fully engaged in the challenge. She knew just where she could get the equipment she needed, and with a few adjustments with tools she already owned, it should be a piece of cake. "Come over Wednesday and we'll give it a test run."

"Isn't Wednesday cutting it close?"

"No. We'll be fine," she responded.

"You're the expert," Chantel said, then pranced off like a child who'd just been given a present to open.

Kyra sat back in her chair and closed her eyes for a

moment. It wasn't the world that had gone crazy. It was her. She just hoped that she hadn't gone off the deep end so far that she couldn't get back.

Thursday will tell, she thought, and went back to work before she ran after Chantel shouting, "I've changed my mind!"

By the time Wednesday came, Kyra was ready. She had stopped by RadioShack and purchased two walkie-talkies, a receiver and an earpiece.

She'd tested out each component individually, not quite sure she was doing the right thing. But the challenge of rigging electronic gear thrilled her, as projects like that always did. And she was confident that the system would work well.

Chantel rang the intercom at six fifty-five. Their meeting was scheduled for seven.

Kyra glanced out the window and waited at the door. Instead of being out of breath like usual, Chantel was barely winded by the long staircase to her apartment and entered as if she'd just won the lotto.

"You ready for me?" she asked, not sitting down.

"Ready," Kyra said. "Come on in to the computer room."

Chantel followed behind her and yipped like a puppy when she saw the equipment on a small table.

"Oh, my gosh!" Chantel said, in a voice Kyra barely recognized.

"Calm down, girl. We still have to test it first."

"Okay, okay!" she said. "Wow, this looks like something from a James Bond movie."

"Not hardly," Kyra said. "I got most of this stuff from RadioShack. It's akin to what news producers use to communicate with their anchors. I'm sure Oprah has something similar, but hers is probably top-of-the-line."

Chantel frowned. "And what's this?"

Kyra held out her palm. "About eighty-four fifty. Hand it over."

Chantel counted out five twenty-dollar bills into her friend's hand. Kyra put the money in her pocket.

"Okay, first put on the necklace. The necklace transmits the signal from my walkie-talkie to your ear," Kyra said, turning the on switch on the small credit-card-sized box.

"Next, put the earpiece in. They had different sizes. I got one that was considered a medium. If it doesn't fit—"

"It will fit," Chantel said, and pushed the earpiece into her ear. She turned. "Can you see it?" she asked.

Kyra looked carefully. "A little. You'll have to wear your hair over your ears."

Chantel nodded. "What's next?"

"Then I turn on my walkie-talkie and talk."

Kyra turned on the final piece of equipment. Then she did her best impression of the Verizon guy. "Can you hear me now?"

Chantel's smile took up her whole face. "Yes."

"Okay, then let's try it. You stand there. I'll sit over here and read a poem. As I read it, you say it. It might take some concentrating on your part."

"I'm up for it!" Chantel assured Kyra and she was right. Chantel had no trouble at all repeating Kyra's words. She got through an entire poem with no word fumbles. However, her delivery was terrible. She looked good, but she had no stage presence. Kyra had watched enough *Def Poetry Jam* and *Spoken* to know that stage presence was everything. Even the most well-written words would fall flat if the delivery sucked. She sighed. This wasn't going to be a piece of cake after all.

"You've got the repetition thing down."

"Told you!" Chantel said.

'Now, we just have to work on your delivery."

Chantel blinked. A pained expression rode her typically fashion-model features. "What do you mean?"

Kyra decided that she could show Chantel better than she could explain it to her. So, for the next two hours, they watched Kyra's DVDs of the documentary *Slam Nation*. She wanted Chantel to get a feel for the performance aspect of reciting poetry for today's live audiences. When they'd finished, the concern on Chantel's face had turned to worry.

"I've seen that," she said, "But I don't know how well I can do it. What I'm saying is, everybody doesn't have to have stage presence, do they?"

"Look, I'm letting you perform my poetry. Now, if you're going to do it, then do it right. Don't step to the stage and do it half-assed. Now, do you want this or not?"

"I want it," Chantel said.

"Then you're going to have to work for it."

For two more hours, Kyra coached Chantel, but it was as if she were talking to herself. She'd once heard that the best way to learn something was to teach it. Well, she sure learned a lot about performance poetry in that short amount of time. And she learned something else. She learned what her poetry really meant. And

she'd had to admit that to Chantel in order to make her
understand the feelings and emotions that needed to be
conveyed by the piece.

Chapter 18

After a long ride in Chantel's fast car, Kyra wondered if she'd be able to read her poem into the walkie-talkie. Chantel was driving so fast, the wind whipping across Kyra's face stole her breath and left her gasping.

"You drive like a maniac," Kyra said, when they finally walked to the door.

"Why buy a car like that if you don't intend to drive it? Otherwise, I would have gotten a Volvo or something."

Before they went in, Kyra stopped Chantel to ask her the question that had been nagging her brain since Chantel first asked her to help her this way.

"There's no slam tonight, right? We're not going to be accused of anything if we're caught, are we?"

"No. I made a royal fool of myself at the slam. This is just an open mic. No contest." Chantel smiled. "And no worries either. I know the manager. We dated for a hot second. Remember Nick Griffin?"

They stepped inside the club and Kyra realized the other reason why she'd hesitated as they entered. The place looked like a large living room. Plenty of comfortable places to sit, muted lighting and lots of space. She'd promised herself the last time she was there that the next time she came in, she'd come in to read on the stage. Well, she was coming in to read, all right. It was just from afar.

"Yeah, I remember Nick. He was the one that walked with a limp and claimed his balance was thrown off by his large—"

"That's him, girl!"

The two shared a laugh and had a look around. Nick was nowhere to be found and neither was Race, thank goodness.

"Wait here," Chantel said.

Kyra was content to do so. She studied the half-empty room of patrons and the stage she stood before. Speaking in front of people was a stupid fear. But it had been one of the reasons computers had been such an easy choice of careers. You didn't have to stand in front of people and talk when you worked with computers. You just had to program or debug or rebuild a motherboard. Those things you could do on your own.

The truth was, Kyra wasn't good with people. Her track record of being a team player extended only as far as her family, Chantel, and a few friends she knew from computer clubs. Other than that, she kept to herself and focused her attention on the miracle boxes that wouldn't tell your secrets, make up stories about you or hurt your feelings. Kyra was comfortable with people, but she was just as comfortable—and maybe even more so—in her apartment with herself and her gadgets.

"Kyra, Kyra. You lookin' good, girl."

"Hey, Nick," Kyra said. She'd been so deep into her thoughts, she hadn't heard Nick and Chantel walk up.

She and Nick exchanged a hug.

"Chantel told me about you guys's set up, tonight. I'm not feelin' it entirely, but since Chantel's my girl, what can I say?"

"Thanks, Nick," Chantel said and gave him a kiss on the cheek.

"I can already tell I'm going to have to spend the rest of the night reminding myself that I'm engaged."

Chantel's face fell just a bit. "Engaged?" she asked.

"Yeah. RayLisa and I are having a winter wedding." He paused, then added, "Her idea."

"Congratulations," Kyra said for both herself and her friend, whom she could tell was speechless.

Strangely, Nick didn't say thank you. He just smiled strangely and gestured to the management offices just off the front entrance of the club.

Kyra and Chantel followed behind him and got a good look at his...limp. Kyra choked down a laugh and nudged Chantel in the arm, but they didn't share a laugh. Chantel was smiling strangely, too.

Even though the two were involved with other people, Kyra wondered if Chantel and Nick had residual feelings for each other. The kind of feelings that "running into each other" can stir up.

Well, she couldn't devote too much time to that

question right now. Right now she had to get somewhere close to the stage, someplace where the audience
couldn't see her, and make sure that her equipment
worked, and pray that no one else within two miles was
using the channel that she and Chantel would be using.

"This place used to be a...well...one might call it a
filling station. During slavery, there were hundreds of
slaves that came through here. It was a first stop on the
Underground Railroad.

"The original owners, a couple named Philip and
Agnes Roberts, thought that the key to a successful
escape to freedom was if a slave started out well-fed
and was given food and directions of where to go. To
the slaves they hid from being found, they fortified a
crawl space right above their living room."

Kyra's heart beat a strong rhythm in her chest. Until
that moment, she'd had all kinds of reservations about
what she was doing. But hearing that, knowing that
she would be reading her poetry from a space that once
served to hide her ancestors from harm...well, it just
seemed fitting. She was honored beyond belief.

"Of course, over the years, the space has been
cleaned out and updated somewhat. The previous
owners of this club destroyed just about all of the his-
torical value of the place. The crawl space is practically
livable now."

"Livable? Why?" Kyra asked.

"I guess they used it the way we use it now, like a
special house seat."

Both Kyra and Chantel frowned at his remark.

"You'll see," he said. "Come on."

They followed him to a door behind his desk. The

wooden staircase behind the door had seen better days. All three of them ascended the narrow stairs to the crawl space.

Kyra didn't know what she'd expected. But she knew one thing, she hadn't expected this. The words crawl space were accurate, but only slightly. Although a person certainly couldn't stand in the space, she could easily balance on her knees. And Nick was right. There was nothing rough or weather-worn about the area. It had been smoothed out by particle board and blue paint. It was like crawling through a wide blue chamber with throw pillows instead of furniture.

"You better be glad I like you," Kyra said. "'Cause this is some crazy-tip mess," she said.

"Uh-oh," Chantel responded. "Look out! She must be serious. She's using slang."

Kyra worked her neck. "I'm just sayin'," she said.

"What would you like to drink?" Nick asked. "It's on the house."

"I'll take a ginger ale," Kyra said. She didn't want to be tipsy and try to complete operation Game Show Cheating. She'd need all her wits about her. As soon as Race walked in, she'd have to call upon every rational fiber in her body to make sure she didn't run down the stairs just to sit on his lap.

Now, wouldn't that be a sight, she thought. She and Chantel sitting at a table with Race, both of them batting their eyes flirtatiously and licking their lips suggestively.

Suddenly the image in her head disgusted her.

"Ky!" Chantel said.

Apparently the discussion had gone on without her.

"Yes," she said, blinking away the nauseating image.

Chantel's face was pulled into a frustrated knot of wrinkles. "Do you want something to eat?"

"No. I'll be fine. Thanks."

Nick crawled back out the way they came. Kyra avoided Chantel's look of concern. "You're not going to change your mind, are you?"

"What? No. Of course not."

"You just look like you're having second thoughts."

"Not at all. I've just been thinking about work." She lied.

"I'll bet Race is involved."

Kyra jumped. Every nerve ending in her body lurched and popped. She nearly pumped her head on the ceiling. "Why would you say that?" Kyra asked.

"Race told me about how all the managers are up in arms behind him cutting their budgets in two."

"No, that's not it. Well...maybe it is," Kyra said, hoping that Chantel wouldn't probe any further. She willed the beating in her heart to return to normal and waited.

"Just hang in there, girl. And if you want me to put in a good word for you and any projects you're heading that need funding, just let me know."

Kyra sighed. "Thanks." Eager to change the subject, she rubbed the palms of her hands together and pulled her pack from her back. "Okay, then. We'd better test this equipment. I wish there was some way for me to watch."

Chantel grinned. "There is. Come take a look."

Kyra crawled the short distance with Chantel to what on first glance looked like a screen. But Kyra understood immediately. It was the painting that hung on the wall near the entrance.

From their vantage point, the painting was transparent. Once they got up close, they saw the front row of tables, part of the bar on the left and the entire stage.

"What do you think?" Chantel asked.

"I think this is the best seat in the house," Kyra admitted. Then it dawned on her that Chantel must have known about this hidden crawl space.

"How did you know you could see through the painting?"

Chantel did everything except pat herself on the back. "Well, girl, you know. I get around."

Kyra didn't say anything, but something told her that her friend had "gotten around *recently*."

"One ginger ale," Nick said, sliding a tray of drinks in front of him, "two dry bourbons."

Kyra slid Chantel an admonishing glance. "Now don't get tipsy and mess up the poem. I've gone to too much work for you to mess this up."

Chantel answered Kyra, but kept her grinning eyes on Nick. "Don't worry. I'll keep my head on straight."

"Good," she said. In the back of her mind, Kyra wondered who Chantel was trying to impress, Race or Nick?

The three took sips from their drinks and chatted for a while. As the place began to fill up, Nick left to do his "I'm the owner" thing, and Chantel left to take a seat as close to the stage as possible and test the equipment.

Even from above, the jazz and poetry club looked homey and comfortable. All of the oversized furniture just lulled people into putting their feet up. Taking it easy. Kicking back. It wasn't nearly as threatening as Kyra had once thought. Threatening not intimidating. Maybe one day, one day soon, Kyra would rise above her fears and not just read her poetry but enter a slam. She had the confidence in her work, just not so much in her performance. She took a sip of her ginger ale and thought that having Race in the audience to focus on and to perform for might be the final lift of confidence she needed to pull it off.

And right then and there she decided she would make it happen. Before the year ended, she was going to recite her poetry on stage.

Kyra turned on her walkie-talkie, checked the frequency and double-checked her spare batteries. All was in order. She was ready. She pulled out the three poems she'd brought—the one she and Chantel had rehearsed with, as well as two others. She didn't know why she brought the others. They were just a couple of pieces that she'd been working on off and on and thought that maybe while she was waiting for Chantel to "go on," they would provide her with something to do. Hearing the voices from beneath her, she realized that she should have brought a book with her to read to pass time.

Kyra looked out through the painting to see that Chantel had snagged the last table in the front row. A small wave of relief washed over Kyra. At least now she would be able to see her in case anything went wrong. She pulled over one of the flat pillows and slid it beneath her. She stretched her legs out in front of her and rested her back against the wall. She got as comfortable as possible and was grateful that she didn't suffer from claustrophobia.

Ready to get the party started, or at least the testing phase over with, she pressed the talk button on her walkie-talkie.

"Chantel, can you hear me?"

Chantel jerked and reached inside her jacket, Kyra assumed, to turn down the receiver. Then Chantel glanced up to the painting and nodded her head.

"Okay. I'm going to try something."

Kyra picked up the poem they'd rehearsed and read a few lines.

"Coming through all right?"

Chantel gave an inconspicuous thumbs-up and smiled wide enough to show off darn near all her teeth.

"Okay, then walk around and I'll keep talking. I want to make sure that you don't get distortion with movement."

Chantel walked around and Kyra talked about the weather. When Chantel returned to her front-row seat with her smile intact, Kyra knew the equipment had passed the test.

"How's the earpiece feel? Is it comfortable?"

Chantel nodded and sat down. She took one of the few remaining sips of her bourbon. She watched intently as the band made final adjustments and tunes to their instruments. One of the guys walked up to the microphone on stage. Kyra hoped there wouldn't be any feedback.

"Mic check, one, two. Check, one, two," he said. Nothing. No feedback or interference of any kind. They were ready to go.

The details of getting ready for this charade had occupied Kyra's thoughts for the past three days. They were a welcome distraction. But in the quiet of the crawl space, her thoughts crawled back to Race. The thought of being able to watch him without his knowledge intrigued her. But the thought of reading her poetry made her nervous. Even if she wasn't reading the poetry herself, her words would expose her and all the feelings she had for him, leaving her raw and open.

She looked at the three poems she'd brought to the club. They all represented soft, tender emotions. Vulnerabilities and desires she didn't know she could feel so deeply. She had written one of the poems so fast, it felt more like the poem had written itself. She stared at it, feeling a familiarity with the words but not knowing at all where they came from. They had just flowed from her one night so quickly, she had trouble keeping her dip pen inked. By the time she'd finished writing the first draft of it, three of the fingertips on her right hand were black with ink. It had taken days for all of the ink to wear off.

Race was like that. Indelible. Lasting. If she passed him in a hallway, ran into him in the cafeteria or, heaven help her, rode with him in an elevator, his strong masculine presence would settle on her like strong arms, holding, squeezing, intoxicating. One time, when there were so many people on the elevator that they had to squeeze together to make room, she'd been sandwiched between him and another employee. It was then that it finally occurred to her why women swoon and why they've sometimes been known to faint dead away. That darn chemistry stuff. Atoms and molecules dancing and moving and crashing into each other. It was…it was…

Kyra decided to change her line of thinking right then and there. Even though the small area had an air-conditioning vent, every time she allowed her mind to dwell on Race for too long, she broke out in a sweat. She was seated right next to it, but it didn't make a bit of difference.

Before she went to bed tonight, she thought, she would say ten thousand "Hail Marys," contact the local food bank to volunteer her time, and read the passage in the bible about "Thou shalt not covet."

"Whew!" she said, wiping the perspiration from the sides of her face. After a few moments, her mind decided to behave itself. She checked the equipment one more time and glanced down to check on Chantel.

Well, well, well, she thought as she waited for a fluttery stomach to interrupt her new calm. Race Jennings, looking good and casual. He looked better in casual clothes than he did in his suits. His muscular frame was much easier to make out in a body shirt and Phat Farm jeans. Crisply pressed Phat Farm jeans that hung loose from the thigh down, but from the thigh up—

"Argggh!" she said, totally disgusted and frustrated with herself. *I am not a good friend. I am not a good friend.*

She turned her attention to her poetry. And even though she'd written it about Race, she would not think of that…much. Her focus would be the delivery. The performance. The opportunity to see a few people's reactions to her work. That was the important thing here.

Not baring her soul.

Everything that made her a decent woman told her to look away from the couple sitting in the front row. But she hadn't had a decent thought in her head since the moment she saw Race. It had just been all downhill from there.

She watched innocently at first, just observing, looking. But after about ten minutes her interest and curiosity became specific. What are they talking about? Why is he smiling? What did he order to drink? Why do they have to sit so close?

Then her observation turned to fascination. Why does Race look so stiff? Why does Chantel look as if she's trying way too hard? Why had Nick visited their table twice since Race arrived? When her poet's eyes kicked in, she knew she was lost until the end of the open mic.

Kyra glanced at the last of her ginger ale with distaste and then drained the glass dry. Chantel obviously didn't know how to treat a man like that.

A man like that was intelligent and was captivated by intelligent conversation, not long legs and short dresses. He needed to know that a woman could do more than just giggle and fix her hair. Kyra knew if she were down there sitting with Race they'd be talking about world events or tackling the nurture-versus-nature debate, or even planning the most creative, inventive, pleasurable way to drive each other to ecstasy.

Kyra wished she had ordered a real drink.

A drink would make it easier to grasp the realization that while she had the brains, Chantel had the heart. Although Chantel might not be able to tell the difference between an allegory and alliteration, she wasn't the one lusting after her best friend's man.

Kyra sighed, realizing that her friend must be doing something right. After all, Chantel was here with Race and Kyra wasn't.

"How are you doing up here?"

At the sound of Nick's voice, Kyra jumped so wildly, she hit her head against the low, low ceiling.

"Sorry," he said, crawling toward her. "The show is about to start and sometimes things can get pretty hectic around here. I just came to see if you needed anything before all creativity breaks loose."

Kyra smiled. She remembered Nick from when Chantel dated him before. It was a quick, white-hot fling. The two seemed almost too compatible. And aside from the fact that, according to Chantel, Nick was *extremely* well endowed, Kyra thought he was a nice guy. And Chantel had been vague as to why they'd broken up.

"You know what? I'll take a drink after all. A glass of Rosemount Shiraz, please."

"You got it," Nick said.

He crawled backward and disappeared down the stairs. Kyra looked out just as an exotic-looking woman with straw-set hair and a henna tattoo on her upper arm took the stage. She wore a thin, soft-looking brown dress that clung to her body from her shoulders to her ankles. A wide multicolored beaded belt hung low against her small waist and wide hips. The toenails of her feet were short and unpainted. Kyra thought she looked like an African-American fairy. All she needed was wings.

"Good evening," her smoky voice said. "I'm Setra and I'm the host of Open Mic at The Griot."

Kyra sat up, got ready. "Chantel, what number are you?"

Chantel kept her eyes on Race. He was talking about something. He was smiling and explaining something with an up-and-down motion of his hands and arms. Kyra laughed. She wished he could see himself from her vantage point.

She turned her attention to Chantel, who was rubbing her shoulder with four fingers.

"Four!" Kyra said. "We've been here since the band set up. I thought you'd be the first one."

Chantel shrugged, almost imperceptibly, but obvious to someone who was looking for it. Kyra sighed just as Nick returned with her wine.

"Thanks, Nick," she said.

"No problem," he said. "Enjoy the poetry. The people around here are pretty good. You know, Chantel showed me one of your poems once. It should be you up there reading tonight."

Kyra smiled and took his words as a sign.

"When's your next slam?" she asked.

"Next month on the fifteenth."

"I'll be here," she said.

Nick smiled. "I'll get the trophy ready."

Kyra raised her glass in salute and then took a sip. Nick disappeared once again to join the activities down below.

I should have eaten dinner, Kyra thought. The easy burn in her stomach told her without a doubt that the wine she was drinking would go straight to her head. If that happened, she would be left with nothing but her heart.

Kyra blew out another breath and took another sip.

"Give the band some love, yaw," Setra said.

Had the band played a song? Kyra hadn't heard it.

"Now it's time to bring the first poet to the mic.

Now, if you don't know this lady, now you know her. She's always number one on our open-mic list. One day you're going to tell a sister how you do that, girl. Everybody, put your hands together for Ms. Venita Gray."

One poet reading, two more to go, Kyra thought. She took one more sip and realized that she'd better get started if she was going to finish the poem she was going to read.

She picked up "Loves Me Like Rain" because as her entire insides warmed up, it finally dawned on her what was missing from that piece, and once she added it, it was the piece she wanted to read for the open mic.

By the time she added the last word, Chantel was on stage and had been standing there for a while.

Chapter 19

All evening at the club, Race had seen Chantel but had been thinking of Kyra. When he had joined Chantel at the table, he could have sworn he smelled Kyra there. Her perfume…her essence.

He'd sat down and immediately asked, "Is Kyra here?"

Chantel's eyes widened as if he'd just asked her to pay for dinner. "No. Why would you ask that?"

And what could he have said? "Well, I'm asking because I smell her, at this table, on you. Or is it on me? Maybe she's in me. In my system. And damn it, I can't get her out."

But he didn't say any of those things. He'd just said, "You two are friends, I just thought she might have come with you."

His body hadn't cooled off since then. It hummed with the particular resonance and pitch it did when he was around her. That wonderful, beautiful, computer-fixing, Techie Kyra. He wondered if he would ever move beyond his strange sense of honor and take Kyra to dinner. Or better yet, tell her how stupid he thought it was that they walk around electrically charged and tuned in to each other's frequencies, yet do nothing about it. It was ridiculous.

But suddenly not as ridiculous as Chantel standing on the stage and not talking. She looked as if she wanted to say something, but was waiting for a sign.

His heart plunged for her. He didn't want this to be a repeat of a few weeks ago.

"Chantel," he said, wanting to take away her discomfort. She was obviously trying to impress him. And it was unnecessary.

"You don't have to do this," he said. And then a miracle happened. She started into a poem and a performance that he would never forget as long as he lived.

Race blinked his eyes several times because he could not believe the transformation of the woman on the stage in front of him. After a few very long moments of stumbling, stammering and what looked like to be a pained expression of utter embarrassment, Chantel opened her mouth and delivered a soul-stirring performance. Race didn't know what had gotten into her. Gone was the woman who stood on the stage before, begging for him to hand her a copy of her poetry so that she could read it. Her delivery was darn near flawless. It was as if someone else had stepped inside her for a moment and was talking for her. She was channeling a great poet.

"Warm wet fingers," Chantal said, "fallin' all over me, drops beat like drums, my soul pulses to his song."

He'd ordered a cognac. He took a sip, believing that if Chantel's poem wasn't over soon, he would gulp the whole thing down and order another.

Her performance was hot. Sultry. Magnificently so.

"I taste his thunder, he loves me like rain, like a cloud full and open and misty gray, my sky is blue no more."

He didn't think it was a call-and-response piece, but men responded nonetheless.

"Talk about it, baby!" one man shouted.

"Woo! Go 'head!" yelled another.

Chantel's poem was sexy as hell, that's for sure. And it was another thing, Race thought as he took a sip of his drink.

Familiar.

His mind worked furiously to determine why this poem felt and sounded like he'd heard it before. He knew it hadn't been one of the poems Chantel had shared with him over the past few weeks. But the essence of it was familiar.

"His water falls all over me," Chantal continued. "My skin shimmers with the moisture he makes. Listen, can't you hear the storm? Shh, shh, he's touching me again."

Oh well, he thought. It would come to him. Race put all other thoughts away and listened to the poem. As conversations trailed off around him, Race was vaguely aware of cigar smoke, the freezing taste of ice in his mouth, and a drenching sensation. Her words bathed him. Soaked him in metaphor and simile. They seeped inside him, set up shop and staked a claim on his heart.

Although Race wasn't in love with Chantel and was

no longer interested in her romantically, he was, however, in love with her words. Every single one that she'd shown him and every single one that she'd uttered tonight.

"We are a hurricane of backs, arching, bodies twisting, arms groping torrential downflow. Ooo…he loves me like rain, Comes all over me, and I am so thirsty, I gulp and pray for monsoons."

The applause rang out so loudly around him, Race started before he joined in. The bright eyes and wide grin on Chantel's face told him that she was proud of herself. Very proud.

When she returned to their table, he stood and seated her. When he sat down, customers were still clapping.

"Outstanding!" Race said, and took his seat.

Chantel took a sip of her drink and fanned herself. "I was good, huh?"

"That poem was amazing," he said truthfully. "Straight out of brilliance."

Chantel stared at him for a moment.

"That was phenomenal. Almost like you were a different person," Nick said, joining them.

Chantel smiled with her mouth. Her eyes had lost some of their sparkle. "Thank you," Chantel said, finally.

Was it his imagination or were these two staring at each other again? Race wondered. He didn't know Nick, but the man had made a good first impression. Race thought Nick and Chantel could make a decent couple. But obviously they had reservations.

Race groaned. They reminded him of an all too-familiar situation.

"Enjoy the rest of the open mic," Nick said, walking away slowly.

"Is that new?" he asked.

"Yes. Very new."

"Is it a borrowed poem?"

"I didn't borrow it from anyone!" she shouted. Race could have sworn that the confident and beautiful Chantel Mosley had suddenly become afraid. Her eyes grew wide and her expression shocked.

"No, no. I mean the technique, where you use other poems for inspiration or 'borrow' a title, a phrase, or an arrangement. You know…"

But she stared at him blankly, the way she always did as though she had no idea what he was talking about. "Oh, yeah. A *borrowed* poem. That's exactly what it is."

Chantel fumbled with the hair above her ear. She'd been tugging on it all evening. For some reason, it was starting to bug him. Must be nerves, he thought, and decided to dismiss the annoying gesture.

"Would you like another drink?" he asked.

"Sure," she said, then fumbled with her hair some more. "On second thought, let's call it a night. I've got some things to do early in the morning, and I'd like to get to bed soon. That is, unless you'd like to come to my place a little later. I could, give you all the details about the poem I read tonight."

"Chantel…" he began, not sure how to have another I-don't-think-of-you-that-way conversation with her. When he saw the hope in her eyes soften and dissolve into disappointment, he knew he didn't have to.

"It's not going to happen, is it? Not even after tonight."

The earnestness of her comment humbled him. "You are a nice, beautiful woman. Any man would be lucky to have you." His words came out strained and regretful. He'd been on the other side of this conversation before. *I like you, but...* It was painful in that place where your feelings weren't returned.

He felt pain, too. He'd hung with Chantel to be near her poetry. That was wrong. And he was suffering because of it.

He wouldn't do that to her anymore.

"I don't think we should see each other anymore," Chantel said.

Race was going to agree when he noticed the smile softly turning up the corners of her mouth. It wasn't a grin, but it was definitely the opposite of a frown.

"What is it?" he asked.

"I just realized that it's the first time in a long list of relationships and almost relationships that *I've* broken it off with someone. No offense, Race, but it feels good."

Race chuckled. He couldn't help himself. It was the most perfect ending to an imperfect non-relationship. Chantel laughed a bit and that broke all the tension between them.

"Shh," a customer beside them said.

Suddenly, Race felt terrible. After Chantel's poem, he'd felt that there weren't any other poems on earth. Or certainly in the room. Just hers. He'd forgotten all about the other readers.

He stood and extended his hand. "Shall we?"

Chantel nodded and they headed toward the door.

Before they could exit, Nick came up beside them.

The way he swayed when he walked made Race wonder if he had one leg shorter than the other.

"Going to read and run?" he asked.

"Yes," Chantel said. She stopped and the two went into stare mode yet again.

Race knew when three was a crowd.

"Chantel, I'm going to head home."

"You sure?" she asked.

"Yeah. Thanks for the wonderful poetry. All of it," he said, thinking of how much he would miss her creativity.

"You're welcome," she said.

Race ignored Nick for a moment and gave Chantel a quick kiss on the lips. Then he left The Griot still high on Chantel's poem and headed home.

By the time he stuck the key into the lock on his front door, Race was angry. Chantel's poem haunted him, taunted him and mocked him. The words from the poem walked around in his soul, but they were fuzzy. Like he couldn't quite see them clearly. And they were *so* familiar—he couldn't for the life of him figure out how or why.

Exasperated, he tossed his keys on his kitchen counter and checked his caller ID. There were five messages from a number he had no trouble recognizing. He picked up his phone and dialed the number.

"'Bout time you got home. I been callin' you all evening."

"Man, where are you?"

"Where do you think?"

"I'll be right there."

Race grabbed his keys knowing that it was going to

be a long night. He usually called "the guys" when Brax was in town and they would all meet. Tonight he didn't think so. He and his buddy would suck down a ton o' coffee and catch up.

And Race would finally get some much-needed advice.

Chapter 20

Race arrived at Gallery Espresso before he realized it. He must have caught every green light on the way. His car was on autopilot and his mind was on poetry and remembrance.

He caught sight of Brax sitting alone at a corner table. The man checked his watch and looked up with a frown.

"You drive like an old lady."

"At least I don't look like one," Race said.

Brax stood and the two men embraced.

"Why didn't you tell me you were *visiting?*" Race always teased his friend, saying that he didn't live in Savannah, he just visited from time to time.

"If you had a life, maybe I would have," Brax said and allowed a smile to break his stern expression and reveal the deep dimples their women friends fawned over so much.

"I'm going to get a cup of coffee," Race said, "before I say something crazy up in here."

When Race returned with his double espresso, Brax was so lost in thought, he barely noticed him sit down.

"Man, you look like I feel."

"Umm," Brax said.

Of all Race's friends, Brax had been the most guarded. He played his feelings and his life close to the vest. Race had learned early on that no amount of coaxing would pull Brax out of his cave until he was good and ready.

Race saw the closed signs on his friend's expression and in his posture, and knew Brax wasn't ready to talk.

"I hung out with Torrena a couple weeks ago. She will neither confirm nor deny that she's happy, but anyone who knows her would know she's happy."

Brax nodded. "So, you gonna drag this out or are you going to tell me her name?"

"Kyra," Race said, unwilling to drag it out. As soon as he said her name, a small wave of relief hit him. It felt good. Loosened him up.

"Start from the beginning," Brax said, then took a sip from his cup of coffee that was nearly empty.

Race started from the moment he saw Kyra in the men's restroom and ended with the poetry reading that night. Brax listened the whole time, his solid expression never changing. "You're screwed."

Race gulped as if he'd been sucker-punched in the gut. "Thanks. That's just the kind of help and encouragement I needed."

"Look, you didn't call me for my good looks. You wanted my opinion. And I gave it to you."

"All right," Race said, looking at his friend, who was way too big to be this grim. "Who stomped on your heart and left it for dead?"

"Hazel," he said. "She left me."

"Hazel? *The* Hazel? The one who took you to church with her?"

Brax drained his cup. "Yeah."

Race whistled. Loudly. "Let us bow our heads for a moment of silence."

At first, he didn't think Brax was going to laugh. But his friend let loose a laugh that shook his demin-clad shoulders and brightened his entire face.

Then Brax quieted down and took a breath. "I'm not ready to go there yet, though, man. You know how I do. Besides, this is about you. And you got a situation on your hands 'cause not many women want sloppy seconds. And if she does want sloppy seconds, then you shouldn't want *her*."

Race's head throbbed at the temple. "You're not much help."

"What do you want me to say? Go after her?"

"That would help."

Brax sat back, his face a tight scowl. "Go after her."

"Damn right!" Race said, but his voice lacked the conviction he so much wanted to feel. He knew the best thing to do was to cut his losses. No more poetry. No more chemistry. Get back to math.

Damn, he felt as if he were in school.

"This isn't just about my opinion. You want to know if I've forgiven you. And this is your way of asking."

"You don't beat around the bush much do you?" Race asked.

"You know me."

Race scoffed in his mind. Brax was always quick to say, "You know me," but Race doubted if anyone really did. "So…what?"

"No," Brax said. "I haven't."

Race nodded. At least he knew where he stood.

"You took up writing again, huh? How's it going?"

"Not good, and nice subject change."

"Thank you."

Race glanced at his double espresso. It was strong, hot, and almost gone, just like his chance with Kyra. He couldn't see letting it slip away, but what could he do?

"You were a decent poet back in the day. Can't Chantel help you dust off the similes?"

"That's the thing. Whenever I talk to her about it, she acts like she doesn't have a poetic brain cell in her beautifully coiffed head. Now, Kyra, on the other hand, she's been a big help. At least she's gotten me on the literary poetry track."

Brax strummed his fingers against the fake wood tabletop. It sounded like a horse galloping. "Kyra, huh?"

"It's funny," Race said, thinking. Then he remembered a line from Chantel's poem. "It's a gracious quandary." He smiled, and that feeling of déjà vu returned.

"'Gracious quandary'…you come up with that?"

Race searched his memory and for a shocking second he realized that he had.

"Oh my, God!" Kyra shouted. "I was on fire!" She glanced at her friend, who didn't seem happy about what they'd accomplished. Kyra thought she'd better clean up her statement. "You were on fire! We were on *fire!* Did you hear that applause?"

"Yes," Chantel said, and drove carefully back to Kyra's apartment.

"Okay, what's wrong? You never obey the speed limit. Did someone heckle you and I couldn't hear it?"

"No. Everyone loved the *poem*," Chantel said.

Kyra wouldn't be able to wipe the crazy grin from her face for a week. She imagined falling asleep that night with her teeth showing from the big ol' grin slapped across her face. "That was the idea, right?"

"The *idea* was for them to love *me*," she said, taking a corner much more sharply than necessary.

"Hold on, Chantel. Get us there in one piece all right? Now, what's bugging you?"

"You!" she snapped.

Kyra didn't want to get angry, but she felt a pool of anger boiling not too far out of her mind's reach. She had to be careful. "Help me understand something. I just rigged up a covert transmission device for you so you can impress a man that I don't know very well and you're mad at *me?* Somethin' ain't right, sister girl."

"No, it's not right. It's not right that your life is perfect and that you are too smart for your own good and that you have this great amazing talent and I...I have nothing!"

Chantel was shouting, but her voice held a deep edge of pain and sadness. When Kyra saw the tiny, almost imperceptible tear track down Chantel's face, she realized how serious her friend was.

"What happened? Did something happen between you and Race?"

"Of course it did, Ky. You warned me that he would leave me and you were right, because he did."

Chantel stared up at the ceiling as if the help she needed would come from there. "We had a...disagreement. I thought Race should love me and he disagreed. So, I broke up with him."

Kyra waited a beat for some inkling of gratefulness to peek into her psyche. It didn't.

Hmmm. Maybe she wasn't as trifflin' as she thought she was.

"I'm sorry, Chantel."

"Yeah. Whatever."

"I am. Really."

Chantel glanced quickly in Kyra's direction, then nodded. "Thanks," she said.

The darkness had swallowed the eastern part of Savannah like the whale swallowing Jonah. The night was strangely still and quiet as if someone had e-mailed a "be still and shut up" memo to the entire city.

When curiosity got the best of Kyra, she said, "So, what are you going to do?"

"Nothing. Except take your advice." Chantel chewed on her bottom lip and turned the car on to Kyra's street. "I'm so tired of being 'out there.' I always come home hurt."

Kyra sighed and hoped her friend meant it. Chantel was a good woman who deserved a good man. But she wasn't going to find him by hopping from one relationship into the next.

"I've never had any 'just me' time, Chantel admitted.

"I know," Kyra said.

"Guess I'm afraid of what I would find out about

myself if I was the only person I had to hang around with."

"I don't know why," Kyra said. "I think you'd discover that you are a wonderful person."

Chantel pulled into Kyra's driveway. Fresh tears glistened at the corners of her eyes.

"I'm not sure if I can ever be the kind of friend to you that you are to me."

"You better. Otherwise, I'm kicking you to the curb the way you did Race."

They both chuckled at that. Kyra wiped the tears that had finally fallen away from Chantel's cheeks.

"I know you got my back. I know it," Kyra said, feeling as though she were the unworthy one.

Chantel just nodded.

Kyra opened the door, otherwise they both would be crying and neither of them would be any good for the next hour or so. "Call me if you need anything."

Chantel tried to smile, but was unsuccessful. "I will."

Kyra stepped out of the car with her emotions in battle. Part of her was still celebrating from the reading that night. She was one step closer to being able to actually read her poetry in public. That thought made her happy.

At the same time, she absolutely hated to see Chantel down in the dumps. It pained her anytime her close friends allowed themselves to become vulnerable to a man's foolishness, or their own for that matter.

Kyra dropped the bag with the equipment in it on her dining room table and tossed the folder with the poems in it beside the equipment.

She stared at the folder, barely believing what was

inside. Love poetry for a man who obviously didn't deserve it. She hated to put Race in the category of all the other men who had gotten what they wanted from Chantel's body and then tossed her aside like a blow-up doll.

Kyra headed for her bedroom and her jazz. She was definitely feeling *kind of blue* tonight and the honesty in Davis's trumpet mirrored the truth in her soul.

She would never be able to look at Race Jennings the same way again.

Ever.

Chapter 21

Race squinted in the afternoon sun even with sunglasses on.

"Fore!" the CEO said, and with great form sent the golf ball flying toward the seventh hole.

They were at Crosswinds Golf Club. They'd been there since one thirty that afternoon. The ComTel Summer Golf League was in, well, to coin a phrase "full swing." Race had golfed with his previous company, but they always met after work hours. The ComTel league was allowed to leave at one o'clock every third Friday of the month to go golfing. This was his first opportunity since he'd been hired. And what an opportunity it was. Because he'd been trapped in an elevator and missed his meeting with the board, the CEO had singled him out and asked if they could discuss it over eighteen holes.

It was an offer Race knew better than to refuse.

For the past hour, Race and Ken Southmeier had played hole after hole—Ken doing exceptionally well and Race not too far behind. They'd talked some about business, but mostly about current events and every item on a small-talk list they could think of. Race participated and waited. He knew Ken would get around to asking him what he wanted to know soon enough.

"So, Race," Ken said, teeing up at the twelfth hole. "Now that you've had a chance to review our financial status, what do you think?"

Ken swung. He was trying to come over-the-top but forced the ball too far outside. It veered gently off-track and landed near a grove of small trees on the far side of the hole.

"Tough break," Race said.

"Well, every shot can't be perfect," Ken answered.

"I was talking about ComTel," Race said. He stood straight, set his jaw and looked his boss directly in the eye. Race knew he was taking a bad risk. He'd worked in corporate America long enough to know that the CEOs rarely wanted to hear bad news. The people under the CEOs know that, and so they made it their jobs to feed them everything they wanted to hear— even when the company was going to hell in a Humvee. People made sure the CEO was appeased by telling him or her that all is right with the world.

Don't worry; be happy.

The result was Enron, Northern Natural Gas, Arthur Anderson and the like. Race had been without his integrity a time or two in his personal life. And he'd learned his lesson.

He waited for Ken to answer him. The man just looked

on as if Race had suddenly morphed into a fire-breathing dragon and Ken could not believe what he was seeing.

"Really?" the man said, finally. "How so?"

Race decided to take the conversation as nonchalantly as his boss sounded. He pulled out a nine iron. Squared himself to the tee. Took a good look at where he wanted the ball to go and went into his swing.

The ball sailed through the air, hit the ground and rolled to less than three feet from the hole.

"The initial product cycle for ComTel has come and gone. It's time for some reinvention. Quick. Fast," Race answered.

"That's not a financial summary," Ken said. The two walked in tandem to the next hole.

"No. But the numbers don't mean a thing unless I know the business. So, I've been studying the business to give the numbers some meaning."

"And?" Ken said. He didn't break his stride. Didn't turn toward Race. He kept his eyes and gait forward.

"And I believe that ComTel is headed for the iceberg. We can't see it yet, but it's out there. If we act now, we can turn the ship. If we wait and do nothing—well, James Cameron directed a movie about what happens when a big ship hits a big rock of ice."

Race stopped and waited for Ken to stop and look at him. When he did, he said, "It ain't pretty."

"What about your financial plan? The presentation you were going to make before the board?"

"That will help, a lot actually, but more importantly, ComTel needs to turn itself inside out, find out what kind of company it really wants to be, and go for it with everything we've got."

Race thought about Kyra and what she'd said to him in the elevator.

"A colleague suggested that even something as regular as meetings should be evaluated for ROI. And I agree. If we make sure that every effort brings a return, Ken, we'll turn the ship. Not only turn it, but clear the iceberg."

They resumed walking and Ken shook his head.

"What?" Race asked.

"I don't know if you're an idiot or a genius."

"You hired me, so I must be a genius," Race said feigning a schmooze line.

Ken broke into loud, vibrant laughter. He laughed long and hard all the way to the next hole.

Later that week, during an upper management meeting, Ken presented the new fiscal plan for the company and gave Race all the credit for coming up with it.

The reviews were mixed. Polarized. Many company managers embraced the plan with an "it's about time" attitude, just as many others left the meeting discouraged or more importantly, angry. Race believed those were the individuals who cared more about themselves and what they could get than about the company. He hoped they would eventually come around to appreciate the changes that were inevitable if ComTel wanted to survive.

It didn't take long for the trickle-down theory to take effect. The following Monday, when Race was in the middle of an important spreadsheet projection report, Chantel came storming into his office.

"Hey," he said, not quite sure why she looked in such a huff.

"Don't 'hey' me. You cut my budget!"

"Chantel—"

"Don't try to deny it!"

"I wasn't," he said.

The tall woman who loved showing off her legs blinked in surprise. "So, it's true."

"Yes. I cut all ancillary expenses. And this is just the first pass. Once we start reviewing things in more detail—"

"So you just decide that the company doesn't need to reward its employees with recreational activities. The Christmas party and the summer fun day mean nothing!"

"First of all, I'd appreciate it if you'd speak to me like an adult. If you want to holler at someone, find a child. I'm a grown man."

He gave her a look that he hoped conveyed his earnestness. Chantel took a deep breath and then sat down across from him. She slapped the thick folder she carried in her hand across an even thicker thigh.

She was really upset. Where was this emotion when they were trying to write together or when she was up on the stage doing a bad recital of really good poetry? It was as if she were schizophrenic. He was well-aware that many artists were, but since he'd discovered her writing, something about her had seemed incongruent.

If only she had the passionate understanding of words that Kyra had. Hmm.

"Well?" she said, waiting.

She'd been waiting for a soothing word of explanation from him. He'd been in truth-telling mode lately and it had served him well. He decided to stay on that track.

He lowered his voice though, in case anyone was walking past his office.

"Chantel, look, we both know that you are a fixture around here, a beautiful one nonetheless, but you get paid a lot of money to buy and sell on eBay.

"Now, I'm not taking anything away from your events planning. I've talked to people and I've read your post-project reviews. Everyone loves your work. But the fact is, you're living in a palace and sitting on a gold mine of money that the company can no longer afford.

"I only reviewed your project budget. That's what I'm cutting. What I'm not doing is reviewing your salary. For the work you do, your pennies are awfully shiny. Here's what will—"

He stopped talking. He had to. The expression on her face looked as if her heart had just been broken into many, many unmendable pieces. Each one jagged and cutting into her insides.

Oh, lord. The last thing he needed was a crying woman in his office. A crying woman was worse than a yelling woman. If a woman yelled at you, you could yell back or just ignore it. But tears were completely different. Tears didn't go away until you wiped them away. And even then, they left impressions. Deep divots in the soul that said, "You're the cause of this pain."

He hated tears.

"If you're going to cry you have to leave," he said, hoping to make a joke.

She didn't think it was funny.

Quite the opposite, he realized, when she took the file she'd brought in and slammed it on his desk. All the papers inside went flying and his composure with them. He hadn't expected that.

She didn't rise from the chair so much as she uncoiled like a snake awakened maddeningly from its slumber.

"You asshole," she said quietly, almost a whisper.

Race retracted his thoughts. There *was* something worse than tears.

"What gives you the right to talk to me that way?" she said.

Her voice was still quiet. Strangely calm for a woman whose face made her look as if she were having a conniption fit.

He'd begun this journey. He might as well see it through.

"My position and the job I have to do at this company give me the right. And our friendship means that I'm obligated to tell you the truth."

Inside he cringed. He was committing poetry suicide. He knew it. She would stop seeing him. Stop sharing her fabulous poetry with him. Stop inspiring him to pick up his pen.

For a split second he wondered if it was worth it. If doing the right thing professionally would balance out to be the right thing personally.

He didn't know the answer to that. But he did know that ever since he'd been affected by the honesty in her writing, he'd wanted to follow that path, and bring back the truth in his life. The thought of being without her poetry saddened him, but he didn't have any other choice. But not seeing him again would be her choice. He doubted that she would continue to be his muse.

But he could not allow her to continue the sham she was perpetrating on the company. No sooner had he thought the word sham than a montage of images flooded his mind.

Chantel uncomfortable talking about poetry.

Kyra passionate about the subject.

Chantel futzing up the simplest of writing exercises.

Kyra with ink on her fingers.

Chantel stupid nervous on stage.

Kyra lighting up every time he mentioned liking Chantel's *poetry.*

He'd been duped.

"So, I'm your friend, huh?"

"Yes," he said, standing up and looking her almost eye-to-eye in her tall heels.

"Friends?" she said again. Her voice sounded as though she were mulling over the word, discovering it for the first time.

"Is that all right?" he asked, sincerely hoping that it was. He wondered why he wasn't furious with her but realized that all he felt was relief.

"No, it's not all right. Even a friend wouldn't treat me like this."

And then to his horror, she did start crying, but she left too quickly for him to do anything about it.

And what would you have done, he asked himself.

There was no answer. Just the thirty or so poems scattering his desk and littering the floor.

He bent down and picked one up. "Hip-o-crite" was the title.

How apropos, he thought and read the first stanza.

Fear is no excuse.
Being afraid never ended any wars.
Only cowards and fools fight to the death.

He wondered if that was true about him and which one he was: a coward or a fool.

He picked up the poems on his office floor determined not to be either ever again. And he knew just what he was going to do to change his status.

But first, he had to buy a dozen red roses, or maybe just a single white one.

Chapter 22

Kyra stared at her reflection in the mirror, surprised that she looked relatively content. She'd done it. She'd gone an entire week without seeing Race Jennings—at least in person.

He still made regular appearances in her fantasies, and when her eyes closed for bed, the night belonged to him. He'd taken over her dreams in a way impossible to describe or fathom. Every morning when she awoke, she kept her eyes closed and breathed softly while her body still thrummed from the closeness she'd shared with him in her dream. The details of him: his eyelashes, the mole on his chin, his savory brown and jutting Adam's apple. Even the hair near his knuckles and on the backs of his hands. Everything to the smallest aspect of him came to her fresh like a painting not yet dry.

And she was never dry when she opened her eyes. Always wet and in deep, deep, oh, so deep need.

She would jump into the shower so quickly with every intention of washing off the memories of him that still lingered in the morning.

That had been her ritual for the past seven days. It's a milestone, she told herself. And she was going to celebrate. Instead of going to lunch in the cafeteria or fast-food joint across the street, she would walk two blocks to Maggie Moo's and get a sundae. It was 1200 calories, easy, but for the struggle with her lust-drenched emotions and common sense that she'd had this past week, she deserved it.

When she arrived at work and walked into her cubicle, a strange premonition told her not to set her mouth too strongly for the ice cream so soon. Her seven-day reign might be over.

Kyra picked up the rose that was set in a beautiful vase in the middle of her desk and smelled it. The aroma was faint, distant. Barely there. Unlike her attraction to the man she knew was standing directly behind her.

"Long time no see," he said.

Had Race's voice gotten deeper, she wondered. It sounded darker, richer than she remembered.

"Kyra..." he said. He spoke her name and it became a hand, a strong sturdy hand on her shoulder. The hand became arms and the arms became an embrace. Just a word. Her name. But he had enveloped her with it.

They had been apart for too long. This coming back together would be hard. It would be hard not to separate again. Hard not to pull closer.

He stood behind her. They hadn't even touched.

Only in her imagination. But there was no mistaking the truth. They'd become entwined. She felt it.

"Thank you, Race," she said. She was too afraid to turn around. Seeing his face would just be too much. Too overwhelming. Too great of a temptation.

"You're welcome. I just wanted to let you know that I'm still writing. Still revising. You helped me a lot."

"I'm glad," she said. Kyra sighed, closed her eyes. Willed him to leave her alone. She'd made it seven days without...

"Have dinner with me tonight," he said.

She clutched the rose tightly against her chest. Her pulse quickened and her face flushed.

Her premonition was right.

"I thought we agreed to stay out of each other's way."

"Bump that," he said.

The authority in his voice sent a warm shiver down her body. She tingled in all the special places. Places reserved for a man's permission and a woman's pleasure.

"Don't say no," he said, stepping closer.

And there it was, all the attraction and chemistry she'd fought to keep at bay all week. She hadn't tamed it. Just allowed it to simmer like a good meal, or chill like leftovers in the fridge—better the next day. Shame flooded her consciousness. She couldn't refuse him.

"What time?" she asked.

"Seven thirty. My place."

She nodded her consent, unable to speak.

She remained still even though she knew he'd gone. The scent of his cologne faded. But not the memory of their exchange. Before Kyra allowed herself to have one more thought about Race Jennings, she replaced the rose on her desk and headed out of her department. It was time her actions spoke louder than her words.

For the next hour, Kyra didn't get any work done. How could she when, after a bit of coaxing, Chantel had just dropped the mother of all bombs on her.

There had never, ever been anything romantic between she and Race. Although Chantel had wanted it, all Race wanted was poetry and friendship.

The admission had almost knocked her off her feet.

"Knock, knock," she'd said, imitating her friend's familiar greeting only a few moments ago.

"Hey," Chantel said. She was staring at her computer, but Kyra didn't think she was looking at it. Her eyes looked dazed, glazy, watery.

Kyra recognized that look. A wall of dread hit her soul.

"What happened?" she asked, walking over to where Chantel's normally proud shoulders slumped over her desk.

"Nothing," she said.

"Who are you trying to fool," Kyra said. She walked back to the door and closed it. Then went to stand by her friend's side.

"Talk," Kyra said.

"*Nothing* happened, Kyra." Chantel looked up and Kyra understood. She remained quiet, allowing Chantel to get her misery off of her chest.

"Nothing happened. Nothing at all. No connection. No commitment. No boyfriend/girlfriend. No sex."

"No sex?" Kyra asked, ashamed by her relief.

"No nothing. Just your poetry. That was it. I thought it would make him fall in love with me. But he just fell in love with the words."

Kyra waited for the tears. There were always tears at the end of Chantel's relationships. Tears, then anger, then forgetfulness. Chantel would conveniently forget how rotten she'd been treated by the last man she dated so she could get on with being in a relationship with another one.

Surprisingly, there weren't any tears. Just sheer exhaustion.

"I'm tired, Ky," Chantel said, slumping even deeper into her chair.

Kyra stroked her friend's TCBY-permed hair. "It's about time," she said.

Chantel said nothing, which was a good sign. It meant that finally, she was in an emotional place where she could listen.

"You need rest, Chantel. You don't know what it's like to be you. You're always plus one: you and 'fill in latest guy's name.' Spend some time with you. Get yourself together. Find out who you are. When you know that and know it well and know it for sure, the man who will make you a better you will be a lot easier to spot *and* attract."

Chantel nodded and for once, Kyra believed that Chantel might actually be able to change her ways.

Out of the blue, thoughts of her lunch date invaded her mind. She took a deep breath remembering what brought her to Chantel's office in the first place.

"Chantel, I know this is the worst possible time to say this in the history of mankind, but I gotta say it and I gotta say it now."

She continued stroking her hair and sent up a prayer. "I'm having dinner with Race tonight."

Chantel remained silent. Kyra did, too, and let the implications of her words soak in.

It didn't take long. Chantel's body stiffened and she pushed her chair back.

"What are you telling me?" she asked.

Kyra wondered if she'd ever seen her friend in so much pain before. Surely she had. There had been plenty men before Race. Men Chantel had wasted years with, invested months of emotions in with no return. But if that were true then why couldn't she think of any times when Chantel's eyes looked more torn and injured?

Kyra couldn't speak. But she held her gaze. At least she could do that.

"Get out," Chantel said.

Kyra didn't try to argue. What could she say in her defense? Not a damn thing that wouldn't make the situation worse than it already was.

With a pain in her heart that matched the pain she saw in Chantel's eyes, Kyra walked out.

She only made it about five feet before her resolve gave way and she had to lean against the wall for support.

Oh, God, what have I done and why?

She put her head in her hands, but she didn't have any tears, either. Just questions. Questions that could only be answered if she actually met Race for dinner.

What kind of woman am I? she wondered.

Kyra walked back to her cube knowing that in a matter of hours, she would know for sure what kind of woman she was.

Chapter 23

Kyra stared at the sheet of paper laying on her dining room table. She was in the living room as far away from that paper as she could get. But that didn't keep her from staring at it. Or from cursing her hands for printing it and bringing it home in the first place.

Race's address and phone number. He'd sent her the e-mail as soon as he'd gotten back to his desk. And she'd stared at it then, too. Stared at it so long that when she blinked her eyes had gone dry, frozen into place by the terrible realization of what she might do with the information.

And in the end she'd done exactly what she'd feared. She'd printed it out and brought it home.

Finally she closed her eyes, let her head loll forward. Kyra took slow and—she hoped—cleansing breaths and listened intently while the rhythm and bass of Charles Mingus's *Better Git It in Your Soul* settled into her body and reached way down into her marrow from Bose speakers.

She heard the music, but her mind was already made up. Had been made up even when she'd placed the CD in the changer and pushed Play.

She loved Chantel with all her flaws. God knew Kyra herself was far from perfect. But she also wanted Race. Despite how wrong her mind told her it was to want the same man her friend wants, her spirit told her wanting Race was right. Kyra prayed that she and Chantel could move past this rough place in their friendship.

Ah, there it was. Mingus's masterful musicianship toward the end of the song. It took her by surprise every time. The force of it. The intensity. The mastery of notes over the formality of and construct of melody, the staff and scales. Mingus had taken the lines of the musical staff and bent them, twisted them into beautiful black tangles and wonderfully complicated harmonies.

He'd found a way to make all the chaos work. Kyra stood up in the sexiest dress she owned and headed toward the door, wondering if she would ever be able to do the same.

When she arrived at Race's home, she was five minutes early. On the way over, she decided to throw caution and all her good sense to the wind. She was tired of fighting nature that seemed determined to put she and Race together. She also decided to deal with the consequences later.

She walked up the stairs to the door and knocked. When there was no answer, she rang the doorbell. This time when there was no answer, she almost turned around and went back home. The disappointment gripping her was nearly unbearable until the door swung open, and Race stood before her in all white, looking like something she should not wait another second to devour.

Stay cool, she reprimanded herself.

"I thought you weren't home or that I'd gotten the time wrong."

"No," he said, stepping aside and letting her pass. "Actually, I was right on the other side of the door wondering what the night would bring when I let you in and…sweet almighty!"

"What?" she asked.

"You look damn good and you smell like…a word."

"What word?" she asked.

"Yes."

Kyra sighed. Right now, the word *yes* was the most perfect word in the universe. She was ready to say it all night.

He closed the door behind them.

"I don't know if this is even safe. Can we last the night without tearing each other's clothes off?"

"We're adults, Kyra. If we want to rip each other's clothes to shreds, throw each other against the wall and ride each other like lust-crazed lovers who can't stop touching each other no matter what they do, we can do that."

"What are you talking about? You were seeing my best friend. I feel guilty being in the same room with you."

"Seeing is an awfully strong word, Kyra."

"That's convenient," Kyra said.

"It's the truth," he said.

So who was giving her the straight story? she wondered. Her best friend, who claimed her relationship with Race was intact, or Race, who acted like there was no romantic relationship at all?

Kyra decided to trust her best friend. How many times had she heard the line, "A man will do and say anything to get in your pants?"

Too many to count. She hated to think that Race was that kind of man, but she had misjudged men in the past. Look at Turk. He'd turned out to be the biggest—however lovable—dog on the planet. She loved him, though. She actually thought she could help straighten out his canine ways. His heart was good, it was just his private part that was in the wrong state of mind.

"I can't believe I'm about to say this, but here goes… I want you more than I've wanted any man in my entire life. It's like a compulsion. Like breathing, blinking, my beating heart. I can't control it. It's involuntary. It's automatic. It's, it's part of me."

He moved closer. Stroked the side of her cheek. Kyra's libido kicked into overdrive. "Then what's the problem?" he asked.

She pulled back. "There's no problem. I lust for you, but I love Chantel. Simple as that. She's my friend. Always will be. Men like you come and go, but Chantel will always be there for me. I can't betray that no matter what I feel. No matter how strong it is. And no matter what I believe will happen to my spirit if I never know what it's like to kiss you."

Boundaries, Race thought. He understood them...
now. There was a time when he didn't. When his friend
Brax had dated a woman so beautiful, Race had willingly crossed the line and nearly ruined his friendship
with Brax. It took some time, but Brax eventually
forgave him.

Thing was, Race never forgave himself. So if Kyra
thought that being with him was in some way violating
a trust she had with Chantel, it would hurt him worse
than anything he'd ever known, but he would respect
that.

He pulled his hand away from where it was—inches
from her face. "Okay."

Race closed his eyes and shook his head. He had a
lot of writing coming on. He could feel it. Words of
missed opportunities, bad timing and attraction so
strong it held like super glue.

If anyone had seen their faces, they would have
thought that these two people suffered a tremendous
loss, as though a great friend, loved one or relative had
died. In truth, it was the chance at being together that
had passed away. And in a way, they were both in a
strange stage of mourning. Mourning they would both
express though lyric poetry and metaphors—the only
things either of them believed would ease the pain and
heal their tortured souls.

"Come in to the kitchen."

"Kitchen?" she asked, chuckling. "I hope you're not
asking me to cook."

She followed him into the modern-looking kitchen.
With its stainless steel appliances and the hanging rack
of pots and pans, it was a cooking area that would do

B. Smith proud. As a matter of fact, the kitchen looked too good, as if it were for display purposes only.

She noted the array of foods on the breakfast bar: tomato paste, tomato sauce, hamburger, cottage cheese, several bags of pasta.

"Lasagna!" she said, happily taking a seat at the bar. "It's my favorite."

"I know," he said, smiling like a man with a secret he can't wait to tell.

"When will dinner be ready?" she asked, getting comfortable.

"As soon as we finish cooking it."

Kyra laughed heartily until she realized that he was serious. Then she laughed even harder. "I can't cook, Race. And when I say I can't cook, I mean I *really* can't cook. I've never even seen the inside of my own kitchen," she said jokingly. "As a matter of fact, I'm not even sure I have a kitchen in my apartment."

Race's smile was so broad and bright, the brilliance could give a Las Vegas casino a run for its money.

"Me, either," he said.

"Okay, help me understand this. You invited me to dinner at your place, but you can't cook."

"That's right." Race reached behind him for wine-glasses and a bottle of Shiraz. "Wine?" he said.

"Yes! I love Shiraz."

"You don't say," he added, smugly.

"What did you do—drill Chantel for information about me?"

"Yes," he said. The lighting in his house was subdued. Just enough so she could see the flash of his eyes. Kyra realized that Race's eyes were truly the windows to his soul. In the caramel-colored depths, she could see everything about him. He probably had a hard time hiding his emotions. He might be able to keep a straight face, but his eyes would give him away every time.

"I see your mind clicking, techie. What are you thinking?" he asked and poured them both a glass.

"I was just thinking, your eyes are so expressive and emotive. Whatever you feel, think...believe. It is reflected in your eyes, isn't it?"

Race re-corked the bottle and put it back on the counter behind him. "Yes. Especially with women. When I was a kid, my mother always knew when I was telling the truth and when I wasn't. She knew what mood I was in before I did and she told me to guard my heart."

Race's gaze was hot against her cheeks, her mouth, and bored into her eyes. "Because if the woman you fall for doesn't love you..."

"She could use me and manipulate me without even thinking about it."

Kyra didn't look away. She hadn't come over here for love or anything like it. She barely knew Race. She only knew how he made her feel.

But the room warmed anyway, or maybe it was just her.

"So, you wanna go out?" she asked, succumbing to the urge to change the subject and acknowledging the growl in her stomach.

"What for? We have everything we need here."

Kyra took a sip of wine. It was wonderful. The bouquet alone and the vision of the man standing across from her were enough to intoxicate her for life.

"What part of 'we can't cook' don't you get?"

"Oh, ye of little faith. If two heads are better than one, think of four hands. Now, I've got a cookbook right here. Surely a senior systems engineer and a chief financial officer can make a decent meal together."

"You're crazy!" she said and took a bigger sip of wine. Maybe the alcohol would make her crazy enough to try what Race was suggesting.

"Not yet. But if I don't keep my hands occupied, they will be all over you. And you can't tell me you don't feel the same, so to keep sane, I think we should keep busy."

Kyra took another sip of wine, and thought "amen, brother" in her mind.

"And here's the bigger truth. We'd be on each other no matter where we were. Any restaurant we went to would throw us out for indecent exposure in a coat room in the back."

Another sip of wine.

"Careful there. If anything happens tonight, I want you to be of sound body and *mind*," he said, trailing a searing glance down her nearly quivering frame, "when I take you."

"Lord, lord," she said and turned up her glass. It was her nerves making her act this way, she told herself. Her stupid nerves. She knew the wine would shut them down, or at least subdue them for a while. After that, who knew?

Race's eyes told her he liked her response.

"All right," she said and slid off the bar chair. "What do we do first?"

They both smiled at the challenge before them. But

the sentiment "Too many cooks spoil the soup" soon brought frowns.

Like all wars, Kyra's and Race's started off as a small battle.

"Why don't we do this chronologically, based on what has to be done first?" she asked, feeling plenty toasty from the second glass of wine she'd started.

Race disagreed. "These recipe things are meant as a guide. Let's just conquer what looks easiest, like cooking the hamburger."

"Since neither of us knows what we're doing, it's probably best that we do as the recipe says."

"Aren't you into jazz? How can you appreciate jazz without appreciating the art of improvisation? Now, we've got all the ingredients. It's just a matter of putting them together, right?"

"Right," she said, slightly irritated. "Let's put them together in the correct order."

Race blew out a long breath. Kyra didn't like the sound of it. Somehow, he'd managed to make it condescending.

He ran a hand through his thick, wooly hair. "Okay. Why don't I take the hamburger and you take the pasta?"

"Cool," Kyra said. But it wasn't cool. She wondered why they couldn't get in sync to cook just one meal in the kitchen. Everything else about them seemed to fit.

Before long, the two were engaged in an out-and-out culinary brawl.

"Are you watching the hamburger?" she said, letting her words and her exasperation fly.

"Of course!"

"Then why is it burning?"

"Oh, damn!" he said, putting down his third glass of wine to stir the meat in the skillet.

"When was the last time you checked on this pasta?" he asked.

"I'm making the sauce. I can't do everything!"

What they had in the kitchen was a mess. Plain and not so simple. It would take hours to clean up.

It was just lasagna, Kyra said in her mind. No salad. No breadsticks. No dessert. Just lasagna. What in the heck?

"Kyra, do you want me to start separating the noodles?"

"Go ahead," she said, giving up.

And she had to admit, when Race's cries of "Ow, ow, hot, ow!" came moments later, she enjoyed a tiny bit of satisfaction.

"You all right over there?" she asked, pouring the hamburger into the sauce.

"Fine," he said.

They worked quietly for a few moments. Kyra appreciated the silence. They'd been arguing since she stepped into the kitchen. She hoped eating the meal would bring them some peace.

"This dinner is a mess. And the strange thing is, it fits. This situation with us is kind of a mess, too."

"Kyra, Chantel and I never were involved romantically."

"I know that, but I still *feel* funny about it. Because you could have been. I mean, she wanted to. Didn't you ever?"

"For a short while at first."

"Thought so," she said.

Race got up and paced in front of the fireplace. He ran a hand though his thick hair. "I think I could make you change your mind. I'm almost certain of it."

Kyra looked up and wondered what her eyes were saying right then.

"I want to come over there, kiss you till you can't breathe, whisper in your ear, play with your hair."

Kyra sighed. She wanted that, too. Damn if she could almost feel it.

"But I won't."

"Umm," she moaned. Couldn't help it. Had to let it out.

"As bad as I want you," he stopped pacing then and stared at her with his soul revealing eyes, "And I want you bad, Kyra, I won't force you to do anything, least of all be with me."

"Is it hot in here? Can I have another glass of wine?"

"No and no." His gaze didn't falter, nor did its affect on her.

"You ready for me over there?"

"Yes," he said.

It wasn't until they started working together, Kyra pouring the meat sauce and Race layering it with cheese and pasta that the tension between them broke a bit.

"Okay, what *was* that?"

"I don't know, and I don't ever want to go through that again."

"I am a little nervous. At least I was until that wine kicked in."

"Well, I was horny."

Kyra laughed and spilled some of the sauce. "And now?"

"Now, I'm really horny."

"Men," Kyra responded and rolled her eyes.

"Gotta love us," he said. And there go the eyes. And there goes my heart, she thought. No, she knew. One hundred percent gone. Hmm, she thought silently, and wondered if there was more than chemistry going on between them.

They finished the lasagna with sauce-covered hands. As a matter of fact, there was sauce everywhere. Kyra was grateful for her apron.

She opened the oven door and Race put the pan inside. It was choked with noodles and sauce and cheese.

"Are you sure it's not too full?"

"No, I love really thick lasagna."

"Okay," Race said and turned the oven on to three hundred fifty degrees. "It says to bake for twenty-five to thirty minutes."

"Let's set the timer."

Race did as she asked. And then they got a good look at themselves and the kitchen.

"Wow!" Kyra said, shocked that they could create such a disaster. Water, sauce and grease droplets everywhere. Tiny pieces of lasagna noodles on the counter and on the floor. Ground hamburger all over the stove. More dirty pots, pans and utensils than Kyra knew one person could have.

"Where do you keep your sponges?" she asked.

"Sponges?" he said, confusion riding his handsome face. "I've got some kitchen towels," Race offered.

"I guess they will have to do."

This time they did everything together. Cleaning.

Wiping up. Scraping food into the garbage disposal. The kitchen detail was moving along at a good clip when they both stopped and stared at the dishwasher.

Kyra spoke first. "You ever load one of those before?" she asked.

"Never," he said. "It can't be that hard."

"Race, it took us two hours to get the lasagna in the oven. Do *not* underestimate the complexity of a kitchen appliance."

"Are you speaking from experience?"

Neither of them had moved. They just stood still and continued to stare at the dishwasher as though it were a spaceship that had just landed from a galaxy far, far away.

Kyra scratched her head. "The first time I used my ice maker, I ended up with tiny slivers of ice all over my kitchen floor."

"How did that hap—?"

"Don't ask."

They both took a deep breath at the same time. Finally, Race said, "I think I have the owner's manual somewhere."

"That would be good."

Race went to the other side of the kitchen and riffled through a drawer full of papers. He placed each piece of paper neatly on top of the counter. Then with a disgruntled huff, he placed them all back inside the drawer.

"I take it that's a *no*."

"It's a *no*," he said and resumed his place beside her. He stroked his chin absentmindedly. "What do you think?"

"Well, I ain't washing these puppies by hand."

"You got that right," he agreed. "I say we go in."

Kyra nodded. "After you."

Fifteen minutes later they had the dishwasher loaded and running. All that was left was to wipe off the counter where they'd stacked the dishes before putting them into the dishwasher.

"Good as new," Kyra said, admiring their handiwork.

"I'll say, and not a moment too soon."

Just as the words left Race's mouth, the timer went off signaling that the lasagna was done.

Again, they worked together and set the dining room table. A couple of times Kyra had to remind herself that she and Race hadn't been doing this very thing for years. That this was a new experience for her, for both of them.

But it seemed too comfortable. So fitting. So meant-to-be. Kyra despised cooking and everything that went with it, after having seen her mother sweat over a hot stove nearly all day and night to feed their family and the extended family of relatives that were living with them at any given time. Every time Kyra even attempted to cook, it reminded her of all the times her mother was cooking and couldn't talk to her or play with her or read to her. The memory was fresh every time. Except tonight. Tonight, she hadn't thought once about that until after she finished cooking. Kyra smiled at the thought. Her mood lightened with the breakthrough.

"What?" Race asked.

"Nothing," she said. "I'm just ready to eat our masterpiece."

But it wasn't a masterpiece.

They served themselves on a nice set of dishes that

Race admitted he never used. They carried their plates to the table, sat down across from each other, said grace and dug in.

Kyra's reaction was immediate. "Oh, my God!"

Race simply spit his mouthful into his napkin and gulped down his glass of wine.

"It's terrible!" Kyra said.

"As in god-awful," Race agreed.

Kyra used her entire glass of wine to wash the taste out of her mouth. "Any more?" she asked, raising her glass.

"Sure," Race said and got up to get them both refills.

"I don't get it. We followed the recipe."

When Race returned, Kyra saw that he'd filled their glasses completely.

"Actually, we didn't. You protested cooking like jazz, but in the end that's exactly what we did."

"But it smells so good."

"It does. And a brother is *hon*-gry right about now."

Kyra felt a little light-headed from the wine, but still in control. "*Now* do you want to go out to eat?"

"No. I mean, yes. But we better not."

"Why?" Kyra asked with a hiccup.

"Because I don't think either one of us is in shape to drive."

Kyra thought about that. When she took a good look at Race, he seemed to be swaying in his chair. She was definitely tipsy, because a part of her wondered if Race was still and it was she who was swaying back and forth.

The thought of that made her giggle. Then Race started laughing, too.

Suddenly, Kyra felt totally at ease. She had no misgivings about being with Race at all. She felt at home in his presence. Oh, the attraction was still there. It had not tempered or eased. But even that had become familiar, like something that should and always would be there.

Like breathing.

Did he feel the same, she wondered. She checked his eyes. They were even more open now than before the wine. A cold finger of fear touched her heart.

What Kyra saw in Race's heart was not lust or magnetic attraction. It was love. Plain. Simple. And obvious.

Chapter 24

Race wasn't drunk, but he was what his friends would call "stupid zooted." He and Kyra had opened yet another bottle of wine and ordered Chinese. By the time their moo-sho pork with curly noodles and empress shrimp arrived, they were good and happy. They'd talked about work, hip-hop, five-dollar cups of coffee and humidity. Kyra was against them all. Especially hip-hop, which she had pegged as the demise of western civilization and African-American culture. Race hadn't said much. He didn't have to. She had talked enough for both of them. And he wasn't mad. He could listen to her sweet, sexy voice for…ever.

He did have something to say, however. But he wasn't sure how she would take it or what she would do afterward. The most important thing he wanted her to say was, "Race, I wrote the poetry, not Chantel."

He wasn't the CFO of a major corporation for nothing. If he couldn't add two and two together and come up with four, he didn't deserve his position or anything that came with it.

Even though he had enough evidence to call a poet a poet, he wanted her to admit it. He didn't want to accuse her of it. He wanted her to come clean and clear the air, so that they could start fresh with no misunderstandings, lies, or deceptions between them. They needed to clear the air about Chantel, too. Because Race believed that no matter what happened that evening, no matter if they shared each other or not, everything between them had changed. The moment Kyra accepted that rose, they were different. And it was beyond physical. He hoped she could feel that. It was beyond *physical*, too.

Please, God, don't let me stand in this room alone wanting.

Just because he wanted her to be up front, didn't mean he couldn't do a little probing.

"Thank you again for your suggestions about my poetry. They really helped."

"I'm glad."

Her loose and giggly posture changed to a more rigid and guarded one.

"Would you like to hear a new poem?"

"Sure."

I got your "sure," he thought. "You know what, never mind. I know you're not much of a poetry person. I don't want to impose."

"No, I'd love to hear it!"

Gotcha, he thought. "In that case, I'll be right back,"

he said and left to retrieve the poem from the spare bedroom he used as an office.

"Here it is," he said. "You can read it yourself or I could read it to you."

Her eyes widened. "Would you read it?"

"Yes," he said.

"Americans," he began. "In nineteen sixty-eight—against water hoses and police dogs—bowed backs dared rise like the sun, weary feet goose-stepped on black-topped streets, and riots too numerous to count ordered us to forsake the status quo and ask: what kind of people are we?

"I borrowed a little bit from Etheridge Knight, but I think it's good."

"I didn't hear much Etheridge Knight. I got a lot of Baraka though." The look of *oops* on her face was so stark, Race used all of his resolve to choke back laughter.

"You like Etheridge Knight?" he asked, taking a seat next to her. She was uncomfortable, almost jittery. And he was having way too much fun.

He decided to torture her some more. "Of course, Knight is okay, but he's no Saul Williams, and everybody knows that spoken word is the ultimate in poetry."

Kyra frowned. "Spoken word?"

"Yes." He took his time in continuing. He knew she'd be a purist. The same way she was about jazz. She probably thought Kenny G was a hack. "Spoken word is when the performance of a piece is just as important as—"

"I know what it is," she said, irritation clipping her words.

"You do?" Race drew out the words, tempted to brush the tips of his nails against his shirt.

"Well, Chantel told me about it."

"I see. What did she tell you?"

"Not much, really. But from what I can tell, it's not that big a step away from rap."

He smiled smugly. "And look how big that is."

Her succulent lips curled with disgust. Oh, he'd ruffled her feathers. He could tell.

"You can't be serious. How can you compare a person with a rhyme scheme—off-rhyme at that—and an attitude to Maya or Kalamu ya Salaam? I mean, pssch," she said, working her neck and rolling her eyes. "There really is no comparison."

"So you're telling me that Paul Laurence Dabney—"

"Dunbar."

"Whatever. And Beau Sia aren't in the same league. Or that the woman who wrote 'We Real Cool'—"

"Gwendolyn Brooks."

"Yeah, her, couldn't stand on the same stage with Sonja Sohn."

"I'm telling you that what they do is different. Spoken word is acting. Poetry is literature."

He grabbed her hand and held out her nails where they were stained with the ink with which she wrote her beautiful poetry.

His eyes drilled hot intensity into hers. "And what makes you an expert?"

Kyra's hand shook. She glanced from her trembling fingers to Race's probing glance. Suddenly the room swallowed her air and the world tilted. The Chinese food they ate was nothing like the disaster they had to throw out, but her stomach felt queasy nonetheless. Needing a moment to steady herself, she got up, walked to the breakfast bar and held on tight while she thought.

"You know, don't you?"

Race got up. Stood behind her. The heat of his body warmed her skin and if she took a deep breath, they'd be touching.

"Of course I know. Did you think I wouldn't see who you are? You glow with poetry! All the time. I mean look at you. Right now you got Rita Dove and Ishmael Reed just drippin' down your hips. Sonja Sanchez swinging all off your hair. Jessica Care Moore dancin' in your eyes."

"No," she said and turned to face him. "I've got you in my eyes."

"Now that's the best poetry I've ever heard," he said, then bent to taste the mouth that could speak such delicious words.

After their kiss, Race struggled to get his mind right and to breathe as if he had some sense. "You *are* poetry," he whispered and kissed her again. This time like he meant it.

"So are you," Kyra said when they pushed away for air.

He pulled her against him. Pressed the side of his head against hers. Kyra felt the earth shift inside her.

They clung to each other and didn't move. Couldn't move. It just felt so damn good to finally embrace, the intensity riveted Kyra to the spot. In his arms. Touching him was the most beautiful bliss washing over her. She was wobbly with delight and so light that a soft breeze against her body would have lifted her off the ground.

Yet she was so heavy with need that she couldn't think coherently.

When Race rubbed his hands across her back, her behind, Kyra moaned with the sheer exquisite force of it—a quick flash of sensation that made her close her eyes and pray for more.

Her body trembled softly. It was amazing what a mere connection like this could do.

"Kyra," Race whispered.

She didn't want to pull away from him the slightest bit. Not even to talk.

"Look at me," he said. Desire had deepened his voice, darkened his eyes.

He was so sexy then, it was hard to keep her lips off of him.

"Say something," he said. "Right now...stop me."

Now she stroked his back, kneaded his butt and thighs with eager hands.

"Ssss," he moaned, closing his eyes with the feeling.

Kyra closed her eyes, too. "Umm."

Race rested his forehead against hers. Pulled her closer. His hardness throbbed against her.

"Sss-oh," she said.

He lifted her into his arms. She clung to his neck and softened into his embrace.

"Just remember, techie, I gave you a chance to prevent this."

They kissed as he carried her up the stairs. She pulled her head back and stared into his eyes.

"Hurry," she said.

But he didn't hurry. He took his time about every-thing. Getting to his bedroom, taking his clothes off, undressing her. By the time they were both naked, Kyra was quivering with need like a junkie who'd waited a lifetime for a fix that was only seconds away.

Race walked his beautiful body, all muscle and sinew, over to his side table, and retrieved protection from the drawer.

When Kyra clasped his hands and helped him sheath himself, he thought he would explode right then and there.

He stopped her hands from their deft massage, wondering if he could withstand their joining.

He knelt on the bed, bent down and kissed her ankles.

"No," she whispered and started to shake.

He massaged her thigh and licked her calf.

"No, Race," she pleaded, trembling.

His hand trailed a path up her body and headed toward the tightened pebbles of her breasts.

She moved his hand away. Her hips undulated on the stark white sheets. Her eyes were half-open. She bit a knuckle on her finger and reached out for him.

"No foreplay?" he asked.

"We've been doing that since the moment I saw you," she responded.

Her words intensified his desire. He didn't waste another moment. He simply moved on top of her silky body, spread her legs apart with his own and entered her softly, slowly. Deeply.

They both cried out. Loudly. The joined sound of their pleasure reverberated off the walls. Race had no idea he could even make a sound like that. Kyra struggled to catch her breath that came to her in ragged, sex-imbued gasps. It was her insides that trembled now.

Race moved slow, slowly out, withdrew so exquisitely, so heavenly a movement, Kyra clung tighter and screamed.

When he slid himself just as carefully back inside her, the groan that came from deep inside him filled the entire room.

He licked his lips. Residue from Kyra's skin tasted like sweet red wine. He licked again, then returned to the source and drank. Quenching and quenching again and again, yet knowing he would never have his fill. His mind grew dizzy with pleasure.

He gasped for a quick breath and went back under waves of pleasure that threatened to drown him and give him life at the same time.

He couldn't stop touching her.

The head of a match that existed deep inside him had been struck—the flame overdue and luminous. His skin felt like nothing would cool it and it would blaze liquid fire forever.

Each breath he took drove him deeper inside her. His emotions rolled on the currents of their pleasure. Made him crazy. Drove him so far over the edge, he couldn't see it anymore. Just her eyes. Just her soft cheeks. Just her juicy, succulent lips. Her big pillow lips that he wanted all over him. He thought if she stopped kissing him, he would die.

He pushed inside her. Deep and deeper. Felt her whole body gasp. He thrust sure and long. Brought her to life as she grew strong against him, thrashing and rolling and grabbing him closer.

Like a montage of pleasure: her breath against his neck, her hands stroking his back, his sweat falling against her face, her waist grinding up to his.

He sank in and moaned. The sensation was too much for him to bear, and so, crazed beyond all reason, he stopped.

"Umm-oh, sss, Race...pleee-ase..."

Her eyes were closed. He kissed each lid. "Kyra," he said, his voice a deep rumbling in his chest.

Her eyes opened slowly, but not all the way. She looked drugged, lustful. Done right.

"This...what we're doing," he said, careful not to move and come, "it's not sex, Ky. it's meditation, it's prayer, it's—it's serious lovemaking."

She kissed his chin. Licked the skin there until he moaned.

"Ky, if we finish this, it means something. You understand?"

Her eyes rose to meet his, so full of lust, so drunk he didn't know if she could recall her own name.

"I know," she whispered and let a single tear trickle from the corner of her eye.

He caught the tear in his mouth. He softly tasted the salt. Kyra trembled against him and hugged him even tighter.

Oh, God she felt so sweet and special and meant-to-be. He moved again, deliberately, steadily, rhythmically. The pleasure took his words and his sanity. He went somewhere inside her body and it told him everything he needed to know.

She was so soft. So supple. So beautiful. He didn't want the feeling rushing and churning inside him to go away. Ever.

If he wasn't careful, it would be over too quickly. So he was careful. Very careful.

Everything about their joining was elemental. The two of them together created every combination of pleasure possible.

First he moaned. Then she moaned. Then they both moaned together and there was no stopping their beautiful noise. The sensation of moving inside her was too great. Too acute. Too fine. Too perfect. He was so hard, it hurt.

"Aw, um—" He bit his own lip, squeezed his eyes shut against the weakening force of it. But not before seeing the way she looked at him. Her eyes told him everything. She was surrendering all. Her being. Her soul. Not just her body. Everything she had to give, she'd offered up on a golden platter.

He accepted it greedily.

It was her eyes that triggered it. Her eyes and the aroma of the passion they shared. It took him to a place where poetry could only come to the edge.

> No more dreaming
> I close my eyes to be
> awake
> in your arms
> where I find the words
> to say everything
> like the way you taste: coffee
> your hips: the ocean
> breaking me open
> where there's only you
> nested and nested again
> inside each version of me
> slid cracked and parted

and riding on this wave
bring me to your shore
swell, baby, please and crash with me

It was too hot and too perfect. He felt like he reached the top of a mountain that he'd been climbing since the day he'd been born.

"Sssa, ah, Race," she whispered and let her head fall back.

All he could hear was their breathing—labored and wrenched from deep inside. He was in another place, where reconnecting with the earth meant flying.

He'd pinned her down. He stretched her arms out to her sides. He entwined his fingers. Ground his hips. Made her scream.

Yes, he thought. Hell, yes.

"Race, wait," she pleaded.

"No."

"Please."

"No."

"Race," her voice whimpered. "It's too much."

He kissed her mouth. "Then hold on."

"Race…"

"Hold on to me," he demanded.

Her arms reached up. Crossed behind his head. Pulled him tighter.

He wasn't going anywhere except deeper.

She was so open for him. So accepting. So wanting.

He'd been forewarned the moment he saw her that touching her body would be profound, like an out-of-body experience. Well, he was out of his body, all the way, and into hers as deeply as possible.

The taste of her, exquisite on his tongue. Like he'd been waiting ten thousand nights to become himself and was doing it through Kyra.

He kissed the wine from her mouth. He pulled the pinot noir from her lips. He let them both breathe and then dove for more. He didn't think he would ever be able to stop kissing her. She would have to throw him off her body.

He reached for her again and again in the night. Each time she came willingly and completely. He couldn't catch his breath or think sensibly, nor did he want to.

Maybe they would have time to do it right the next time, the time after or the time after. Now, he had to be inside her. Touching her in all the ways that mattered.

Her heart beat so hard and so wildly, it scared her. She didn't know the extent of her own excitement.

She wanted him on top of her where a man should be. Forget all the foreplay. She was much too aroused for that.

He touched her anyway. First with his lips and tongue. On her neck and down until she sucked in a quick breath and surrendered. Then when his lips played with her belly button and his tongue danced inside it, she let a quick scream escape and a tiny orgasm burst inside her.

He seemed on a mission. Down, down and down with his tongue.

"No," she begged. "Please."

She lifted his head, knowing that his destination would have thrown her overboard before she'd experienced all the selfish pleasure she wanted.

"I want you inside me, Race."

His gaze bore like the tips of hot irons into hers. "Are you sure?" they asked.

"Yes," she whispered.

He took his sweet time, his leisurely sweet time entering her. The deeper he took her, the tighter she held on and the longer she moaned.

"Race," she said.

She was so wet, she could hear him sliding in and out of her. And that sound. That wet, excited, aroused sound, thrilled her even more.

Of all the things she was afraid of, sharing herself had been the scariest of them all. But in Race's arms, under the sweet weight of him, there was no fear.

Everything about Race's touch told her she was safe and protected.

And home.

He wanted all of her. Every part. Every nuance. Every drop. And she was ready to give in and turn herself over to him.

She'd been bound in her own skin for far too long. She wanted to know what it was like to offer herself, all of herself, freely and not worry about being rejected or dismissed.

Race's eyes said everything she needed to know. He wanted every inch of her and God help her, he loved it. Every aspect of her being.

Aw, the chemistry.

Even if she wanted to leave, and she didn't, she couldn't. Her head and heart wouldn't let her.

Chapter 25

Kyra breathed slow and easy. She couldn't have been more relaxed if she'd taken the most potent sedative, been dipped in silk and levitated on air.

She let her head drop to the right and took in the sight of the man who'd brought her to pleasure beyond her deepest desires and had taken control of her body with his mind, willing her to ecstasy again and again.

His deep brown and well-muscled chest rose and fell quickly as if he were catching his breath. Kyra, on the other hand, felt nothing but drunken bliss.

"That was good," she said. Her orgasm even reached her eyes. She saw Race through the haze of her euphoria. He looked like an angel.

"Thank you," he said. He didn't move. He kept his eyes to the ceiling, his strong hand against his stomach. His wonderfully naked body lying still beside her.

She rolled over on her side. Pressed her fingers gently into his side and slid them up toward his chest. She kissed the trail her fingers had made, licking the salty sweat of his body on her lips.

"I mean it, Race. You were…"

He took her hand. Kissed the back of it then turned toward her. "So were you," he said. And she could tell he meant it. His eyes had turned the darkest shade of ochre she ever seen them. Smoldering, steamy brown. A brown that promised he would take her again, soon.

She smiled. "Now *that* was poetry."

"Hmm," he moaned and kissed the tips of her fingers. Then he brought one into his mouth. Sucked and teased it with languor. His warm, moist tongue circled lazily around each knuckle. Kyra relaxed even more and let him have his way.

"Good?" he asked when he'd paid the same long, gentle attention to every finger.

Kyra lay back, eyes closed softly. "Yes. Your mouth can do no wrong."

This man is lovin' me every which way but wrong and he's doin' everything except stopping.

As if he heard her, he said, "Hold on to that thought," then lifted himself on top of her and kissed her sweetly on the mouth. From her bottom lip, he kissed a straight line down the center of her body, massaging her breasts and nipples as he went.

"Race, no," she said when he got close. "Please, it's too much. I can't come anymore."

After the way he'd pleasured her body, she doubted if she had any orgasms left.

His tongue flicked against her feminine opening.

"That's like telling a thirsty man not to drink," he said and proceeded to have his fill of her and guide her deftly to one more delicate explosion. When she finally toppled over in ecstasy, she could only whimper and sigh while the muscles of her core tightened and released for seven beautiful minutes.

"Now *that's* poetry," he said again, falling beside her. The smile on his face was as wide as an ocean.

Kyra reached up to clutch her chest and see if it was heaving like his. Race caught her hand and held it. He stared at it as if he weren't quite sure what it was. She watched him with fascination.

"I'll be right back," he said, hurrying out of the bed and leaving her hand floating in the air.

Just then, Kyra had a terrible thought. The past few hours had gone so perfectly, it was time for something bad to happen. What if Race turns out to be crazy or weird? What if he's going to get some kinky gadget that he wants to incorporate into their experience?

Stop it! she chided herself. She had a habit of thinking the worst as soon as her life seemed to be going well. And usually, she was right. Most things that she believed were perfect were really too good to be true.

Her attention never wavered. She kept an eye on the doorway, wanting to know the moment he stepped back into the room with her. When he finally entered, he came in with a tray, two bowls of water and a tall bottle of lotion.

Kyra sat up. "What's that for?"

"It's for me, actually." He smiled and, although he had a wonderful smile, Kyra fought with herself to keep her eyes on his face and not on the rest of his body that he hadn't bothered to cover. Thank God.

"Will you indulge me?"

Cautious, Kyra responded, "Indulge you how?"

He placed the tray on the nightstand beside the bed and knelt beside her. "Let me massage your hands," he said.

That was not the answer Kyra expected. Curious, she persisted. "Do you have a hand fetish?"

"Maybe," he said, taking her right hand in his, laughing.

"What?" she asked.

"Is this the hand you write with?" Race asked.

"Yes," she said.

His eyes darkened again. "Then I have a fetish for this one."

She chuckled. "You better do them both."

"Don't worry," he said. "I'll do any body part you want me to."

Once again, Kyra found herself closing her eyes and letting Race have his way with her body. True to his methodical, analytical nature, his massage was just as thorough.

"I want to give your hand as much pleasure and enjoyment as it has given me. I know this one massage can't come close, but—"

"Yes, it can," Kyra said, honestly. Her hands were so limp and relaxed, she didn't know if she would be able to hold a pen ever again.

Race warmed the lotion in his hands before clasping her left hand and massaging with measured strokes. His hands moved as though they were practiced and trained. He knew what he was doing.

Kyra sat back against the pillows, no longer wanting to hold herself up. She only wanted to succumb to the waves of contentment rushing over her.

When Race finished with her left hand and started working on her right, the sensation sent her floating. He rolled each finger in his palm, applied lotion generously, kneaded the skin and pressed the flesh of her palm until it was supple and cooperative. Just like her mind, her body, her spirit had been made supple and cooperative by the way Race touched her.

"This is the hand that touches my heart," he said, massaging and kissing each finger. "This is the hand."

Kyra drifted. His touch sedated her. Made her woozy and brought her to a deep sleep. During the night, she awoke only slightly. Long enough to realize she was in Race's bed and he was sleeping beside her. She snuggled close, draped an arm across his belly. In turn, he wrapped his arm around her shoulders.

When she awoke, she hadn't moved from that spot and didn't want to ever again. The chemistry between them had proven true. Two bodies had come together to form one. The thing between them lived organically inside their hearts and outside them in the breath they released and the air they breathed. It was alive and changing and bonded them together. It was sent. Meant to be. Inevitable, and with care, she hoped everlasting.

"Good morning, beautiful," he said.

"Good morning, handsome," she replied.

He rolled toward her. "Give me those lips," he said, angling toward her.

"Morning breath," she protested, turning away.

He pulled her face back to his. "I'll get used to it."

Kyra didn't know if he stole a kiss or if she gave it freely. Either way, it felt good and the right way to start a morning.

He sprang out of bed the same way he'd done the night before. "I have something for you," he said, leaving her alone.

Kyra frowned. It was too much of a good thing. The voice in the back of her mind said, enjoy it. Get used to it.

He returned quickly and sat on the bed next to her. She sat up and stared at the softcover book in his hand.

He didn't have to say a word. She knew a literary journal when she saw one.

He handed it to her and her hands trembled so she could barely turn the pages.

The trade-paper-size book was white with a multi-colored painting of hands on the front. Hands of all shapes, sizes and ages. Much like the hands of those whose work lay inside, waiting for eager eyes like hers.

Flipping to the table of contents, she scanned the page for a title she recognized. Even if Chantel's name was after it, it would still be her poem.

Her finger stopped on the words *"If You Have to Get Out Fast"* and her breath caught at the sight of the name after it. Kyra Douglas.

"Race…how?"

He smiled and his eyes sparkled like stars. "I made a phone call."

Joy washed over her in waves so big, she could hardly breathe. She stared at the book in her hands. Something she created had found a home. Her hands shook and she nearly lost hold of the journal. All my life, she thought. I've been waiting all my life.

"Oh, Race!" she said and threw her arms around his neck. He tumbled back on the bed with the force of her affection and she covered his face with kisses.

He didn't talk or move. It was his turn to let her have her way. The pleasure in his eyes told her he enjoyed every lip smack against his skin.

When she let him up, he placed a kiss on her cheek. "Read it to me," he said.

She did as he asked.

She flipped gingerly to page twenty-four, where a poem she wrote sat in the middle of a page of linen paper in one of the leading literary journals. She read what she felt and with tears in her voice, expressing all of the emotions she'd put into the poem. She looked up a couple of times to see if Race was listening. The emotion in his eyes proved that he was paying attention and feeling every word.

He really, truly felt her poetry. And the sun in her world had just come out. Race had made her happy beyond words. She could neither move nor speak.

"Come on," he said. "Let's try to make breakfast."

Chapter 26

"No, no!" Kyra shouted and sprinted toward disaster.

"Margaret, wait!" But it was too late. She had already turned off the computer.

"Did I do it again?" she asked.

"That's okay," Kyra said, pushing away the irritation threatening to come through in her voice. "I'll fix it."

After the wonderful night she spent with Race, Kyra was floating on every cloud in the heavens. Nothing could get her down. She cheerfully turned the computer back on and hoped that once again the recovery program would save Margaret's file from being lost.

Margaret had a habit of finishing a computer activity and then turning off her computer instead of saving the file she created and waiting for the next lesson. Sometimes the recovery program would keep the file and load it to be saved and sometimes it wouldn't.

This time it did.

The white-haired woman looked up at Kyra with eyes that said, "I mean well, I just like to turn things off."

And she did. Margaret would turn off the lights, other people's computers, ceiling fans. Anything that was running, she would either turn off or unplug. She got on most folk's nerves; Kyra just thought she was funny.

"All right, Margaret. Here is the letter you typed. Let's save it and then we'll get on the Internet and you can send it to your son."

Her eyes lit up like sweet stars. "Thank you, honey."

Kyra wondered where her parents were. They were never late for class. Now that she'd gotten them to be regulars, they were more like her assistants than two students. She'd been counting on them to help her keep everyone in the same place when it came time to attach documents to e-mails.

Oh well, there was always Marta. She knew her way around a computer.

"Okay. Has everyone finished typing their letters?"

Kyra got several nods and yeses.

"Then I'm going to have you go ahead and open up your search engine. Can someone tell me where the search engine is on your desktop?"

Before she could get the answer to that question, Natria, the community center receptionist, poked her head into the computer lab.

"Ky, call for you."

"Thanks," Kyra said.

"Marta, will you take over class for me while I answer this call?"

"Sure," the older woman said. She slid slowly and effortfully out of her chair and stood in front of the class.

"Excuse me, everyone," Kyra said, sounding a lot calmer than she felt. Her heart beat a hard and deep rhythm in her chest. It thudded in her ears and made her dizzy as she exited into the lobby. With her spirit full of concern, Kyra approached Natria's desk and picked up the phone.

"Hello?"

"Ky, it's Dad. Your mother was just admitted to St. Joseph's. She had a heart attack."

The bottom dropped out of her entire world and Kyra's stomach knotted with fear.

"Is she all right?"

"You know your mother. Of course she's all right."

Her father's words didn't alleviate her fear. "I'll be right there."

"What's wrong?" Natria asked.

"My mom's in the hospital. I've got to go."

"I'm so sorry, Ky. Don't worry about the class."

Kyra dashed into the lab just long enough to get her purse, tell the students she had an emergency and dash back out.

Natria called after her. "I hope she'll be all right."

"Me, too," Kyra said, and ran out of the building.

When she walked into her mother's room at the hospital, her mother was sitting up in the bed eating strawberry sorbet.

"Mom?" Kyra said.

She didn't realize how nervous she'd been until she

reached out, hugged her mother and sobbed uncontrollably.

"Be careful, now. You'll squeeze me so hard, I'll have another heart attack."

Kyra wiped her tears and pulled back, but only a little.

"What happened?"

"Your mother said she didn't feel good and kept complaining that her chest felt tight," her father said. "I got tired of hearing it and brought her to the emergency. When they did the EKG they saw some blockage."

"They gave me some kind of 'clot-buster,' which is supposed to increase blood flow and hooked me up to a heart monitor. Now I feel fine and I'm hungry. They brought me this kiddie food, and what I really want is a Wendy's double cheeseburger."

Kyra was so relieved that her mother was alive and feeling pretty good that she laughed. Ever since Kyra could remember, her mother had loved Wendy's hamburgers. Their treat on Sunday's was to go to Wendy's for dinner. It was like a tradition in their family for years.

"Mom, I don't think you'll be eating too many more hamburgers after this, from Wendy's or anywhere else for that matter."

Her mother took another spoonful of sorbet and frowned. "I guess not," she said.

"I want to talk to the doctor," Kyra said. She was determined to find out everything there was about her mother's condition.

"You'll probably have to wait until tomorrow

morning to speak with a doctor. There are plenty of nurses to go around though. Annie is your mother's nurse. She should be back any minute to look at the blood pressure readings. They've been taking them every fifteen minutes since she came up here."

Kyra nodded. She still hadn't moved from her mother's side. And she had no intentions of leaving her alone in the hospital overnight. If the staff wanted her to leave, they were going to have to kick her out.

"Portis is on the way," her father said.

Kyra nodded. Still in shock. Still numb. She couldn't believe that her mother could have been gone from her life just that quickly. She couldn't believe it. And her heart couldn't believe it, either. It was still beating like a jackhammer. If she wasn't careful, she would have a heart attack of her own.

She took a deep breath. Then another. By the third one, her mother was stroking her arm. Comforting her.

"I'm okay, baby. See. I just have to stay here until they get my arteries unblocked. Then I can go home."

Kyra nodded. She didn't want to start crying again. "I love you, Mom," she said.

"I love you, too, sweetie," her mother said.

Her dad moved from where he'd been standing against the wall. "Hey, what about me?"

And for a moment that wasn't nearly long enough, three members of the Douglas family embraced with heartfelt emotion.

The next day, when Kyra and her father awoke to the sounds of doctors making rounds, they had a chance to speak to her mother's physician.

He'd ordered a series of tests and recommended that she stay in the hospital for two more days of monitoring. If everything stayed the same during the next forty-eight hours, Kyra's mother would be released and she could return to the hospital for further tests if needed.

"I recommend aspirin therapy and a cardiac rehab program."

Kyra had heard of cardiac rehab. One of her coworkers had been on it once. It was a regimen that retooled the patient's mind, body and spirit for healthful living.

"The program works best if the spouse also participates," the doctor said. "Your mother was fortunate this time, and I don't want there to be a next."

"But I don't understand, doctor," her mother chimed in. "I'm not overweight and I'm active."

"But your cholesterol level is too high. For some, high cholesterol is in the genes. So, there are other things you need to do to make sure that you get your numbers down and keep them down."

"Like no more Sundays at Wendy's."

"I wouldn't say that. Just order the Wendy's salad with fat-free dressing."

"Yuck!" Kyra's mother said.

"I'm also going to prescribe Lipitor to help you lower your cholesterol."

"Great. More medication."

"I know," the doctor said. "Getting older can be a challenge, but I'm on Lipitor myself."

Kyra and her parents stared at the doctor, who looked the picture of good health.

"High cholesterol runs in my family."

"I'll make sure she sticks to the program, doctor," Kyra's father said.

"Good. Do you have any other questions for me?"

"Yes," Kyra said. "Where can I go to get a decent cup of coffee around here?"

The doctor laughed. "Starbucks," he said. "There's a vendor cart in the lobby."

Doctor Carroll patted Kyra's mother on the shoulder. "I'll see you in the morning to sign your discharge papers."

"Thank you, doctor," her parents said.

Although her father looked as if he'd just jumped out of his own bed and showered, Kyra had no such fresh and perky feeling. She'd been worried about her mother all night and it had manifested itself in the dreams that had broken her sleep. She felt as if she'd been stepped on and ground into the floor.

"You look tired, sweetheart. I'm fine and James is here."

"She's right, Kyra. Go home. Get some rest. You can come back later after you've had some sleep."

"What about you?" she asked, worried that her dad was in the same worn-out state.

"I'm fine," he said. "You go on."

Kyra nodded, kissed her mother, hugged her softly, and went out for air. She had no intentions of going home. And she had no intentions of being alone.

She drove through the early morning Saturday traffic straight to Chantel's house. It was funny. During all their years as friends, Kyra was usually the one providing the shoulder. It felt strange to her that this time, she was the one in need of comfort.

She fumbled with her cell phone. It had been turned off since her computer class last night.

The loud honk startled her. When Kyra looked back at the road, she's strayed into the lane next to her. Quickly jerking the car to the left, Kyra realized that she was too tired and distraught to concentrate on more than one thing at a time.

"Let me just get there in one piece," she said. "Please God, let Chantel be home."

Well, they say God is good, all the time. And pulling into Chantel's driveway, Kyra saw Chantel's red sports car parked in her driveway. She waited for the wave of relief to wash over her, but the car parked next to Chantel's prevented it.

The car belonged to Race.

It was eight thirty in the morning. Why would Race be at Chantel's house this early unless he'd spent the night?

Could he be that much of a dog, she wondered. Sleep with me one night and sleep with my friend the next.

Kyra didn't want to believe it. When she parked behind his car, she didn't want to believe it. When she walked up the stairs and took Chantel's spare key out of her purse, she didn't want to believe it.

There had better be a good reason for Race to be here, she thought as her heart raced a mile a minute for the second time in twenty-four hours—like work or just a friendly breakfast. But if he were here betraying her, she would call him everything but a child of God, tell Chantel she would explain later and go home to cry… again.

She let herself in and listened for voices talking

about budgets and projects; she sniffed the air for platonic breakfast smells.

There was neither.

There were sounds though. They came from upstairs.

Kyra climbed the stairs, not caring if they heard her.

"I'm sorry, Race," Chantel said. "I'm sorry I got you mixed up in this."

"Stop talking crazy. I'm here because I want to be."

"You're a wonderful man," Chantel said.

At her words, Kyra stopped short on the staircase, before she reached the top. What was Chantel saying about Race being wonderful?

"So, are you going to look at it or what?" he asked.

There was a long silence, then Chantel's worried voice broke it wide open.

"Oh, God, Race!"

"Let me see," he said, and then, "Holy smoly. You're pregnant."

Kyra's stomach lurched and she nearly threw up right there on Chantel's multi-loop Berber. Catching herself and her stomach before it went heave-ho, she turned and ran down the stairs.

Before she could get going good, she stumbled. Kyra grabbed at the railing, but it was too late. She landed hard on her backside and stubbed her toe in the process.

"Ow," she said, and scrambled up.

"Who's there?" came Chantel's weak and fright-filled call.

Kyra was up and nearly out the door before she heard the voice that almost stopped her.

"Kyra?" Race said, some ways behind her.

She didn't stop, didn't turn around. Her toe hurt like

hell, but she kept going until she was in her car and headed down the quiet suburban street in the early morning.

"Kyra!"

She heard Race call again.

"Asshole!" she shouted back, but she doubted if he heard her. She was too far gone.

"You two deserve each other!" she said out loud.

She steered her car back toward the hospital. Her brother would be getting in soon. It would be nice to be at the hospital when he got there.

She wiped at her face, but was surprised. There were no tears. Just anger. It had arisen from the center of her soul and flooded all parts of her body.

Wow, she thought. This time it's me. I got dogged by a man, and the worst part is not the fact that I got dogged but that I don't have anyone to lean on and help me ease the pain.

Maybe she deserved it.

Well, she had enough to think about now without letting her mind fill up with thoughts about a trifflin' man. She had a mother who needed to be nursed back to health.

And if she didn't see Race again or Chantel again for a long time, that was just fine with her.

Chapter 27

Maybe the whole world hadn't gone mad, but all of the PCs at ComTel America had gone crazy.

If they weren't breaking down completely, they were suffering from a virus. Nearly one third of ComTel's PCs had become infected with a virus. Kyra had managed to track the origin of the virus to the news specialist in the marketing department. He'd downloaded a fun fact from the Internet that came complete with a Trojan horse. When the news specialist e-mailed the daily-employee news bulletin to all employees, those who opened the bulletin right way infected their PCs with the virus. By the time Kyra's department figured out what had happened, seven hundred PCs had been infected.

Kyra and her team quickly quarantined the virus and sent those with infected computers a program to run to clean their hard drives. It worked for some. For others, their entire hard drive was wiped clean.

It had been a busy morning.

And on top of all that, Race Jennings had seen fit to make it known that he was having computer problems once again and requesting her services to fix them. Kyra had done a good job of ignoring his requests all morning. When Sam stood outside her cube with the pained expression of a man who'd just lost the biggest poker hand ever, she knew her minutes of ignoring Race had come to an end.

"Sam, I think this virus is more important than one man's PC."

"You won't if we have to have a reduction in staff and your name gets thrown into the hat."

Kyra spun around in her chair and stared Sam straight in the eye. "What are you talking about?"

"I'm talking about the CFO's cost-cutting crusade. He's trimming the fat everywhere and we're as lean as we can get around here. So, he might just suggest we start trimming away people. So, I want to do everything I can to keep that man happy. Including getting him what he wants, which is a working computer."

"I don't believe you. I've got seven hundred infected computers."

Sam shoved his pen into his mouth and chewed on the end. "All right, then. Just go see if his computer is a quick fix. If it is, fix it and get back here. If it isn't, tell him he's second in priority only to the virus."

Kyra didn't say a thing. She was too upset with her boss for choosing position over production. And too mad at herself for caring in the way that she did. She knew a substantial part of her objection was the fact that she never wanted to see Race Jennings again.

When she arrived at his office, he was pacing back and forth. Staring out the window, then pacing some more.

"Race?" she said, entering his office, ego first.

He jerked in her direction. "What took you so long?"

"Didn't you get the message? There's a virus infecting PCs."

"Now just exactly how would I get that message if my PC isn't working?"

"How about your admin? Isn't that what you pay her for? To keep you appraised of things?"

He stared at her. The frustration melted from his features and was replaced by a deep glow of pleasure. The temperature in the room increased by ten degrees.

Kyra walked to his tower. "Did you open the daily bulletin? You probably have the same virus as everyone else."

"Did you read my problem description? I couldn't turn my computer on this morning. So there's no way I could have the virus."

Kyra sat down in his chair. She was used to sitting there. As usual, it felt wonderful. She wondered if she would voluntarily get up without being pulled up.

"You don't have any more magnets sitting on your PC do you?" she asked, looking around.

"No," he said.

His voice sounded relaxed. Playful. Not nearly as stern and serious as usual.

Just as before, Kyra checked connections from the wall to the PC. Everything was in order. She was about to try turning on the PC herself, when she noticed the LCD clock stuck on the side of it, which started a huge wave of incredulity crashing through her. She pulled off the offending device.

"Race!"

His eyes sparkled mischievously. "Yes?" he said. "Did you find something?"

"Of course I found something. This clock," she said, trying to keep her voice even.

"I like it, don't you? I picked it up at the hardware store the other day when I purchased a new garden hose."

Kyra was about to speak, when images of she and Race drenched with water, sweat and lust played like a four-star film in her mind. Thirsting for a cold drink of water, among other things, Kyra snapped herself out of her vision. "You see this?" she asked, pointing to the small black metal square attached to the back of the clock. "*This* is a magnet. A *mag*-net. Remember the problems you had because your pendulum was magnet-ic?"

"Oh, yeah," he said, stroking his chin.

"Well you're going to have them again if you insist on shorting out your computers with them."

Kyra couldn't believe he'd done it again. "You're so concerned about everyone else around here cutting costs. Just think about how much you have cost the company in IT equipment and time. The next time you want a de-partment to drastically cut costs, think about that."

Kyra's hand flew to her mouth. She couldn't believe how she'd just spoken to the CFO of the company. She'd let those words fly as if she'd known Race for years. She was feeling way too comfortable with him.

If her boss got wind of her behavior, there's be no telling what he would do.

"I'm sorry, Race."

"Don't be. You're absolutely right. I shouldn't be wasting the company's money like this."

Kyra loaded up the cart with PC parts. Broken PCs saddened her a little. Kyra hated to see a good PC go bad. As she loaded the CPU, keyboard and monitor on the cart, she thought she must have some small idea of how paramedics felt when putting people on to stretchers and carting them off for more treatment.

"No more magnets, Race. Please," Kyra said. She realized that she was speaking about more than just the magnets. And she hoped that he got the message about both.

For the next two weeks, not a day went by that she didn't run into, get on an elevator with, or sit in a meeting with Race Jennings. He seemed to be everywhere she was. And what was worse, he was sexier than ever.

At first, Kyra thought it was her imagination. Race had forgone the ultraprofessional attire for more relaxed suits that, while putting on a business sensibility, were quite sensual. Softer fabrics, hitting him snugly in all the right places. And on casual days, the top two buttons of his shirts were undone exposing the upper part of the most exquisite chest Kyra had ever seen.

And it wasn't just his clothing. He'd changed colognes. What he wore now had the power to levitate her and could easily have her drifting on air behind him wherever he walked. The aroma was raw and sensual, like the man. It seemed to fill up a room, or maybe just her nostrils. Along with his open collar shirts, he'd started wearing small diamond studs—one in each ear. He looked so good, Kyra didn't think she could take much more of this sexy metamorphosis.

Every evening, Kyra would come home, take a cool shower and moisturize her skin with lotion she kept in the refrigerator now. It was the only way to keep her libido in check.

Turk had started calling her more frequently. She couldn't talk to him for fear of losing her resolve once again and shouting into the phone, "Get over here and do me!"

So she threw herself into her poetry and teaching her computer class. It was almost the distraction she needed.

Finally, when she'd "run into" Race three times in one day, she stopped him.

"Are you following me?"

"Why would you say that?"

"We just keep running into each other. It just seems so…"

"Intentional?"

Her heart seized up and nearly bent her over with weakness. This thing she felt for Race was far more than an attraction. And she was realizing it for the first time.

"Yes. Intentional."

Race let his eyes travel the length of her and then back to her eyes.

"Hmm," he said, giving her the vaguest response possible.

"I've gotta go, I need to, to go," she said, fanning

herself with the folder she was carrying. She'd long since forgotten what was in the folder or where she was going with it. That information had been lost in Race's eyes.

St. Augustine, she said in her mind as she moved quickly down the hallway. She needed a prayer about lust that worked. Kyra decided to purchase a St. Augustine medallion for herself before she went home that evening. Her longings for Race were stronger than ever and she knew that only God could help her now.

In Kyra's poetry, Race was never far. He was always around, no matter where she went or what she did. She had no idea how much life could imitate art until Race showed up at one of her department's project-update meetings as a presenter.

With his smoky eyes, sensuous mouth, tall muscular body and business-casual white suit, he looked every bit the antithesis of an officer of a telecommunications company. He looked like he'd just stopped by after a walk on a beach in Barbados.

"Race Jennings has been making the rounds with the practical points of our new justification process and he's here to identify steps we can take on an individual basis and to answer any questions you might have." Sam couldn't have been happier that he and the CFO were actually in the same room. Sam actually looked as if he had some sense and was a halfway decent manager. Kyra might have had an outburst of laughter if it hadn't been for Race's eyes, which had been on her for most of the time he'd been in the meeting with them. Without thinking, Kyra got up, walked to the thermostat, adjusted the temperature down to sixty-two degrees and retook her seat. None of the other ten employees said anything, just gave her a few curious glances and then turned their attention to Race.

When Race began his presentation, Kyra didn't hear a word he said. She just watched his lips and imagined what he could do with them. As if he knew she was watching, he licked them periodically and folded them in once or twice for good measure. Kyra had to stop herself from purring or making some other sound that would belie her attraction and embarrass the heck out of her.

Her eyes never left his face, except to stare at his Adam's apple, his broad shoulders and firm hips. Periodically, she heard him say things like, "Reduction in travel, taking on more responsibility and future hiring freeze." But overall, she just memorized every movement his lips made, every gesture his hands created. And the startling way she could smell Race, the man, beneath the captivating layer of cologne he wore, and how the "Race the man" aspect of him intoxicated her.

She realized that she had to do something to break the spell. She leaned over and asked her friend Sheila if she was going to finish her iced tea. Sheila whispered *no*, so Kyra took it, removed the lid from the plastic cup and turned up the cold liquid to her lips. She gulped freely and quickly.

When she drained the last drop, she mouthed *thank you* to Sheila, picked up her pen and pretended to take notes.

By the end of Race's presentation, she had the bulk of a poem written.

She didn't know how, but Race had managed to raise

the level of her writing again. Even in a meeting. She couldn't wait to get home and work on the piece. If she had to stay up all night, she would get it into decent shape to share with Chantel the next day.

At least this thing between Race and I is good for something.

As her team members filed out of the conference room when the meeting was over, Kyra felt Race's eyes on her. He was behind her. Closing in. She walked quickly down the hall. Instead of waiting for the elevator, she dashed inside the stairwell. She needed to get some fresh air. But first she needed to work Race Jennings out of her soul.

After the first flight of stairs, she discovered that he wasn't about to let her do that.

"Wait!" he called after her.

Keep going, her mind shouted. But her feet wouldn't obey. They stopped and waited for him and Kyra wondered what on earth Race could possibly want.

"Are you my shadow?"

"Kyra, slow down," he said, but he didn't mean it. His legs were long enough to catch her easily.

"Race, you're wrong for this," she responded, stopping on the twentieth floor landing. "We're wrong for this."

Her eyes pleaded with him to leave her alone. But how could he? The attraction between them wouldn't let him.

"What's wrong with us talking about something besides broken computers?"

"Because it won't end there, and you know it."

Kyra paced a bit. Avoided his eyes. Looked hot enough to drink like coffee.

He took a step closer. She held up a halting hand.

"I keep saying it to myself. Over and over and over. Maybe it's time I reminded you. You are dating my best friend."

Race's heart nearly stopped beating. He felt as though he'd just been sliced with cold steel. "Dating? I'm not dating Chantel. Not for a long time. We just hang together now and talk about poetry. But we're not seeing each other."

Suddenly the space in the large stairwell shrunk and took all the air with it. Kyra could barely breathe. "You're, you're not, not seeing each other?"

"Didn't she tell you? It's been weeks."

Kyra didn't think she could stand anymore so she used the wall of the stairwell to brace herself as she slid down to the stairs. Shock did not adequately describe what she was in, but it was close enough.

They weren't seeing each other.

"You're not lying to me?" she asked. Her words echoed softly off bare walls.

Race sat on the step next to her. He took a deep breath and then took her hand. The energy that surged between them was almost visible. Kyra gasped with the power and intensity of it.

"Does that feel like a lie to you?"

Kyra slowly looked up into his eyes. "No."

Race pushed a strand of hair away from Kyra's face. Any excuse to touch her with his other hand. Her hair was strong, silky. Just like Kyra herself. He didn't want to stop touching her hair or her. He wanted to plunge his hand deep into her locks, comb them with his fingers, toss and tousle them the way he felt tossed and tousled every time he looked into her eyes.

"We need to talk," he said. "Come over."

She opened her mouth to protest. He hushed it with a sweet kiss that was quick and over before everything he'd been thinking about for weeks happened right there between the twentieth and twenty-first floors.

"Tonight. Come tonight," he said, still twisting the strand of hair around his finger. "We'll have dinner. You don't have to say anything. You don't even have to eat if you don't want to. Just show up."

The lump in Kyra's throat wouldn't let her speak. She just nodded instead. Nodded like a crazy woman.

"Good," Race said and helped her stand. "Seven thirty," he said and couldn't resist one more kiss. This one a bit longer.

Kyra's lips tasted as sweet as strawberries and were every bit as plump and juicy. He groaned to keep his knees sturdy.

He decided he'd better go back to his office immediately. He turned and headed back up the stairs.

Kyra watched him go. Her body throbbed so strongly with excitement, she didn't know how to make it stop.

She continued down the staircase, now and then touching her lips where his mouth had been and feeling the heat that still radiated there.

Seven thirty will take an eternity to get here, she thought.

Chapter 28

There was no doubt in his mind what Kyra had assumed. He didn't even wonder how much she'd heard. Obviously, she'd heard enough to make her run out without a word.

He took off after her, only pausing long enough to tell Chantel that everything would be okay and that he would call her later.

Race followed Kyra through the Savannah traffic, which was unusually light for a Saturday morning. He wondered where she was going. Traveling through the south side of Savannah, he knew she wasn't on the way home.

He dialed her cell number hoping she would pick up. He got her voice mail.

"Kyra, it's not my baby. Ask Chantel. She's been trying to reach you all night. When she couldn't catch up with you, she called me. She's freaking out and needs someone to talk to." He paused. "For that matter, so am I."

He hung up and kept up with her as she weaved through traffic.

Wow, that woman can maneuver through traffic, he thought, then realized she could maneuver around his heart, too. If she couldn't, he wouldn't be chasing her halfway across the city.

When she turned into the hospital parking lot, his chest got heavy with concern. What was she doing here, he wondered.

He followed her to the parking lot and parked only a few cars away. He got out quickly and jogged up beside her.

"I don't associate with liars," she said without breaking stride.

"But it's okay for you to be one," he snapped.

She stopped short then and he begged his stupidity to be cool. It did no such thing.

"I don't have time for this, Race, but for the record, I didn't lie to you."

The Savannah sun spread its rays between them and cast shadows on the sidewalk before them.

"Didn't you? The last time I checked, 'I don't know much about poetry' coming from a poet like you is probably a 'bald-faced lie.'"

She started walking toward the door. "I'm not going to do this here."

Race stopped short, astonished that she would not even give him a chance to explain. "So that's it? You don't want to hear from me about anything?"

"What is there to hear, Race? The sexual position you used to get her pregnant? Spare me the details."

Her voice sounded tired. Washed out. She was upset about much more than the conversation she'd overheard.

"Why are you here? Are you visiting someone?"

She didn't answer. She just kept going. She kept her head down and her pace fast. She reached the door and disappeared inside in no time.

Race wanted to go after her. But his mind was boiling at full force. *She* didn't trust *him*. Considering all that she had concealed from him over the past few months, he had every right to believe that it should be the other way around.

Tell her that, he screamed to himself.

"I think I will," he answered back and jogged into the hospital.

He caught up with her at the elevator bay. "Kyra!" he said, just before she could step onto the elevator.

"Leave me alone, Race, or I'll tell the security guard you're harass—"

"Ky!" a male voice called from behind Race.

A man ran up beside Kyra. His eyes were red and puffy. His hands shook at his sides.

"Did they revive her?" he asked frantically.

"Calm down, Portis. Mom's fine. They're just going to run some tests."

"No. I just got off the phone with Dad. He said Mom couldn't breathe all of a sudden and then she passed out."

"Oh, my God!" Kyra said.

Race's heart shriveled in his chest as if someone had reached inside him and squeezed it.

As soon as the next elevator came, Kyra and her brother got on. Race watched helplessly as the doors closed and the two embraced with fear and sadness as large tears ran down their faces.

It was a long time before Race moved. He wanted to be by Kyra with every ounce of his will. But he knew that in her present state and current frame of mind, she would neither accept his support nor want it. At the same time, he couldn't leave.

When he'd gathered his thoughts, he went to the receptionist's desk and got the room number for Kyra's mother. After that, he went to that floor and took a seat in the family waiting area. He knew that what he was doing didn't add up. For once in his analytical life, two and two equaled a new number. Something he'd never thought of.

And the sum was love.

While his heart and his mind raced, one clear thought came through and he knew what he had to do. He pulled out his cell phone and called Chantel.

Twenty minutes later, she stepped off of the elevator and was headed in his direction. He'd been sitting in the waiting room, numb. He wanted to comfort Kyra so badly, it twisted his stomach into a fist-sized knot.

"How is she?" Chantel asked.

"The nurse said she's stable now, but if she has another episode, they're going to move her to ICU."

Worry made Chantel's eyes look large and liquid. After the baby and now Kyra's mother, there was another piece of news Chantel needed to know. Race just wished he could have told her under better circumstances.

"Chantel," Race said. "Before you go back there. I need to tell you something."

Kyra had finished one prayer and had just started on another when Chantel walked through the hospital room door. The sight of her friend opened the pit of emotions churning at the bottom of her stomach and she burst into tears.

Chantel rushed to her side and held her tight.

And not a moment too soon. Kyra had been through too much and the stress had weakened her. She needed to be held and comforted by someone who understood her and cared deeply.

No matter what, she needed her best friend.

"Chantel, she was doing fine. She was eating ice cream and cracking jokes and—"

"Shh," Chantel said. "Don't cry, Ky. Moms is going to be all right. Just wait. She'll be back to telling us all what to do and where to go in no time."

Kyra just hugged Chantel, too tired to talk.

"What did the doctor say?" Chantel asked.

"He doesn't think it was her heart. He believes she had a panic attack," Kyra's father said.

"The nurse gave her a sedative and she went right to sleep."

"Thank God," Chantel said.

Kyra sat up straight and found her voice. "They're still going to run tests tomorrow to make sure."

Chantel patted Kyra reassuringly on the shoulder and studied her friend, and then her friend's brother and father. They all looked spent, like they'd been beaten down and back up by a relentless tormentor. Kyra's father looked as if he hadn't slept much. Kyra's brother looked as if he would never sleep again. And Kyra just looked. Chantel knew that Kyra and her mother were very close.

"You all need to get up and stretch."

"We're fine," Mr. Douglas said.

"No, you're not. You all look like you're about to fall out. Now, I'll stay here with Moms while you get up walk around. Go get something to eat or a cup of coffee. Stretch your legs."

Kyra shook her head. "Thanks Chantel, but—"

"But nothing," she said. "Now what good are you to her if you're so tired you can't function?"

At their silence, Chantel continued. "At least five minutes. Get up and walk around."

The Douglas family hoisted themselves up reluctantly.

"Come on," Mr. Douglas said. "Let's get something to eat."

His children didn't respond. They just followed him out of the hospital room. Before leaving, Kyra mouthed the words *thank you* to her friend and then joined her family in the hallway.

Without speaking they walked toward the elevator. When Kyra saw Race Jennings sitting in the family waiting room, she stopped short and her breath caught quickly.

His gaze bore into her and he stood slowly. Kyra's father and brother stopped and turned around. They glanced at the man staring at her from the waiting area, then turned back to her.

"Ky?" her brother began.

"It's okay, Portis. I'm not hungry anyway."

"Call me if you want me to bring you something," Portis said.

While her father and brother resumed walking, Kyra stood still and allowed an errant thought to drift to the cell phone in her purse. She'd gotten it out to call her aunt Muriel to see if she was coming to the hospital when she discovered two missed calls. One of the calls was from her aunt saying that she was on the way. The other was from a frantic Race Jennings telling her he wasn't the father of Chantel's baby.

Kyra had been too concerned about her mother to react.

A frayed ball of emotions rolled around inside her. A tenuous mixture of sadness and relief.

Race stood before her as tall and as handsome as ever. His eyes beseeched her for a sign. Instead of waiting another moment to give it to him, she walked straight into his arms.

It was the embrace she'd waited an entire lifetime to feel. Solid. Strong. Unwavering. Committed. Chemical. Right.

"How is she?" he whispered.

"Resting," she whispered back.

Race's hands encircled her, rubbed her shoulders and arms reassuringly. He'd been there. The whole time. Waiting for her. That thought broke open inside of her like a small sun, warming her soul. He filled a space inside her she'd never known was empty.

"Race," she whispered. "Oh, God, Race."

"I'm here, Kyra," he said, squeezing her tighter. "I'm here, forever."

His eyes filled with worry and regret and hope all at the same time.

She squeezed back. "I love you, Race."

"I know," he said. His heart filled up with joy and contentment. "I love you, too."

Chapter 29

After more tests than Kyra could count—electrocardiogram, echocardiogram, CT scan, MRI—the doctor confirmed his suspicion of heart disease. "This was a warning," he'd told them. "Your heart is telling you that you've been taking it for granted. This was just a small protest. If you don't make the changes we discussed, next time your heart is going to go on strike and refuse to work. You got me?"

"I got you, Doctor."

"Good," he said. "Now, I don't want to see you in here again under these circumstances. And remember, Wendy's has salads, too. Now, you all take care, Angela."

"We will, doctor," Kyra's father said.

For the next week, Kyra was so happy to have her mother out of the hospital, she spent nearly every moment with her. She'd gotten family medical leave from ComTel in order to take care of her mother until she healed completely. And unlike when she first arrived at the hospital, her mother didn't pretend that nothing was wrong. She took all the help that Kyra and her brother offered her. She rested when she needed to and took everything slowly, obeying her doctor's orders to a T.

Going into the second week, Kyra felt just a tad bit guilty. She spent all of her time with her mother and had only spoken with Race on the phone twice.

One evening, when she dragged herself home at eleven o'clock at night, Turk was on her doorstep, looking like a lost puppy.

"Turk, what are you doing here?"

"Looking for you. What else?"

"I'm fine and I'm tired. Can we talk another time?"

"No," he said, following her inside.

Kyra threw her purse on a table in the entryway, kicked off her shoes and plopped onto her couch.

"Umm," Turk said, giving her a once-over. Kyra closed her eyes and didn't care what he did, didn't care one way or the other about what he wanted. She was much too exhausted.

She heard him walking around in her kitchen, opening doors and drawers. Running water. Pouring something.

He came back with a wineglass filled to the brim.

"What's that?" she asked.

"Some of that Shiraz you had in there. I mixed in some Sprite, a pinch of sugar, a dash of lemon juice and poured it over ice."

Kyra was too tired to smile, but she managed to reach for the glass. "Thank you," she said.

The cold drink slid down her throat with a welcome coolness. The warming in her stomach reminded her that she'd only had a piece of toast and a banana all day.

"That tastes great," she said.

Turk sat beside her. "Are you sure you're in a committed relationship, because I got something that goes with that drink."

Kyra stared at her friend with eyes that were half-open. "Race is nearly a foot taller than you. He's probably got forty pounds on you and I'm sure he wouldn't stand for anyone talking to his woman the way you're doing. But more importantly," she said, touching his hand lightly with hers, "I won't stand for it. As of today, all comments like that, stop. You understand?"

Turk dropped his head, then looked up slowly. His eyes held a fighting mixture of happiness and sadness. "You're really serious about this one."

"I am," she said, regretting that she hadn't spoken to Race in two days.

"So why isn't he here?" Turk asked.

"I don't know," Kyra said. She took a large swallow of the wine drink and placed the glass on an end table. She closed her eyes and let her head fall back against the couch.

"Here," Turk said, rising.

He helped her lie down on the couch. When she was comfortable, he went into the closet, got a thin blanket and covered her with it.

"Thank you," she said, already drifting.

"It's all right. I just wanted to make sure that you and Moms were okay."

"Yeah," Kyra said.

"You want me to stay?" he asked. His voice sounded so far away, Kyra wondered if it were real.

"No, I'll be fine."

"Good night, Ky."

"Good night," she whispered.

When she awoke the next morning, she decided to take a detour before going to her mother's house. She missed Race with a fierceness and it was time he knew it.

Race uploaded the revisions for ComTel's cumulative projects budget to their Intranet site for the fourth time. He waited as the cursor turned into an hourglass and the progress bar got longer and longer. Just as before, the bar stopped three quarters into the upload, the hourglass turned back into a cursor and he got the same error message.

Inappropriate action for file type. Upload unsuccessful.

He grit his teeth and stopped himself from hurling his computer across the room.

What good is technology when it was so volatile? He'd have better results with an abacus, squid's ink and papyrus than he was having with the five-million-dollar Intranet site the company swore was the latest and greatest.

Out of exasperation, he shut down his program and stood up. He didn't have a meeting for another hour. It was a nice day. Walking might clear his head.

It could also help him put things into perspective. He couldn't blame everything on technology. The truth was, ever since he and Kyra admitted their love, he hadn't been able to focus clearly.

And the one person who could help him focus had been busy taking care of her mother. He understood that. Respected it, and at the same time, wanted to see Kyra every day. Talk to her every day. Make love to her every day.

He wondered if their relationship was ending or simply slowing down before it even got started. He took one last look at the computer he wanted to rip from the wall and thought that yes, a walk was a very good idea. Otherwise, he was going to lose his mind with worry, want and frustration.

"Leslie, I'm going out. I'll be back in about—"

He caught a glimpse of Kyra out of the corner of his eye. The sight jump-started his heart, which he realized hadn't been in the right place since he left Kyra at the hospital that night.

Without a thought in his head, other than he had to see her, he followed her.

"Kyra," he said, opening the door.

Startled at first, she turned and gave him the warmest smile he'd ever seen.

Relief washed over him.

"Race," she said, then frowned. "What are you doing in here?"

He looked around. He was in the women's restroom. *Oh, well.*

"What are *you* doing here? I thought you were on family medical?"

"I am. But I had to see you." She lowered her head a bit. "It's kind of windy outside. I decided at the last minute to make sure my hair didn't look too crazy before I stepped into your office to see you."

He leaned against the wall. Partly because he thought he might look good doing it and partly because he was so happy to see her, his legs weakened. "Damn, you look good."

"Thank you," she said. She turned to the mirror and tussled with long, thick hair that could never look bad as far as he was concerned.

"How's your mother?"

"Much better. She hardly gets tired at all anymore. She has a doctor's appointment tomorrow."

More relief. "I'm glad to hear she's doing better."

"Yeah, me, too."

"So, how are *you* doing?"

It was a long moment before Kyra answered that question.

"Changed," she said.

Good thing he was leaning against the wall. That word nearly toppled him.

"Changed how?"

"Like all my life I've been acting as if life is forever. That close call with my mother was like a slap on my mortality. I mean, tomorrow really isn't promised. It's made me appreciate her, my entire family and friends so much more."

Race realized that what she was saying was either really good or really bad.

"I'm changed, Race. And I know it's clichéd as hell, but I just can't afford to take anything for granted anymore." She paused for a moment and then said, "Even my love life."

Race took a deep breath and decided to bite the

bullet. "So, that either means life is too short for you to be a one-man woman or—"

"Or," she said, taking a step toward him, "I've found the man I want to spend the rest of my life with."

He didn't allow another second to go by. Instead, he walked up to her and embraced her tightly. These past few weeks, gave him the inside dope on how Superman felt when he was exposed to Kryptonite. Having Kyra in his arms again gave him his strength back. All of it. He held her close and she snuggled into his body.

"Race?" she said without moving.

"Yes."

She took a deep breath. Held him tighter. "Will you marry me?"

He sucked in a breath as wave after wave of contentment hit him. He was so happy, he laughed. "Isn't that supposed to be my line?"

"Yes, but I've read your poetry. I'm much better with words."

He laughed again and then answered her. "I'll marry you under one condition."

"Name it," she said, still holding tight.

"That you give me a lifetime of free technical support on my computer. I'm having problems again."

The laughter coming from the women's restroom on the twenth-seventh floor of ComTel America that day was heard throughout the entire floor. It was spirited, full of joy and when it cut off suddenly, everyone wondered what happened. Except Kyra Douglas and Race Jennings, who kissed each other until they were half dizzy and could barely breathe.

Chapter 30

"If you're too tired, we can go," Kyra said. Her mother fidgeted with a glass of orange juice mixed with Diet Sprite on ice. Kyra hoped bringing her out tonight wasn't too taxing. Angela Douglas had been recovering wonderfully well since her heart attack and Kyra wanted her health to stay in good shape.

"Ky, I'm fine. My heart attack was two months ago, not two days ago."

"How's everything here?" Nick asked. He always checked on every table in his club and tonight was no exception. He'd been to their table twice since they arrived.

"Everything's fine," Race answered.

Thinking about that, Kyra would have to agree. And it wasn't just that evening at The Griot. Everything in her life had been going well. She was back to work. After Race's favorable report on her service of his computer, Kyra's boss told her he was reviewing her proposal on observation again. Even if it didn't go any further than that, Kyra believed that Sam was actually giving it real consideration this time. Chantel's baby was healthy, although Chantel herself struggled with morning sickness at all hours of the day. But she was happier than Kyra could ever remember her being. After a heart-to-heart talk, Nick had broken off his engagement and proposed to Chantel. Chantel still hadn't given him an answer, but the couple seemed to like the idea of becoming parents together.

Kyra glanced around the club. It looked different tonight. Only a handful of people. In addition to Chantel, Race and her parents, Race had invited his friend Brax and Kyra had invited Turk and Orlando, her friend from work.

The band was not only hot, it was sultry. Apropos for celebrating the force that drew she and Race together.

Chemistry.

If someone would have told her that she would find the love of her life that way, she would have called them crazy. There is no love at first sight, she could hear herself saying to such a suggestion. You can't possibly know that you're perfect for someone by the way they make you feel at the moment you first see them. But, by goodness, that's just what happened to her. Sometimes the person you're made for doesn't have to grow on you. Their essence has already grown *in* you since the moment you were born. And both your lives are waiting for that moment, for that most perfect juxtaposition in time and space when you meet and your eyes engage and your souls connect in a way that only God can cause or explain.

And there was absolutely no denying the truth.

Kyra glanced at Race, so comfortable in his skin, so giving and so loving, talking easily with her friends, and knew even without the three-carat diamond shining on her ring finger that she would be with him forever.

"Our first poet tonight is someone I've been trying to get on this stage for some months. Her presence honors us so much, I had to introduce her myself."

Kyra's mother's eyes went liquid with pride. Race rubbed Kyra's back and planted a kiss on her cheek.

"You ready, techie?"

"Please welcome to the stage, Kyra Douglas."

Kyra smiled, kissed her mother's cheek, winked at Chantel and mouthed *I love you* to Race, then took the stage.

She glanced out at the audience. The people she loved were there. Her newfound determination and their presence didn't take away her nerves as she thought they would. So, she used her nervousness and put all that energy in the delivery of her poem. A poem she wrote for Race the first day she saw him. She never imagined that she would read it, but since the day they met, her life had been everything except something she could imagine. Kyra smiled and thought, I hope it never will be again.

If you have to get out fast
you stop
wondering if there's time for you to grab
what's important
then you realize
your important stuff
is all over the place

like the smoke pushing out
good air.

If you have to get out fast
you remember
fire drills
when you were in the sixth grade
and appreciated any excuse
to get out of school
and stop learning
and you wish that just once
you had pretended there was an emergency
to help you figure out which way
your feet should go.

If you have to get out fast
you think of photos of your mother
that you never copied
the insurance papers shoved in a desk drawer
and the safe deposit box
you always wanted but never got because
if you had to get out fast
you believed you wouldn't hesitate
to save yourself.

Dear Reader,

Thank you for picking up this book about Kyra and Race. I had such a fabulous time writing their story. By combining my love of poetry and romance, my goal was to bring you a sensuous and touching story that is also uplifting and inspiring. For those of you who've read my previous novels, you know these are new characters. I'm turning a new corner and I hope you will turn the corner with me. Many of you have sent me e-mails about Brax. Thank you for those. You'll be happy to know that Brax is getting his own story—tentatively titled *Ever Wonderful*. So stay tuned. It's coming up next!

As always, I appreciate your continued support and am honored and humbled that you read and appreciate my work. Please contact me anytime and let me know how you feel about my stories. I'd love to hear from you!

Peace and blessings,

Kim

**Bestselling author
Brenda Jackson
introduces
the Steele Brothers
in a brand-new
three-book miniseries**

Solid Soul

by Brenda Jackson

AVAILABLE JULY 2006
FROM KIMANI™ ROMANCE

Love's Ultimate Destination